Siberian Secrets

By the same author

TO KILL A TSAR, by G. K. George (a.k.a. Alfred J. Rieber)

THE KIEV KILLINGS, by G. K. George (a.k.a. Alfred J. Rieber)

Also by New Academia Publishing

Russian History/Culture

REAL AND PHANTOM PAINS: An Anthology of New Russian Drama compiled and edited by John Freedman

CULTURAL CABARET: Russian and American Essays for Richard Stites, David Goldfrank and Pavel Lyssakov, eds.

THE RUSSIAN NANNY: Real and Imagined, by Steven A. Grant

PASSION AND PERCEPTION: Essays on Russian Culture, by Richard Stites

MOSCOW BELIEVES IN TEARS: Russians and Their Movies, by Louis Menashe

RUSSIAN FUTURISM: A History, by Vladimir Markov

WORDS IN REVOLUTION: Russian Futurist Manifestoes 1912-1928 A. Lawton and H. Eagle, eds., trs.

IMAGING RUSSIA 2000: Film and Facts, by Anna Lawton

BEFORE THE FALL: Soviet Cinema in the Gorbachev Years, by Anna Lawton

WE'RE FROM JAZZ: Festschrift in Honor of Nicholas V. Galichenko Megan Swift and Serhy Yekelchyk, eds.

PETS OF THE GREAT DICTATORS and other Works, by Sabrina P. Ramet

NEW PERSPECTIVES ON SOVIETIZATION IN CENTRAL AND EASTERN EUROPE AFTER WORLD WAR II, Balázs Apor, Péter Apor and E. A. Rees, eds.

THE INNER ADVERSARY: The Struggle against Philistinism as the Moral Mission of the Russian Intelligentsia, by Timo Vihavainen

RED ATTACK WHITE RESISTANCE, by Peter Kenez

RED ADVANCE WHITE DEFEAT, by Peter Kenez

Memoirs

THROUGH DARK DAYS AND WHITE NIGHTS: Four Decades Observing a Changing Russia, by Naomi F. Collins

JOURNEYS THROUGH VANISHING WORLDS, by Abraham Brumberg

See inside the book at www.newacademia.com

Siberian Secrets

by G. K. George

ILLUSTRATIONS by

George O. Linabury

NEW ACADEMIA PUBLISHING | SCARITH

Washington, DC

New Academia Publishing, 2014

Printed in the United States of America

Library of Congress Control Number: 2014948133
ISBN 978-0-9906939-0-1 paperback (alk. paper)

 An imprint of new Academia Publishing
P.O. Box 27420, Washington, DC 20038-7420

 www.newacademia.com
info@newacademia.com

To the memory of my parents
Albertina George Rieber
John J. Rieber

Prologue

Ivan Fedorovich felt a storm was brewing, although the sky, a dome of deep blue like a Ming dynasty bowl that had once been his many years before, gave no sign. He knew such things because he had special knowledge, and he had lived long enough in Siberia to be aware of changes in the air around him. He had never been wrong about the storms, just slightly off in his timing. Recently, his senses had grown more acute. His predictions about the actions of men had likewise become more reliable over the years. The wrong predictions had been made decades ago, before he had the special knowledge. In his youth at Moscow University, Professor Pavlov had told him that his head was the perfect barometer. He was tempted to reply: well, then professor, with people like me around why did they ever invent the instrument? I and those like me could perform the same function; our gift, if you wanted to call pain a gift, might have kept some poor devils gainfully employed, those who were dismissed from service because they suffered from dizziness or headaches. But he kept such subversive thoughts to himself. Perhaps that had been the start of it, the seed from which the special knowledge had come. He had been prepared for it.

Of course, it was one thing to be prepared and another to be fulfilled. If he hadn't been exiled to the far reaches of Siberia, he would never have been fulfilled. Now his predictions were almost always right and not just about the weather. His rational voice still argued, although more weakly as time went on, that his predictions came true because whenever he predicted something, it would happen because people would believe it had to happen and they would make it happen. He always wanted to write something for the Ethnographic Society about it, but repressed the idea as too dangerous. He was lucky to have been able to leave the farthest reaches of Siberia and come back almost to Russia, to a milder climate, though still severe enough.

He estimated he had a couple of hours before the downpour turned the garden into a quagmire. He hated to write when the headaches threatened; one was already lurking along the left side of his face. And why the left side? An ideological reminder of his radical past? He smiled to himself.

He sat down at the rude wooden table, carved by his own hands, and smoothed out a sheet of foolscap. He examined the nib of his pen. It was wearing down. Had he really put it to such hard use? He wrote "Chapter 26" on the top of the page and in the lower left hand corner he wrote a number. Why did he wish to recall such unpleasant subjects when the sky was tinted the color of a Ming dynasty vase? Better to take a walk, or see how the tomatoes were faring. They might be knocked down if the storm was a strong one, as he felt it would be. Anything but the misery of the subject he had set himself to write about. He put down his pen and left the cabin. He stood for a while staring above the line of birch and larch trees at the eastern horizon. That's where the monster would come from. He sighed and went back into his cabin, rummaged in the bin by the oven and pulled out a burlap sack. He carried it into the garden and filled it with the juiciest tomatoes he could find. As he picked each one, he would sniff it, fully understanding the danger. The pungent aroma would trigger an avalanche of memories; that was part of "the gift." They would be etched so sharply and flit by so rapidly through his mind that he would lose his bearings. No matter! Let the sensations take over. He stood still for a while—how long he would not remember. The memories suddenly receded. He held a tomato up to the Ming sky; a lovely contrast! Of course, he would have liked to have let them ripen on the vine for another day or two. In their present state, they were just a shade under done.

By the time he had finished and glanced up again, a ragged gray line had appeared on the horizon. He cursed it idly and went inside. He put up shutters against both windows and dropped the wooden bar across the cabin door. Suddenly, it was very dark. He lit a candle and lay down on the bed to wait out the storm. A visitor would have noticed immediately that there was no icon in the corner. Ivan Fedorovich did not believe in God or not in the Christian God.

He must have dozed until he heard the groans of his cabin protesting against the gusts of wind that struck with mounting violence. He reached down in an automatic gesture to comfort Kiki, his dog or whatever she was, only to remember with a pang how she had died a week before and how he had buried her just inside the garden fence. He knew it was the loneliness of an exile living by choice far from the nearest village that made him sentimental about the animal. But she was a beauty, snow white with a single gray stripe running round her neck. She had turned up as though she had dropped from the sky, the same kind of intense blue sky that now heralded the storm. He found her one morning squatting at the door, her tongue lolling, her bushy tail undulating in an almost sensuous way. He inquired of the village elder, did she belong to someone? The elder stared at her for a long time before shaking his head. Ivan Fedorovich had never owned a dog and didn't know what to call her. After a while he noticed how she loved to play tricks on him, harmless, playful little tricks like hiding one of his slippers or pulling off his bedclothes in the middle of the night, but never when it was cold, and always gently and stealthily so that he didn't notice until morning. She was always clean, keeping her fur glossy by licking it almost like a cat, or going off to bathe in the nearby stream, or in winter rolling in the snow and shaking herself until she was shimmering. Other times she would disappear completely, though how that was possible in the open steppe he could not imagine. It was as though she were playing hide and seek. He realized he could not call her back because he had never given her a name, just called her 'dog.'

When he related all this to the peasant elder who visited him once a week, the man shook his head again; "she's a regular Kikimora." Ivan Fedorovich remembered what they had told him in the East. Kikimora in Siberian folklore was a mischief making demon married to the forest spirit or *leshii*. "Some o' them they can wreck a household. But yours, it seems, has taken kindly to you. She'll protect you, but you mustn't ever scold her," the elder said.

So Ivan Fedorovich had taken to calling her Kiki. She continued to play harmless tricks Then one night when he had fallen asleep with the candle lit, she wakened him with fierce barking, pulling on his trouser leg. The flames had just caught the curtain and he was able to dose it with a bucket of water he kept as a fire precaution just as the peasants had taught him. No red cock for him; that's what the peasants called the dreaded fire that could burn a cabin, a man and his family in a flash. Now he missed her. Her protection was gone.

It was a sturdy cabin but the storm was fierce. Though the logs fit well, they had not been recently tarred. The rising wind blew in strongly and snuffed out his candle. He thought about just lying in the dark, but then decided to light another candle. He got up and went to the carved wooden cabinet hanging over the stove next to his drum when he heard the pounding on the door. For a moment he could not imagine any living thing having been caught by the storm in his remote corner of the world. A wild animal? No, the pounding was too regular, too insistent like the throbbing in his head. For one frantic moment he thought it might be Kiki coming back. Was he going insane? He groped his way to the door, un-barred it and threw it open. A vision of Hell greeted him.

Chapter One

The two Russians and the two Americans had been making good time along the Siberian post road until the storm threatened to overtake them just beyond the boundary marker between Perm and Tobolsk Provinces that announced the beginning of Siberia. Riding in the lead *tarantas*, a heavy four wheeled carriage drawn by three horses, Inspector Vasili Vasilievich Vasiliev of the Moscow City Police leaned forward, peering at the gray clouds massing ominously in the east before turning to his companion, Sergeant Serov.

"We should tell the driver to pull up the hood or we'll be drenched before we get to the next post station. Wouldn't do to have our guests washed away."

He jerked his head back in the direction of the second *tarantas* following close behind. He noticed that the two men were also leaning forward, perhaps because they were not accustomed to the hard seats, or they may also have seen the signs of the approaching storm. He wasn't really worried about them. Although they were Americans, one of them, the journalist, George Kennan, had spent some time in Siberia a few years before and had even written a book about his adventures. The other man, a Mr. Frost, was an artist who had accompanied him to sketch the landscape and perhaps other things as well. A novice to Russian life, he was having a harder time of adjusting, but he never complained which endeared him to Vasiliev. For the past few *versts*, the Great Siberian Road had been deeply rutted and they were badly shaken up. Could American stagecoaches be any more uncomfortable?

Transport wagons

Vasiliev signaled to them that they would stop at the next post station. Before they arrived the wind was already gusting as they passed a bivouac of transport wagons drawn up on the side of the highway under a stand of pines. The leader must be an optimist, Vasiliev thought, to expect shelter from the downpour that was sure to come. Just as the storm broke, the post station came into sight, a collection of weather worn wooden buildings crouching close to the ground as if expecting another beating from the forces of nature.

The Americans were laughing as they ducked their heads to enter the log cabin of the post master.

Vasiliev smiled in return. "What's so amusing?" he spoke to them in their own language, a slightly accented 'Oxford English', as Kennan playfully called it.

"I was just thinking that we might meet Pushkin's *kapitanskaya dochka* or rather her grand daughter." Kennan spoke back to him in slightly accented Russian which Vasiliev playfully called the 'Baltic Baron's Russian.'

"Alas," said Vasiliev, "in all my travel around this country I have never caught sight of a beautiful post master's daughter or her granddaughter."

"Just bad luck, my friend."

"You're still a bit romantic about Russia, aren't you, Mr. Kennan? I'm afraid you may be cured of that charming trait by the end of this trip."

"Perhaps. But if I do I'll just think of you and Sergeant Serov and my feelings will return."

"Always the master of compliments."

"Easy when the subject is so attractive."

"You see what I mean!"

Vasiliev laughed displaying his crooked teeth; it was part of his charm in Kennan's eyes, the crooked teeth in the face of an aristocrat. Well, they did say he was the illegitimate son of a Count and a peasant girl.

The post master did indeed have a daughter, but she was not the ideal subject for a poet's verse. She served the four travelers a frugal meal, for which they paid an exorbitant sum, and she prepared a rude bed of damp straw mattresses for each, but none of them was tempted to share it with her. They agreed to rise early in hopes the rain would stop during the night and that the road might be passable in the morning. As it turned out, a muddy track was not the main problem facing them in the light of morning.

Vasiliev was sleeping less and dreaming more the closer they came to the Tiumen Forwarding Prison. He was desperately afraid of what he would find there. His last word of Irina had come to him in a roundabout way a year ago. She was working in the prison hospital with 'Letchik', the Healer as they called him, her comrade from the revolutionary organization known as Land and Liberty, or the Partition of the Land. They had been arrested shortly after the assassination of Alexander II although they had not been involved in the conspiracy. Vasiliev replayed in his head a hundred times their last meeting in a Moscow prison. They had cut her beautiful auburn hair and dressed her in drab prison garb, but they could not strip her of her noble bearing, her calm demeanor, her tough realism. "No romantic gestures," she had told him. She would survive Siberia, she assured him, until he obtained a pardon.

He stared into the darkness and silently cursed the departmental heads, the court notables, the Tsar himself for their stubborn refusal to pardon her. And what was her crime? She had done everything in her power to help him try to prevent the assassination of the Tsar, supplying him with details of the plot until the very last moment. "The white handkerchief will be the signal," she had let him know, and she was right; he was there—he saw it flutter at the end of the Quay—but he had failed to save the tsar. Irina, the "Swan" was her conspiratorial name, had been condemned for revolutionary propaganda, for belonging to an organization that preached socialism to an uncomprehending peasantry. They should have given her a medal. Now he was determined to free her.

He dozed off but suddenly woke with a start. Another bad dream? He could not recall anything more than feeling a vague disquiet. His mouth was dry. He got up quietly and thought about going out to the pump for a drink of water but was afraid of wakening everyone. Instead he stole into the kitchen. Perhaps there was some water left in the samovar. Anything would do. His hand closed around a jug. He sniffed the contents. A strange bitter-sweet odor. What the Hell, it couldn't be poison. He took a deep draught. Was it fermented? He couldn't tell, having never tasted anything quite like it. He replaced the jug and crept back to his bed.

He heard Frost mutter in his sleep; Kennan was breathing quietly. What strange company for his mission. They had no idea of what he had in mind. They knew nothing of Irina or of her exploits. Somehow, Kennan had received permission to examine the Siberian exile system. The authorities must have been mad. What did they think he was going to write after he saw the real conditions that had been hidden from the world? But Vasiliev no longer cared about Russia's reputation. Somewhere along the line he had lost his faith in the possibility of reform without being converted to a new faith, that of revolution. Now he thought only of helping or saving the good people. The idea of justice seemed too abstract, too remote, unattainable. He wondered why it had taken him so long to reach that simple conclusion.

His assignment to accompany the Americans had been engineered by his old friend Ivan, known in Petersburg society as the Iron Colonel for his ability to survival wars, bureaucratic in-fighting – and worse. He was a force to be reckoned with, though he had lost some of his influence. Still loyal, even though the new Tsar, Alexander III, had disappointed him by turning away from reform. What Ivan did not know was that he, Vasiliev, no longer felt himself to be a defender of the realm. There was only one thing that was driving him now: to find and free Irina. After that, he was not sure. But his thoughts were beginning to move in a direction that surprised him. A year ago, he mused, he could not have imagined it. Was he really prepared to flee the country with her? If so, that's where Kennan would be useful. Vasiliev laughed to himself. Unsuspecting Kennan! Little did he know what might be in store for him. There would have to be a careful plan. It was no joke to cover two thousand miles of rough terrain, mostly wilderness just to arrive on the shores of the Pacific. And then what?

He had been talking to Kennan about the United States. Kennan called it the land of opportunity. Well, he had heard those words applied to Siberia too. He was more interested in how the law worked. Kennan was a mine of information. Vasiliev was convinced he could get the American to help him reach the United States once he had crossed the Mongolian frontier. They might be leaving the country as fugitives. "No romantic gestures," Irina had said. Well, this one would stagger even her imagination...if it worked.

He turned again, trying to make as little sound as possible. But Serov lying next to him was alert to his every move and interpreted his every sigh. It had always been that way, ever since their childhood together in the village, he the son of a count, Serov a serf boy, freed only in 1861. That was the other problem that worried Vasiliev. What would Serov choose to do? Go with them or stay behind? It was unthinkable to Vasiliev that Serov would break the tie that had bound them together; yet it was equally unthinkable that he would leave Russia. These thoughts tormented him until he fell into a light sleep toward dawn.

Chapter Two

Irina lay on her cot, unable to sleep, staring up at the ceiling somewhere above her in the darkness. She dreaded the nightmares. They seemed to lie concealed just below the level of her conscious mind as if gathering strength for a sudden furious outbreak when she least expected it. The worst visions recalled the terrible incident that had begun her transformation from a naive and docile daughter of a strict but benevolent father, a colonel in the Guards, to a revolutionary despised and expelled from the family nest of gentlefolk. She could still envision down to the last detail the birching of a young recruit under her father's command. She could hear the crack of the birches as they fell on his bare back, raising welts and leaving bloody wounds. She could still hear her father's stentorian voice, unaccustomed to her ears. "Seven times seventy," he barked as he sat astride his bay mare, slapping his riding crop against his boot. She had ridden out to visit him, a surprise on an early day in spring and stumbled upon this outrage. She had fled in horror.

Later there had been the arguments, the shouting on both sides, his savage dismissal of her protest as infantile sentimentalism. Her mother shrank from intervening, and over the next few days the quarrel mounted in intensity. Finally, he had ordered her out of the house to stay with her grandmother until she came to her senses. But she surprised the family and perhaps herself as well by coming to a different kind of sensibility.

She had good reason now to recall how her fellow student, already a revolutionary with the appropriate nickname of Magician, had stoked and guided her anger into a realization that her father represented something bigger than a cruel officer. Rather he became for her the embodiment of a vicious system where corporal punishment had been outlawed but soldiers like real criminals were forced to run the gauntlet a thousand times until, if they survived, their bodies and spirits were broken. Magician introduced her to the literature of the Land and Liberty Party, an underground movement of which she had been unaware, with its non-violent program of preaching socialism to the peasants. She wondered occasionally whether she had not just moved from one kind of naivete to another. But she took strength from the comradeship of the small group to which she had belonged. At least their ideals were pure. She had even nurtured hopes that she could use her old family ties to influence some of the reform minded bureaucrats. Another case of naivete? The alternative was worse; the revolutionaries had split. A terrorist wing had carried out the assassination of the tsar who had liberated the serfs and in whom high hopes were placed for further reforms. She had played her small role in the attempt to prevent it; that had brought her together with Vasya again, her girlhood idol and love. But they failed. Magician was killed, the group broken up and only she and Letchik survived to be sent unjustly into exile. What else could she have done?

It was six months since she had left the Forwarding Prison and a year since she had begun her exile. She often wondered how she had survived the thousand mile trip, trudging on foot from Moscow across the Urals and through much of western Siberia to Tiumen. The convoy included common criminals as well as politicals like herself and Letchik. Most of the prisoners were manacled, but she had managed to have hers removed by bribing the head of the convoy. Having a little money enabled her to buy food from the peasants in the villages through which they passed. Letchik was less fortunate, though he too managed half way along the Great Siberian Track to get rid of his ten pound manacles. When the head of the convoy dislocated his shoulder falling from his horse, Letchik had come forward to reset it. As a reward he too had been freed from the cursed manacles which produced terrible sores on the ankles that never healed. It was the first time he realized that his medical training might spare them both the ordeals faced by the other prisoners.

She stroked the back of her left hand, feeling the roughness of her fingers, as she mechanically peeled off the dead skin until she became aware of what she was doing. She quickly balled her fingers into a fist which she pressed against her side. How terrible the first days in Tiumen had been! She remembered her relief when Letchik came to tell her that they would be working together in the dispensary. Dispensary! That was the word he used as if to conceal its raw and primitive appearance. Only later did he mention that he had insisted on her being his assistant, refusing otherwise to become 'the physician in residence' as he ironically called himself. He patiently taught her how to care for the sick. Strange how she began to feel needed, almost indispensible for the first time in her life. And the director of the prison, that strange man, Krasin, had assigned them each a small room, hardly more than a cupboard, so that they could have some relief from the exhausting work of caring for his prisoners. A humane policeman? Or was it that he just wanted to cut the number of deaths in his official reports to St. Petersburg? "Well," she thought, "I mustn't be too harsh, though God knows there wasn't much concern for the humane treatment of anyone in Siberia."

Letchik had been a good comrade in the short time she knew him in the underground. But now they were like brother and sister. She had gotten back the brother she lost in the war. Slowly her fists unclenched. Had she dosed off? Another memory came to her, of Vasya standing mute and distraught on the veranda of her home, holding in his hands her brother's sword. As took it from him, she had felt his reluctance to give it up. Gazing into his eyes, she had yearned for him to embrace her. But the sword came between them. He had bowed and left. Where was he now, her beloved Vasya?

An urgent rapping at her door startled her; a voice rasped, "Irina Nikolaevna, quick, they're calling for you,"

She vaulted out of bed. Shocked by the contact with icy floor, she hurriedly threw on her clothes, shivering all the time, and rushed into the dispensary. She never cased to be stunned by the noxious odors that assailed her. She bent over the feverish form of an ex-officer who had been exiled fifteen years earlier for having been part of a conspiracy in the Imperial Nikolaevskii Military Academy. He had long suffered from malaria but recently was wasting away from some internal ailment that Letchik could not diagnose.

"I am here, Fedor Grigorovich," she whispered, mopping his brow with a fresh towel. In the semi-darkness, his eyes seemed to glitter with an inner light.

"How is it, you are always here?" his attempt to smile turned into a grimace.

"Listen carefully, my dear," he coughed harshly and for a moment caught his breath. "Ah, but you always listen carefully. So, listen very carefully. We have been watching you for some time, you and that wonder-working young orderly. And we have heard about you. No need to tell you how. But the others are now gone. I am speaking to you as the last in line here. It will break unless you take it up. Yes, the last in line and it is breaking."

He coughed softly again, drew a long breath and continued. "So, we trust you. No mean thing these days." He paused again. "Long ago we began to construct a network. Good people like yourself. A network of information. To collect and disseminate. Information about this system, the exile system. Statistics, stories, a full picture. We decided, the last few of us, that the time has come to get it out to the world. But we need couriers. You see where I am going. I fear I haven't enough breath to tell you everything. Foolish man, I waited too late. Did I think I was able to delay death by waiting?"

Irina dipped the towel in a cup of water and brushed it against his lips.

"Always anticipating the needs of the dying! I would ask God to bless you, but I don't think He is listening any more." He coughed again, violently. Irina held his shoulders until he stopped. He took a deep breath and went on in a cracked voice.

"So, you will understand the rest. We still have a contact in town. Shpelev, the pharmacist. You probably know him. You will identify yourself by reciting to him the first few lines of Pushkin's 'Deep in the Siberian Mine'. You know it? He is our repository. But there is more. The real blow against the regime is being prepared in Omsk. Somehow you must get there."

Irina had to bend low over him, her ear almost pressed against his mouth.

"The contact there is Pestov…he…has…more, a big affair…tell him Lermontov sent you…" Fedor Grigorovich fell silent.

Suddenly Letchik was beside her, a hypodermic needle in hand.

"He is dying," said Irina, "let him go in peace." Letchik turned away. Irina kept mopping Fedor Grigorovich's brow as his breathing faded until she could not hear it any more.

Chapter Three

It seemed to Vasiliev that he had just fallen asleep when he felt Serov gently shaking his shoulder.

"There's been some trouble, Vasili Vasilievich. The elder is waitin' for you in the stables." They left the cabin without waking the Americans. The elder was standing next to the post master under the eaves of the stables. He was holding the reins of a shaggy pony. The rain had stopped much earlier, but water was still dripping from the eaves of the buildings. Ragged clouds were scurrying across the sky as if in a hurry to catch up with the thunderheads that were rapidly vanishing in the West. Vasiliev was surprised that the elder looked so young, a sturdy fellow with flaxen hair and a short, neatly trimmed light colored beard. His eyes were pale blue. He had the picture book looks of a Great Russian peasant. His alert look marked him off as a figure of authority. He was wearing a belted, short jacket that looked almost new and highly polished boots spattered with mud. A real *Sibiriak*, more confident and self-assured than the peasant elders Vasiliev was used to seeing in the central provinces.

The elder inclined his head in Vasiliev's direction, no obsequious bow for him. He introduced himself as Dmitri Ivanovich.

"Sorry to disturb you, Your Honor. The master here told me you was stoppin' here by chance. Luck thing too. I was countin' on a good long ride to the telegrapher at Chernaia griaz. Now you've saved me the trouble." His voice was deep and somber. The post master looked frightened. The elder paused as if expecting this police officer to respond. Vasiliev said nothing, waiting for the man to explain. He never asked questions unless it was absolutely necessary. People would say what they had to say in their own time. He had learned that much playing in the village with Serov years before.

The elder cleared his throat. "There's been a killin'." Vasiliev nodded his head. The elder seemed surprised. Still no reaction. This was a cool one, he thought.

"I've just ridden' over to tell 'em." Vasiliev knew that "them" meant the authorities.

"Now you can tell me," Vasiliev broke his silence.

The elder shook his head and began to stroke his beard, then let his hand drop. He looked Vasiliev straight in the eye.

"It was Ivan Fedorovich that got killed. Looks like an ax split him in half. I was goin' over to his place, 'caus it's Thursday, the first Thursday this month. It's always been my day to visit him. Was a political, you know, but served his term. A learned man. Well, what do they expect? He's been there for as long as anybody can remember. Came before my daddy was elder. I was a small boy. For us, he's always been there. Greets us with tea and sometimes a small cake he's made. Tells the peasants how to grow better. Some listen, most don't. The ones that listen get better crops. Now he's dead. Will you come and see about it?"

Vasiliev asked how far the telegraph station was. He wrote out a message handed it to Serov. "I've asked for a return message. When it comes, read it and make any arrangements that have to be made before you ride back. I'll wait for you here." Serov picked out a fresh mount and saddled her himself.

"You can take me over there now." Vasiliev turned to the post master and for a moment he felt slightly dizzy. "You have another good mount?"

The door opened and Kennan stuck his head out. "What's going on?" he asked. Vasiliev said only there was some trouble. He had to ride out. Maybe the road would be too muddy for the tarantas. "But you'll see. Whatever happens, I'll catch up with you, if not in Tiumen than beyond. Serov and I can ride fast, so don't worry if you don't see us for a few days."

"What trouble?" asked Kennan.

"Peasant problems," said Vasiliev. "I'll tell you how it turns out."

He went back into the cabin and finished dressing, took out his revolver and checked the chamber. Serov was gone by the time he emerged. Kennan was shaving and bid him goodbye.

Vasiliev and the elder took off cross country avoiding the track which was still deep in mud. They rode silently side by side. By the time they arrived at Ivan Fedorovich's cabin, the sun was blazing and the air felt fresh. The sky had that peculiar washed out color that follows a violent storm as though it had been drained of its vitality. Was that the reason, Vasiliev wondered, that he found it difficult to focus on the horizon? It seemed to approach and recede in waves.

The cabin stood alone in a large garden with a row of apple and pear trees shaded by a grove of larches and birches. At a distance Vasiliev could already see the flowers in the window box. As he drew nearer he could distinguish different varieties; fuchsias and oleanders predominated. The windows of the cabin overlooking the garden gave out an iridescent glow which he had noticed before, a peculiar effect of the glass made in the region. As they drew nearer the windows seemed to be flashing a signal as the rays of the sun struck them at an oblique angle.

Abruptly, the elder lifted his face to the sky and slowed his pony to walk. Vasiliev followed his gaze. The elder, shading his eyes, seemed to be staring straight into the sun. Vasiliev saw something black hovering at the edge of the corona, something resembling a bird, but he could not make out which kind. He thought it strange that he had not seen it before, flying towards them. It floated very high above them in an empty sky, moving in and out of the bright center of the sun. The elder bowed his head, reined in and made a sign of the cross.

"Go on ahead, Your Honor. I want no more part in this."

Vasiliev glanced at him in astonishment. The man appeared to have undergone a transformation. He had lost all vestige of a sturdy Sibiriak. He looked almost frightened.

"Wait here then," Vasiliev said and rode on, keeping his eyes fixed on the cabin. As he rounded the edge of the house, he immediately noticed the door was wide open. He dismounted, drew his revolver and cautiously approached. He peered in the windows, but the translucent glass only reflected the giant larch tree that towered over the cabin. He eased his way toward the open door when he heard the buzz of insects. He called out, "Ivan Fedorovich? It's the police. I'm coming in." But he hardly expected Ivan Fedorovich to answer. What he saw he also had not expected, and it turned his stomach.

The figure of a man, no longer young, lay stretched out just inside the threshold. His head and the upper part of his torso had been cleaved in half by what must have been a powerful blow. The man's arms were extended to both sides of his body, giving the impression of a splintered cross. Vasiliev had witnessed ax killings before, but never anything like this. The insects were all over the bloody mass. They rose from the ruin of the man's face and began to swarm around Vasiliev. He waved them angrily away. He holstered his revolver and knelt down to examine the man's wounds, covering his mouth with his face cloth, fighting down his nausea. Blood was spattered on the far wall and had formed a huge pool around the dead man's head. Then he saw it; another horror rocked him back on his heels. The man's trousers had been ripped open and his genitals had been sliced away. The dismembered parts were nowhere in sight. The stump had bled some, but the man must have been dead, thought Vasiliev, when the wound was inflicted. What kind of a madman...

Suddenly, he was aware of a whirring noise over his head. He ducked and half turned, automatically reaching for his revolver. A flapping close to him, brushing the crest of his hair. The next instant he felt as though he were being pressed to the earth. He slumped against the doorpost, the sun momentarily blinding him. Then he was plunged into darkness. He heard, or did he see something perched astride the dead body? A hoarse cry pierced his ear, the image blurred. Another whirring, and whatever it was had gone. The buzzing of the insects had stopped; they too had disappeared. Vasiliev felt dazed. He staggered to his feet and reeled into the full sun. He searched the sky, clutching the butt of his revolver but he saw nothing. The wisps of clouds were gone, the pale blue dome was empty. He thought he might have seen a speck at the center of the sun. But the glare was too strong and he turned to look for the elder. Only a few moments could have passed since he left the elder, sitting astride his pony, his head lowered. Vasiliev ran to the back of the cabin and scanned the broad sweep of the grasslands. The sharp line of the horizon was broken only by the copse of trees. There was no human figure to be seen.

Vasiliev wiped his face on his sleeve. He felt his whole body had been drenched in sweat. He found the pump in the garden, stripped off his shirt, and doused himself with the pure, fresh water. Was it the cold water of the deep well or something else that made him shiver? Something reminded him of the contents of the jug, a bitter-sweet odor. He shook his head.[1] Never mind, he would figure it out. He sat down on a wooden bench, surveying the neatly planted rows of tomato plants devastated by the storm; and beyond them flower beds knocked about but recovering quickly, their bent heads straightening up heroically, even as he watched. He picked up a bright red tomato from the muddy soil, washed it off and bit into it; the juice came running down his chin. He had rarely tasted anything as good. It almost seemed life-giving like the water. Silly thought, he rebuked himself. All right, there was a murder to solve. As for the other matter, that would have to wait.

He looked around him. Everything was peaceful, or better, he thought, at peace. Why did he want to put it that way? Because he felt that way, curiously at peace. He sat for a long time, letting his mind wander idly. Good moments in life flashed by; hunting with Borka in the foothills of the Urals, forgetting that he too was dead killed by the Gendarmes while trying to hunt down the men who were planning to kill the Tsar; dinners with Ivan at the Strelnya; the quiet times with Irina and her brother, lying on their backs on freshly mown hay before her brother too had gone off to war with him and not come back. Then as if his mind was nothing more than a lantern slide projector, new, darker images flashed by, images of the dead. A long shadow from the larch tree had fallen on him. He started, recalling where he was and what he was supposed to do. Had so much time passed? He glanced at his watch. Impossible! Several hours had gone by since he rode up with the elder. He felt his pulse. Strong, regular. For a moment he feared he might have suffered an attack of some sort. Not that, no. Yet how to explain what had happened or what he had imagined. The horror of the mutilated body, the strange reaction of the elder, the blinding sun and…What else could he think of that was rational? And then there was the strange reverie, like a nightmare in broad daylight.

Reluctantly, he went back to the open door. He half expected the body to have disappeared. But things had not gone that far. He entered the cabin, carefully stepping over the pool of blood. He found a long canvas coat hanging from a nail in the wall and spread it over the body. Then he surveyed the interior of the cabin. A desk, homemade by the looks of it with a number of quills, an ink stand carefully aligned. He opened the two desk drawers. Empty. Odd, there were no papers of any sort. What did the man write on? Above the desk, two shelves of well-worn books crowded together, arranged by subject. The poetry caught his eye right away, and he nodded in approval. He ran his fingers over the leather bindings of old editions, Pushkin and Lermontov, newer ones of Fet and Nekrasov. A man of taste. But judging by the second row of books on horticulture, also a practical man. He read the titles: a monograph on seeds; another on grafting fruit trees; texts on pharmacology, Planchon's *Traité practique de la détermination des drogues simples*; and Pereira's *Elements of material medica*. Over the stove hung a carved wooden cabinet and a small drum, apparently made of deer skin. He opened the drawers. Candles, a half empty box of matches and a flint; underneath a passport. He flipped through the pages and read Ivan Fedorovich Golitsyn, enrolled in the nobility of Perm *gubernia*. That was right across the provincial boundary line. Born 1798, entered the army in 1813, just in time to take part in the last campaign against Napoleon. Retired from service in 1823, a major. Promotion was fast in those days as casualties were heavy among the officer ranks. Exiled in 1826 for participation in the conspiracy of December 1825 against His Imperial Majesty, Nicholas Pavlovich. So a Decembrist after all! The original place of exile was a village near Irkutsk out by Lake Baikal. In 1856 the new Tsar Alexander II had pardoned the Decembrists, but not allowed all of them to return to European Russia. So Ivan Fedorovich obviously came as close as he could, and probably near his ancestral home somewhere in Perm *guberniia*. Vasiliev slipped the passport into his pocket.

Vasiliev wondered whether his political past had anything to do with the elder's weekly visits and always on a Thursday. But then he dismissed the idea. This had nothing to do with surveillance or politics of any sort. The man was eighty-two years old; surely no longer a threat to the regime. Perhaps the elder was just a kindly man, bringing provisions or checking on Ivan Fedorovich's health? He would find out soon enough.

He continued his search. Of course, something could always be hidden in plain view. He thought of Poe's purloined letter. Nothing so simple here. The desk top was empty, swept clean except for the writing materials. If nothing hidden in plain view then perhaps secreted. Before examining the books more closely, he thought, let's try something else just as obvious, the existence of a secret compartment. He pulled out the drawers again and measured their length. Sure enough one was shorter than the others. He reached underneath and found the trigger mechanism that opened the compartment. A bag of gold coins fell out. They dated from the reign of Alexander I and were in mint condition. That ruled out robbery as a motive, although Vasiliev had never given much consideration to that possibility. The place did not even seem to have been searched, let alone ransacked. But let's not be too hasty, he thought. He kept coming back to the fact that there was no paper yet plenty of writing materials.

He crossed into the pantry and found the usual dry provisions, bags of flour and sugar, salt and smaller containers filled with pepper and aromatic spices. Along one shelf a line of tightly sealed glass jars was arranged, a few filled with preserves: berries, apples and pears; probably what was left from last year's harvest. Others were empty, waiting for their turn to be filled when the fall fruits ripened. A fishing rod stood in the corner and on a shelf a box of home made flies. Vasiliev examined them one by one; the man knew what he was doing. No gun, of course; not for an exile even a political who had served out his sentence. Or else he had been pardoned but forbidden from living in either of the two capitals— Moscow or St. Petersburg— even if he wanted to. Vasiliev went into the bedroom. An old fashioned bedstead, ornately carved, dating from the end of the last century. Was he able to salvage this from his estate which presumably had been confiscated, its contents sold? It was a beautiful piece. Vasiliev ran his fingers over the carving. He recognized the style, just like the furniture in his father's bedroom. He wondered for an instant if their paths had ever crossed. After all, the Golitsyns were a high-born family with princes scattered all over the social landscape. Vasiliev tried to remember. Had papa ever mentioned a Golitsyn? Perhaps in passing, but the name of Ivan Fedorovich did not register. Now it was too late to ask. The old Count had died, his heart attack probably induced by the false news from Kiev that his only son and heir, Vasili, albeit a bastard son, had been killed by terrorists.

Vasiliev wondered too whether Ivan Fedorovich had any close relatives left. Would anyone care at this point to learn that an old man who had been in exile for almost six decades had been brutally killed?

The bed was made, but Ivan Fedorovich had left the impression of his living body on the bedclothes. He must have been lying down during the storm, but not ready to turn in for the night. Then he had gotten up to go to the door. What had summoned him and persuaded him to open up in the midst of a storm? Vasiliev went back into the entry way and examined the drawn up bar that had secured the door. No forced entry. Ivan Fedorovich had opened the door of his own free will to admit his assassin. Had he know who it was? Or was he just responding to an urgent knocking, a mute appeal for help? Someone lost in the storm? It seemed strange to Vasiliev either way.

He searched the cabin thoroughly but found nothing else until, on impulse, he opened the oven. In the ashes of a recent made fire, there were a few scraps of charred paper. They crumbled at his touch. With a wooden spoon he carefully lifted out what remained and laid the pieces gently on the desk. He could just make out a few words giving a hint of what had been the subject of the writing. One was the word "prison" although the end was so burned it might have been "prisoner;" the other was "night soil." Too refined, this Ivan Fedorovich, Vasiliev mused, to write "shit." Prison and shit, a pungent combination, thought Vasiliev ruefully. But perhaps this was a fragment of a letter and not the writing of Ivan Fedorovich. But if he had correspondents, then surely he would have paper to write letters in return. And the writing materials were all there, neatly arranged on the desk. Vasiliev tucked the fragment carefully into his wallet.

There was nothing else to do but notify the local justice of the peace and be on his way. He had been counting on the elder to help. Where the devil had the man disappeared to? And what the hell was I doing when he did? Vasiliev asked himself. Dreaming of strange apparitions? He spat out a mother curse. The coarse speech of a peasant came back to him with force when he felt angry with himself.

Chapter Four

Vasiliev closed up the cabin. He hesitated about burying the body, but decided the justice of the peace would want to examine it. At least the insects were gone and the wild animals couldn't get in. As he rode back to the post master's station, he kept turning in the saddle, looking for a sign of the elder. Every once in a while, he would glance at the sky, less eagerly to see whatever had been hovering over them. The sun had passed its zenith as if tired out from its hard work of drying up the track and the fields. It was still light when he saw the outlines of the station.

Postal *telega*

As soon as he dismounted, he knew that the Americans had left and Serov had not returned. The station master was standing on the threshold of his cabin. He had just seen off a postal *telega* heading east; the imperial mail took precedence over everyone no matter how high his rank.

The station master was hoping no other travelers would show up. He didn't have a fresh mount for an impatient officer who could make life miserable if the man had to sit around the station, drinking huge quantities of tea and waiting until one of the horses was rested and ready to go. Vasiliev felt weary, but he was impatient to find out as much as he could about Ivan Fedorovich from the station master. He wondered why this was important to him. An inner voice warned him not to give in to his habitual curiosity. After all he would be leaving as soon as fresh horses were available, and then it wouldn't matter any more.

The station master's daughter served them steaming bowls of soup, a home made brew which was very tasty. She kept glancing at Vasiliev with a half-expectant look.

"That's the last of the fennel," she said, wiping the table again, although it looked spotless to Vasiliev.

"I think I saw some in Ivan Fedorovich's garden," he said.

"Yes, he was the only one who could grow it. He used to send us over the seeds and I'd mash them. But..."she broke off and ran into the kitchen holding her apron up to her face.

"He was greatly loved in these parts," said the station master breaking off a chunk of black bread and dipping it in his soup. "They say he was an aristocrat and used to own many souls, but freed them before he entered the army in 1813. He was only fifteen then, but already master of his estates. He fought against the Emperor of the French in the last campaigns. Then came the misfortunes." The station master sighed deeply and for the next few minutes devoted himself to his soup.

When the dishes had been cleared, Vasiliev offered a cigar and the station master made much of lighting up and puffing, savoring the rich tobacco.

"Ah! Vasili Vasilievich, I haven't tasted Turkish tobacco like this since the war."

"Which war was that?" asked Vasiliev.

"Why in the Crimea. It was the French again, and this time they had the English with them, all backing the Turks. Shameful, Christians like that together with the *basurmany*, heathens. They say there were some Italians too, from Piedmont, but I never saw any."

"Well, mine was a later war, '77 and '78. We fought the Turks too."

"Gave them a real hiding, you did. But you know, you didn't have the French and English on your backs as well."

"True enough. So here we are, you and I and Ivan Fedorovich, all having fought for the motherland. You wonder though sometimes, what it got us."

The station master nodded. "Well, we was defending the Orthodox way."

"Tell me, my friend, was Ivan Fedorovich *pravoslavnyi*, a believer in the holy Orthodox faith? I saw no icons in his cabin."

"I'd be telling you an untruth to say he was. He had nothing good to say about our local *popy*, our village priests. Thought they were sucking the blood of the peasants. Well, who knows…but I'll say one thing. He really hated the sectarians. No argument there."

"Sectarians? I didn't know there were any in the area."

"Oh yes, about twenty versts due north, some of them, *skoptsy*, castrates you know. Not a pleasant people."

"Well, that all depends…" Vasiliev let his sentence hang.

"Not with these, it don't *depend* as you say." The station master seemed content to let the matter drop. Vasiliev was not.

"Funny, I used to see a lot of them in Bucharest, you know in the Principalities, during the war. They were coach drivers. Left Russia because of the persecution. Round, puffy faces, beardless like the Turkish eunuchs. Harmless bunch."

"Skoptsy eh? Well, I tell you I'd like to see a little persecution, as you call it, around here. They're crazy people. Why I've heard tales…" he got up and peered into the kitchen where the clashing of pots and pans had ceased. "Go finish up, Daria, and get to bed. We'll be getting up at dawn tomorrow." She came in, curtsied awkwardly to Vasiliev and rushed off blushing.

"You were about to tell me some tales."

"Well, all right, seeing as you have this idea of them being peaceful and all. Around here they still believe that their leader, what's his name?" The station master rubbed his head. "Selivanov, that's it. They still believe he's alive though he died years ago. Wandering the earth, they say. And you know why? Get this. He has to wander the earth until they finish their work of recruiting. Some recruiting eh? And you can't imagine how many they've got to recruit. Can't guess. Eh?"

Vasiliev shook his head, though he had a pretty good idea.

"One hundred and forty-four thousand! And who's counting? I ask."

The station master sat back in his chair with a look of satisfaction on his face. He repeated the number several times.

"Sounds like an army corps," said Vasiliev.

The station master broke into peals of laughter, growing red in the face. Then he suddenly became sober.

"Well, they're not content to persuade people. They'll go hunting. They've paid poor people to have their private parts cut off, and gotten children in their hands as well. Always counting toward one hundred and forty four thousand."

"So Ivan Fedorovich had a special dislike for them."

"And rightly so, I say. Once he told me that he went over to a neighboring village to hear them preach. It was disgusting he said. They had this clever way, you see. They wouldn't come right out and tell you what to do. Oh no! They'd say things like 'Here is my sword you shall chop the deadwood and sins off many trees.' So, we all know what that means."

Vasiliev thought of the mutilated body of Ivan Fedorovich. He wondered whether cutting off a dead man's private parts counted toward the magic number of one hundred and forty-four thousand.

Chapter Five

The next morning Vasiliev had just finished a breakfast of buckwheat oats and strong coffee, when he heard the voice of the station master calling from outside. The sun was still slouching on the horizon behind a veil of haze as though it was unwilling to rise. And why should it? mused Vasiliev. Just to witness a man split in two?

He came out on the porch and saw the station master pointing to the west. In the distance he could make out a figure on horseback leading two ponies behind him. He knew in an instant that it was Serov. He was moving at a slow pace. As he came closer, Vasiliev saw the tiredness in his eyes, the sweat and dust streaking his face, and guessed that he had been riding most of the night. He was astride the post horse; but why the two ponies?

Serov gave his mock salute and dismounted. His first words were to the station master. "Sorry uncle for wearing out your good horse. It was a long ride. I never drove him, you ought to know. Fed him well; but I expect you'll want to rest 'im for a while." The station master shrugged and led the mount into the stables.

"For the love of God, Vasili Vasilievich, give us a strong tea. As it gives me strength, I'll tell you all."

They sat across from one another, the samovar gurgling between them. Daria, unasked, had brought Serov fresh rolls and a pot of a deep brown honey. Serov winked at her in appreciation. Vasiliev told his part of the story, only omitting what he could not easily explain. He kept trying to banish the hallucination, or whatever it was, from his mind. Only once before had anything remotely like it happened to him. When he was a boy, Foma had led him deep into the forest to witness of ceremony of the Jumpers, another of the radical sects that the Holy Synod had condemned as pernicious. What he saw had haunted his dreams for months. But this was different; he was not a witness but a participant. If he couldn't get rid of the feeling of foreboding, at least he could bring it under control.

As he spoke to Serov, he decided that his mind had played a trick on him. Or rather, he thought in a flash of inspiration, it had subconsciously woven together a number of unrelated impressions, reversing its normal way of functioning. He was always fitting together bits and pieces, as Serov like to call them, fragments of a larger picture in order to solve a crime. In this case, the bits and pieces were so bizarre and fell around him, as it were, so suddenly and unexpectedly, that his rational way of puzzling things out was by passed or short circuited. The elder's strange behavior – what did he want no part of? Then the strange object in the sky, the curious effect of the sunlight reflected off the windows made of local glass, the shocking sight of the slaughtered old man, the insects and the fluttering sound; what was it, a bird of prey? It had all come together mixed with whatever lay deeply buried in his memory. Yes, he thought as he watched Serov react to his story; that was the explanation he would settle for, until something better occurred to him.

Serov normally accompanied a Vasiliev monologue with a string of grunts, whistles and sighs, but with his mouth full of fresh rolls generously smeared with honey, he was forced to rely on an ocular repertoire, rolling his eyes, blinking and squinting, lifting his eyebrows and shutting his eyes altogether. Serov's performances never failed to amuse Vasiliev in spite of himself. Wasn't that Serov's aim? Somehow to make the terrible more prosaic or even to reduce it to absurdity, to save them both from sinking into the morass of human iniquity. Or perhaps, Vasiliev sometimes wondered, he was simply attributing the effect to the intention.

Serov scooped up the crumbs, licked the honey off his fingers and swallowed the last mouthful of tea. He folded his arms as a sign that he was ready. He slyly apologized that his story couldn't compare with Vasiliev's; but it had its own devilish twist. He drew a telegram out of his tunic pocket, handed it to Vasiliev, and studied his face for his first reaction. He was rewarded with a deep frown.

"I'd had the feelin' you'd not be pleased," said Serov.

Vasiliev restrained the impulse to crumple it in his fist. The message read:

> Request you assume full authority over case of murdered exile. Our resources strained to limit. Cannot, repeat, cannot spare experienced officer. Local justice of peace seriously ill. Minister of Justice informed concurs. (Signed), Deputy Governor-General of West Siberia.
>
> A.A. Orlov

"So! The Ministry of Interior assigns me to accompany Kennan and Frost and the Ministry of Justice lifts me up and puts me down in an entirely different place. And what do I do now? Send more telegrams? Get involved in a bureaucratic tangle?"

"Well, there's always ways of sayin' the message strayed along the way, you know, got blown off by a sudden puff o' wind, or rained on so that you couldn't read it. There's always ways."

Vasiliev thought for a moment of the unburied body of the murdered old exile, the ferocity of the killing, the beautiful garden and the fuchsias in the window box. He thought of how the justice of the peace would get well and blame the local peasants because he couldn't think of anything else to do.

"Shit," he said. And Serov knew that meant Vasiliev would take the case

Serov nodded his approval, though he hadn't been asked for his opinion.

"I bought the two ponies from a Tatar at the horse fair," Serov said.

Vasiliev stared at him. "You knew I'd take the case, you rascal. Where did you get the money?"

"My orders, you remember Vasili Vasiliev? I was to make arrangements. That's what you told me to do. Well, that's what I did."

"Did I order you? I thought I never ordered you to do anything. It was just a suggestion. Well, never mind let's see whether your Tatar horse dealer cheated you or not. We'll ride out to the cabin. I've an idea about how to go about this. You might even approve."

As they rode Vasiliev thought about his decision to stay. It was not just the pull of duty and serving justice. If they cut and ran, as Serov had suggested they might, he would jeopardize all his plans to free Irina. He didn't even know where she was now being held. A rumor had reached him that she had been sent farther east, away from Tiumen, which was after all just a transit prison. Siberia was vast and the chances of finding her quickly were slim. On an official mission, he could move around freely. He couldn't afford to break away yet. Perhaps he and Serov would get this case solved quickly. But his intuition told him this was not to be.

The station master came back and led the ponies away. Once they had been fed and watered, they were ready to go. Tough, these Siberian ponies. Still, they did not spur them on; a gentle canter was sufficient, Vasiliev thought. No immediate hurry at this point. Again he was proven wrong.

From a distance something appeared to be different. The ponies sensed it first and began to toss their heads. He couldn't tell what it was until they were within a few hundred meters of the cabin. He had to hold the reins tight to keep the pony from shying off to the right. Serov had dropped a couple of lengths behind, struggling to keep his mount under control. Just as Vasiliev made out what it was, he heard Serov's cry. Perhaps he had been prepared at some deep level for another such surprise; but the sight of it stunned him nonetheless. In an instant, he recovered and recognized it for what it was. A human form lay across a bed of thick branches high in one of the birch trees. For the first time, Vasiliev observed that the birch trees formed a semi-circle of sentinels around the clump of larches. Perched on the body was a gigantic bird, an eagle from all appearances. It was pecking away at the breast, pulling off strips of flesh. Serov drew up beside him, his hand fumbling at his holster. Vasiliev leaned over and gripped him firmly by the wrist.

"No," he said in a hoarse voice. Serov stared at him in wide-eyed horror, resisting the pressure for an instant, then giving in.

"My God," he gasped, "you're not..." but he choked on his words.

"Listen to me, Serov. This is something that I should have expected. I'll explain. Now quickly dismount. Lead the ponies around the corner of the cabin. Out of sight of this thing."

The door to the cabin stood wide open. The body of Ivan Fedorovich was gone. The blood on the wall and floor had been washed away. Everything else seemed in place except for the drum. It was no longer hanging on the wall.

"We're downwind now. The ponies shouldn't give us any trouble now." They looped the reins around a post. Vasiliev led Serov inside.

"Sit down and listen to me, carefully."

"What you and I have just seen, witnessed really, is the burial of a shaman." Vasiliev raised his hand to check Serov from bursting out wildly.

"I should have known this might happen from what I saw here in the cabin and outside in the trees."

"But you said this was a white man, a Golitsyn, a Russian noble. It can't be."

"Listen to me and I'll try to explain. Please don't interrupt me, not this time Sergeant." Serov's shoulders sagged.

"Ivan Fedorovich's passport tells us he was exiled to the Irkutsk region, a land inhabited by nomadic tribes. They are believers in a magic world, a world governed by their shamans."

"I know this," muttered Serov in spite of himself. Vasiliev ignored the remark.

"When I came into the cabin, I noticed there was no icon. Instead, a drum made of animal hide, probably a deer or reindeer, was hanging over the stove. This is a shaman's ritual object. I don't know the exact meaning. But he beats it as part of the ceremony of entering the other world. Let's stay with that. I should have immediately put two and two together — the place of exile, the drum. But the ferocity of the killing gave me a shock, I admit. That and the mutilation. Then there were the books, the books of a cultured, rational man. From poetry to horticulture. The drum was an anachronism. As I think back, I guess I just assumed it was a kind of souvenir of his exile. Perhaps I wanted to believe it was a momento of something good that had happened to him and he wanted to remember it. What I failed to see or rather to observe, as our English friend Holmes would put it, was the pattern of the trees. As we rode up just now, it jumped out at me — the nine larches surrounded by a semi-circle of birches, the shaman's sacred number of the sacred trees.They look to be ten years old, so he must have planted them. Then there was something else, something I didn't tell you, but should have."

Serov who had fixed his eyes on the floor, looked up. "Holdin' back on me again, Vasili Vasilievich," he joked feebly.

Vasiliev smiled his crooked smile for the first time since the murder. The old familiar Serov was trying for a comeback.

"Yes, always a mistake. I've got a good excuse. I'm still not sure that I know happened to me, or even that it really happened."

"Another mystery; they're pilin' up fast."

Vasiliev told him as best he could about the apparition or hallucination or whatever it was, although his memory of it kept fading as though someone was interfering, mixing in his mind.

Serov shook his head. "And what does it mean?"

"If I were a believer in this sort of thing I would call it a shamanist experience."

"But you're not."

"No," said Vasiliev with less conviction than he wished. "No, not a believer, but perhaps open to suggestion under exceptional circumstances."

Serov shook his head again. "Vasili Vasilevich, there's things I don't understand and want to understand; and things I don't understand and don't want to. You see what I'm sayin'."

Vasiliev recognized he had crossed a line with his faithful friend. Every once in a while, it would become clear to him that much as they shared the ways of the village, from Vasiliev's mother and their times together as children —wrestling in its dusty streets, wandering in the forest, catching frogs in the local ponds —a gap existed between them that could never be closed.

"What's going on outside in the tree is the ritual for the funeral of a shaman. His body is supposed to be laid out in the branches of a birch tree, left there to be picked apart by birds and animals. The more completely the body is devoured, the greater the shaman."

"And then?"

"I don't know what happens to the remains. But it's important that no one interrupt what's going on. You see, for believers, that would be a sacrilege. That's why I stopped you from shooting. What we have to find out now is whether Ivan Fedorovich was killed because he was a shaman, or because he fell victim to the skoptsy, or because he was writing something somebody didn't want him to finish."

Serov gave a slight shudder.

Chapter Six

Vasiliev could tell that Serov was uneasy about staying the night in the cabin of Ivan Fedorovich. He did not feel comfortable about it himself. They had brought a few of Daria's fresh roles in their saddlebags, and these along with a few ripe tomatoes from the garden served as their evening meal. While they ate Vasiliev outlined a plan they had often followed in the past. In the morning he would ride over to the nearest village, following the instructions of the station master, where he would find the elder, Dmitri Ivanovich, and enlist his help in tracking down the skoptsy. Serov would stay in the cabin. Serov was not happy about the plan; he worried about Vasiliev going to the skoptsy alone.

"I'll take my service revolver. No need to worry. I'm not sure yet whether to go as a police officer or in disguise. It will depend on what Dmitri Ivanovich tells me."

Serov made a show of protesting, but he knew the argument was lost before it began. "I'd be a happier man if you was to go as an officer. Less chance they'd try to convert you."

"Less chance, true. And less chance of finding out what we need to find out."

Vasiliev stretched out on the luxurious bed of Ivan Fedorovich. Serov climbed on the broad flat surface of the stove, as if he were back in his village, and quickly fell asleep. Vasiliev was restless. He couldn't get the image out of his mind of the eagle picking the remains of Ivan Fedorovich. Who lifted the body up there? Who knew that was the right thing to do for a shaman? The same person who had taken the drum? He wondered how a white man could become a shaman and still read Pushkin. But then there was always Pushkin's dark side to consider — "The Queen of Spades." The Decembrists were enlightened Europeans, but the court of Alexander I was a refuge for all kinds of mystics. The Emperor himself was drawn in. Vasiliev remembered his father telling him how the tsar had summoned Selivanov, the founder of the skoptsy sect, for an interview; called him out of an insane asylum where Alexander's father Paul had confined him; and how Selivanov had told the tsar that he should transform Russia into a skoptsy ship, a community of castrates. The tsar rejected the plan and sent Selivanov to a monastery to be reformed. Of course, all these mystics were Christians, of a sort. But still…

And then there were the strange rumors surrounding the death of the tsar. Everyone agreed it was unexpected, sudden, and strangely in the town of Taganrog in the far south, a thousand miles from the capital on the edge of the steppe. People said he really hadn't died; he wanted to escape the crushing burden of his duties as tsar; a substitute had been found and buried in his stead. The story went on that he disguised himself as a holy man and wandered throughout Russia; was arrested and beaten and came to Siberia. It was said he lived until 1864 as Fedor Kuzmich. They said too that Selivanov had never died.

Vasiliev slipped off into a light sleep, his head filled with dreams of men sharpening knives and chanting, "your flesh will kill you." He woke with a start. A faint light came through the window. Vasiliev swung his legs down on the floor and rubbed his eyes. It was only the dawn breaking. But there was something else, the neighing of the ponies. He took his revolver from under the pillow and walked barefoot to the door. Serov was snoring peacefully. He quietly lifted the bolt and eased open the door. The sky was covered with a uniformly gray mass of clouds except in the east where a yellowish band was spreading. He approached the ponies and stroked their muzzles, calming them.

A gentle breeze sprang up, rustling the leaves of the larches. In the far distance, the last call of the night jar sounded faintly. He tried to concentrate on the sounds of nature as if that's all they were. But something kept pressing him to check on the body of Ivan Fedorovich.

He turned the corner of the cabin and stared at the branches of the birch for a long time. The body of Ivan Fedorovich had disappeared. He thought for a moment of waking Serov; couldn't he rely on his own senses any more? He dismissed the thought and walked across the cool earth of the garden path until he was directly under the birches. He examined the trunk and saw the marks where the bark had been stripped. Human hands had done this, he told himself. He peered into the branches. Shreds of clothing hung down in a few places. A broken branch hung loosely.

He turned toward the cabin and saw another source of light. It was coming from the river. A fire was burning sending a column of grayish smoke to merge with the sky of the same color. It seemed to Vasiliev as if it were a ladder ascending, to what—heaven? His imagination was running away with him, he thought.

He untied the reins and vaulted on to his pony. He hadn't ridden bare back since he was a boy, but it still felt natural. He dug his bare heels into the pony's flank and galloped down to river. Flames shot up from a raft piled high with branches. The current was carrying it slowly toward a distant bend in the river. The fire would probably burn out before it got that far, leaving nothing but ashes floating downstream. He galloped along the banks trying to see whether there was a corpse or the remains of one lying on top of the burning branches. But the smoke obscured his vision. Was this Ivan Fedorovich's funeral barge? If so, then why another funeral? Or was this just a trick to lure him away from the cabin so they could commit another atrocious crime? He wheeled his mount, dug his bare heels into her flanks, and urged it to race back across the meadow. In the east the yellowish patch had expanded, and the edge of the sun was now visible as it pushed its way higher and higher. Vasiliev had the impression it was rising reluctantly, once again unwilling to greet the day. He quickly reproached himself. What was getting into his head, attributing an anthropomorphic spirit to natural forces? These crazy notions had to stop; he swore to himself.

When the cabin came into view, he felt a wave of relief. Nothing seemed amiss; Serov's pony was still attached to the post; the door was firmly closed. As he approached the cabin, Serov stepped into the yard, still half dressed.

"Vasili Vasilievich, what's happened? My God, I didn't know what to think, you being missin' like that."

Vasiliev took a moment to explain. Then they walked back to the sacred grove of birch and larch and began to search the ground for signs. They moved out in concentric circles but did not pick up a trail.

"Clever bastards, whoever they are. I'll be damned if we'll ride off aimlessly. I'm sorry you have to mount guard here, but I don't want anything else to happen to the place. Who knows? We ride away and come back to a burnt out cabin. Let's get some breakfast and then I'll be off. Just keep a good look out, and for God's sake don't open the door even to someone who claims to be the resurrected Christ."

Chapter Seven

As he rode past the fields of ripening wheat, orchards of apple and pear began to appear. Vasiliev thought again about the richness of the harvests and the poverty of the peasants. He went over the old arguments in his head. The land owners, the agronomists, the socialists all had their pet theories. He had his own. It came from the peasants in his mother's village where he had spent half his childhood. They took him for one of theirs; well he was born there, and they spoke freely when he was growing up before his father, the Count, had sent him off to the Page Corps to be educated as a proper nobleman. When he returned, of course, it was different. But he remembered the early years, the better years. It was the taxes, they said— that's what was killing them —and the redemption dues. They didn't get the land free after the emancipation of '61. "Why we'll be payin' for the next forty-nine years," they used to tell him. "And for the land that's ours. Yes, we plough it and sow it. That gives us the right!" It always finished with the same laments.

But he still couldn't figure out what had caused Irina to join the socialists. She had little contact with the peasants, brought up as she had been in a noble household. Was it just reading books? He didn't think so. She had a passionate nature. It must have been something else, something that happened on her father's estate. A mystery he had never solved. He was sure it had something to do with righting an injustice. But to preach revolution to the peasants! He thought that was a mistake; he had hopes that the tsar-liberator, as they called Alexander II, would push through the reform to its logical end, the distribution of land. But it didn't happen. Bad advisors? Fear of a noble fronde? He was beginning to have doubts even before the tsar was assassinated. But the heir to the throne, Alexander Alexandrovich, held out no hope to right the wrongs. In Petersburg his ministers were already undoing the modest progress which had been made. So what now? Perhaps it was he who was naïve, as naïve in his way as the young people who went out to the villages in the mad summer of '74 preaching socialism to the peasants. Naïve to think that the bureaucrats sitting in Piter could understand the countryside. He had enough trouble understanding it himself.

The sky had almost cleared by the time he arrived at the village. Only a gray smudge remained on the western horizon. Vasiliev immediately repressed the thought of what that really meant.

The broad earthen street was still drying out and the mud in the old ruts cut by the peasant carts made it slow going. The log cabins were old and weather beaten, the thatched roofs in need of repair. A few had collapsed and looked abandoned. He picked his way around a family of razor back hogs, basking in the sun. He would have said it was a gloomy place but for the profusion of flowers in the window boxes, just like at the house of Ivan Fedorovich, but here an even greater variety of them: geraniums and tea roses as well as oleanders and fuchsias. There was no one about; probably everybody was in the fields.

Then he spotted a woman's head behind a wattle fence and heard her berating a gaggle of geese who returned her compliments in force. He dismounted and walked his pony over to the fence. She didn't hear him approach and looked startled when he called out to her. Her hand went up to her mouth.

"Don't worry, auntie, I haven't come to take away your precious little ones. They're beauties all right, well taken care of by the looks of it." Vasiliev fell into his village accent which might have confused her coming from a man in uniform, but the look of alarm faded. She squinted up at him, a lined, toothless face. He smiled and let her have a look at his crooked teeth. That should reassure her, he mused.

"I'm not here to make any trouble for you good people. Just looking for an old friend, Dmitri Ivanovich, the elder, a man of God. Can you show me where he lives?"

Elder's house and barn

The gander who had been giving her an argument, turned his wrath on Vasiliev and began to cackle violently as he marched boldly toward him.

"Well he's better than a watchdog isn't he? Quite the protector." He glimpsed the approximation of a smile turn up the corners of the old woman's mouth.

She pointed wordlessly at a cabin diagonally across the street.

"The house with the big barn?"

She nodded. He thanked her, bowed and led his pony to the elder's place.

The shutters were elaborately carved with fantastic birds and flora, brightly painted in red and green. Vasiliev stood in the yard and called out.

There was a flutter at the window curtain and then the door opened. A young woman appeared, a long wooden spoon in her hand.

"Dmitri Ivanovich is in the fields."

"And where would that be?"

The woman looked at the sky, shading her eyes.

"You'll not find him easy like. Best wait here for him. He'll be back soon. Come in and rest yourself."

An old woman was lying on the strove and two young barefoot children stood in the doorway to the bedroom staring at him. The woman silently served him tea. In about half an hour Dmitri Ivanovich came in. He was startled but Vasiliev thought he covered it up nicely.

"We've got to talk after you've refreshed yourself."

They sat facing one another. The woman left them, carrying out a bundle of wash with the children running behind. The old woman lay motionless on the stove.

"Strange things have been happening, Dmitri Ivanovich. I'm asking for your help. The Governor-General has instructed me to find the killer of Ivan Fedorovich. I can do this quickly with your help. Or they'll send a detachment of Cossacks into the village to find out what has to be found out."

The elder sighed and folded his hands on the table.

"I'll do what I can. But I can't tell you everything there is to know because I don't know everything myself."

"So let's begin with what you do know."

The elder leaned forward as if he were about to convey some dark secrets. Instead he related how Ivan Fedorovich had come to their village many years before. He had just been a small boy, but heard tales of how he got the peasants to build him a house, paid them in real coin, "not those paper rubles other folks were always flingin' about." He would rent a horse and ride over to the station master and bring back bags of who knew what. Several carts appeared loaded with household goods. Afterwards, he planted the trees. A couple of wagons brought the seedlings. Men dressed like townspeople brought the seedlings. He hired the peasants again to plant them.

"Was very partic'lar like about that," said the elder, rubbing his hands together, "very partic'lar he was."

"Particular, in what way?"

The elder looked surprised. Wasn't it enough to know it was partic'lar?

He explained to Vasiliev just how they had to space the trees and plant them just so far apart and all the rest. His father would take him over and he would watch. Sometimes Ivan Fedorovich would give him a sweet.

"And then the strange things began," said the elder. He glanced at his wife who had come back with the children and was now molding dough at the stove. She shook her head, but the elder would not be deterred from telling his story. Vasiliev felt the strong urge to ask about the strange things, but true to his method of interrogation he waited for the elder to speak.

The elder got up and beckoned to Vasiliev to follow him out of the house and out of range of his wife's hearing. He leaned up against the wall of the cabin, reached into his pocket and took out a handful of sunflower seeds which he offered to Vasiliev before popping them into his mouth one by one. He spit out the hulls on the ground.

"Strange, I say. Well, well, Evdokia Vasil'vna's cow is fallen ill. She's givin' no milk. Evdokia's prayin' all the time, and 'specially on her saint's day, you know, March first, *Pliuschikha* we call it because the snow's begun to flatten out, *spliushchivat'sya* like. And she goes to the priest and he says it must be sorcery. But who's to know the sorcerer? And so she prays some more. And my papa goes over to the station master one mornin' and mentions it. And two days later Ivan Fedorovich shows up here, right at the gate of Evdokia Vasil'vna. It's right over there, you see. She's with her geese now. And he says 'Evdokia Vasil'vna, your cow's ailin'. I'll tell you what. Here, I'll buy her from you for silver ruble. Then I'll bring her back cured in a few days and claim my ruble back.' Evdokia thinks about it and agrees. She's got nothing to lose, you see. If the cow dies or doesn't come back she's got a silver ruble to buy a new one. But she'd rather have her old cow back."

The elder looked around and hunched his shoulders.

"And what happens next, do you think?"

"Ivan Fedorovich returns the cow and she gives milk again."

The elder started and almost choked on a sunflower seed.

"And how do you know that?" he gasped

"You just told me."

"Now, Your Honor, you're havin' me on."

"Not in the least. You told me it was a strange story. So the cow had to be cured, or else it wouldn't be strange."

The elder bent over laughing. "Oh, Your Honor, you're too clever for the likes of me."

"But one cured cow does not add up to strange things."

The elder snickered. He went on to tell Vasiliev another long story about how the priest got angry and the village folk began to take their woes to Ivan Fedorovich. And soon the word got round that he was a healer of sorts. But then one bright lad snuck over to Ivan Fedorovich's who was with a sick lamb and when he came back he was trembling with fear. He had seen something he wouldn't ever talk about. And there were others who claimed that Ivan Fedorovich was doing a strange ritual like thing in among his trees. The priest threatened to denounce him. But one night someone or several beat the priest and told him to keep his mouth shut. He had never done anything for the villagers except take their money for the sacraments and then spend it on drink. A week later he left the village and became a wanderer.

"Now, our new priest still drinks but he don't push his mug in where it shouldn't be," said the elder.

"I wonder if the old priest, you say he's wandering now, I wonder whether he's been seen in these parts lately."

"Not so anyone's noticed." The elder fell silent. He kept spitting out shells but seemed to have turned in on himself. Vasiliev knew he would say nothing more.

"And the new priest? Is he living nearby?" asked Vasiliev.

The elder silently walked into the street and pointed to a well-built cabin set somewhat back from the others with shutters painted green and a spacious garden in the back.

As Vasiliev turned away the elder shaded his eyes and looked up into the sky. Vasiliev followed his gaze but saw nothing except some irregular shaped clouds massing to the east.

Chapter Eight

The wife of the priest and a little boy— Vasiliev assumed it was her son—were working in the far corner of the garden, weeding or planting, he couldn't tell which. She must have heard the gate swing open, although it scarcely made a sound. She stood up and shielded her eyes to gaze at him. The little boy imitated her. They did not move or speak. It seemed to Vasiliev that they were expectant, perhaps even wary; he had the feeling a man in uniform was not welcome. A curious reaction coming from a priest's family. He remained by the gate, but no one moved for several minutes, as if posed for a *tableau vivant*. The spell was broken when the door to the cabin swung open and the priest, a tall well-built man with long silken black hair and a luxurious beard to match, hastened to greet him. The woman and the boy turned back to their task. Vasiliev noticed the boy had a slight limp.

"Father, I am Vasili Vasilievich Vasiliev of the Moscow Police, but on a mission to Siberia. I am investigating…" Vasiliev stopped in mid-sentence. The priest was staring at him intensely, and for a moment Vasiliev thought he caught a glimpse of a watchful look before a smile broke the spell. Even then, Vasiliev had the impression that he had just witnessed a great effort to veil a deeper feeling, perhaps even hostility. He brought himself up sharply. Perhaps it was just the angle of the sun as it struck the priest's face. What was it that was feeding his suspicious imagination these days?

Vasiliev estimated that the priest could not have been much older than forty, a contemporary then, but he looked younger, and unlike many priests of Vasiliev's acquaintance he was lean. His cassock could not disguise a powerful frame which seemed to belie the softness in his eyes, the full sensual lips.

"Ah," Vasiliev broke into his own introduction. "I see you already know who I am."

"You might be astonished when you find out just how well I know who you are."

Vasiliev prided himself on controlling his reactions, but he felt his face had given him away.

"You have the advantage..." he began but stopped again.

The priest raised his hand and for a moment Vasiliev thought he was about to bless him, but he simply waved Vasiliev into the garden.

"Let us sit here under the arbor. Perhaps when Marfa has finished her task she will bring us tea." Another surprise. "I am Father Iosifei."

Now the priest was simply beaming. For an instant, Vasiliev expected him to look up into the sky as well. Everyone was doing it these days. But he continued to stare at Vasiliev, as though he were silently interrogating him. Vasiliev felt slightly uncomfortable; this was after all his role and he was not accustomed to have somebody else assume it.

"I apologize for having confronted you with a small mystery, when you are already preoccupied with a more serious one. The fact that I knew you were in the village surely cannot come as a surprise. You understand better than most outsiders — or perhaps I should not even use that term in your case — how news travels among the peasantry. But our acquaintance dates back some years."

"I was not aware..."

But again the priest raised his hand in a gesture meant to convey a gentle but firm reproach. Vasiliev began to see the humor in the situation and decided to play along, but in his own way.

"I see your wife has finished her chore. She seems to be heading our way. You promised tea?"

The priest looked disconcerted, aware that his advantage had irrevocably slipped away.

"Marfa, please, prepare the samovar for our guest, Inspector Vasiliev."

The little boy clung to her skirts as she swept past them, barely acknowledging Vasiliev with something between a nod and a bow.

"Was it Moscow or Petersburg?" asked Vasiliev, smiling broadly to display his crooked teeth.

The priest adopted a more sober tone. "It was the capital. My parents had a house on the Moika Canal. My father had known your father at some point. We were invited to a recital at the Page Corps and you were performing with your fellow students. Do you still play the flute? You played something by Frederick the Great as I recall. A lovely evening. People were talking about your brilliant future. The Guards or an appointment at court. But of course, we did not meet in any formal sense. Later I learned that you had given up your prospects and perhaps the flute as well to join the police. I felt a kinship with you. I too had been expected to follow in my father's footsteps, but after a year at the University I felt a different calling and entered the Theological Academy. So here we are the children of noblemen sunk deeply in the remote provinces, serving the people. Not your average story."

The priest had turned his face toward the sky. At last, thought Vasiliev; but in this case it must be the heavenly hosts he's searching for. The priest's wife appeared with the samovar and silently placed it on the table in front of them. The priest thanked her in a formal way, but she did not acknowledge him and went back into the house.

"I fear Marfa was hoping for a different parish," he sighed, a bit theatrically thought Vasiliev. The tea had a strong aromatic perfume; it was entirely different from the cheap brick tea that he and the Americans had become used to on their travels along the Great Siberian Road.

"My parents, too, had hopes at first that I would enter a monastery, become an abbot, surely and possibly Metropolitan..." his voice trailed off. He sipped his tea. "Well, we still enjoy a few luxuries like this, thanks to my parents. I have no other vices."

Vasiliev was not eager to go down that path.

"Better to be a priest and a policeman than a revolutionary, like our dear departed Ivan Fedorovich, also a nobleman sunk deeply in the provinces."

"A tragic figure; a tragic end." The priest crossed himself.

Vasiliev had finally brought him to the point. But this one, he thought, will need questions set to him. Otherwise God only knows, quite literally in this case, where he would take us.

"I do have to ask you about him. His death was bizarre."

The priest looked up as if he had not heard the gory details. At least that was encouraging. When Vasiliev told him, the priest crossed himself and covered the lower part of his face with his hand, muttering what Vasiliev could only suspect were prayers.

"Did you know him well?"

"I saw him a few times in the village. But my parishioners often spoke of him. Apparently, he had a great quarrel with my predecessor, Father Porfiry, who accused him of sorcery. And other sins as well."

"What were those?"

"Stealing his flock."

"Because of his healing."

"Yes."

"I have a theory about that. You see I think all the shamanist rigmarole was just a form of disguise. Ivan Fedorovich was a rationalist. His healing came from books not rituals and incantations. I saw his library, books on pharmacology and anatomy. I think he created the illusion of being a healer with supernatural powers because it was the only way to convince the peasants to accept his remedies. Curious, isn't it? Our peasants believe in miracles but not in science. But science too is miraculous, or may appear to be so. Perhaps it is because they are kept in ignorance."

The priest nodded and shook his head as to despair of the failings of man.

"I fear you are right, Inspector. I was appalled at the ignorance of my teachers at the Academy. We should understand the laws of the natural world as God's work. I have suffered the consequences of that belief."

"Your exile, here?"

"Exile! Yes, I suppose you could call it that. I was denounced as a heretic. Fortunately, I had powerful protectors. But not powerful enough to prevent my being sent out here."

"Speaking of heresy, what can you tell me about the skoptsy."

"Truly heretical and pernicious. Here I agree with the hierarchy. Their practices are unnatural."

"Would they be capable, do you think, of this outrage?"

"You mean murder? This is hard to say;" the priest sought solace in the sky again.

"What about castration of the dead man?"

"It's not in their doctrine. Or at least never that I have heard of, and I made a special study of them at the Academy. Of course, there is always the possibility of some radical group splitting away from the main body. This is the curse of heresy."

"You've had no relations with them?"

"No."

"So the mutilation may have been a clumsy attempt to put the blame on them," Vasiliev muttered. The priest said nothing.

Suddenly, a thought struck Vasiliev. "Tell me how long you have been the parish priest in this village?"

"Ten years."

"And your predecessor, Father Porfiry, you said, has he ever been seen in the village since he wandered off?"

"Not to my knowledge. But I do not know everything that happens here. There were rumors..." His voice trailed off. The priest frowned for a moment and then he raised a finger to his lips, as if contemplating whether he should add something to what he had already said.

"There was the strange incident recently of the sacramental oil."

Vasiliev was tempted to ask if it had not performed its sacred function, but suppressed the remark as too Voltairian.

"Strange in what way?"

"A considerable quantity disappeared."

"What do you mean? Evaporated or stolen?"

A quick smile passed over the priest's lips.

"Disappeared is as far as I am prepared to go."

"No suspects? Corporeal or spiritual."

The priest chuckled. "Nicely put, Vasili Vasilievich, but you will not draw me out further. Let's see, we were talking about the struggle between magic and religion. I have won back some of the erring flock, but not all. You have to understand how powerful Ivan Fedorovich's 'magic' had become. He handed out all kinds of remedies. Some of the peasants swore by them. I tried one once, just to see the effect. It was a strange smelling, viscous liquid. I just sipped it, but I immediately felt disoriented. But the peasant who used it said it cured 'spiritual troubles.' I told him prayer would do him better."

Suddenly, it all became clear to Vasiliev: the drink in Daria's kitchen, the hallucinations at Ivan Fedorovich's. Thank God, he thought, one mystery solved.

"And Father Porfiry, what kind of a man was he, I mean physically?"

"When I knew him he was a ruin of a man. But he was still very strong. Taller even than you or me, powerful shoulders, though badly sagging. He had taken to drink. A sad story."

A silence fell between them. Were they thinking the same thoughts? Vasiliev wondered.

"Thank you, Father. If your parishioners confide in you and you do not have to break the confidence of the confessional, then please send a message to me at once."

The priest rose and assured him he would. He excused himself for having to hurry off to conduct a wedding in a neighboring village. Then he offered to supply Vasiliev with some fresh vegetables. Vasiliev was happy to accept. They went into the garden together.

"This is all Marfa's work, and the boy's," said the priest bending down to pick some ripened tomatoes.

Vasiliev surveyed the garden. There was a distinctive pattern to the plantings. He was suddenly aware that the garden was laid out in exactly the same way as that of Ivan Fedorovich.

The priest was saying something about the peppers when Vasiliev turned to look back at the cabin. He saw Marfa standing in the doorway pressing a cloth tightly against her mouth.

Chapter Nine

Vasiliev rode slowly down the village street until he saw a cart pick up Father Iosifei and bear him off to his wedding. Then he turned back to the priest's house, tied his horse to the wooden fence and knocked on the door. Marfa opened it almost immediately as if she had been waiting for him. Her face betrayed her fear.

"Father Iosifei has gone," she managed the words with difficulty, speaking so softly he could hardly hear her.

"I apologize for bothering you again. But I forgot to ask about something that has puzzled me." He too softened his voice and smiled at her.

She seemed to hesitate until he proposed walking in the garden. Then she spoke a few words over her shoulder and closed the door behind her.

"The elder seems to think that everyone in the village knew Ivan Fedorovich. It seems he was a good man even though ungodly. I understand he was an expert gardener." She walked beside him, silently, her eyes cast down.

Vasiliev stopped short and let his eyes wander over the garden as if seeing it for the first time.

"You know your plantings are arranged just like his. I can't think this is by chance."

Marfa's eyes glistened with tears. She rubbed them away with a clenched fist.

"You mustn't say anything," she whispered.

"There is nothing to say. Planting a garden is not a crime; not even a venal sin. But it suggests to me that you knew Ivan Fedorovich. He must have shared his knowledge with you, about plants, that is. Perhaps about other things as well. It's important for me to learn as much as I can about him. That way I can find and punish the person who murdered him, you understand?"

She nodded. They had reached the bench where he had sat with Father Iosifei. She sat down heavily. He stood next to her looking out at the garden. A cool breeze had sprung up and the leaves of the tomato plants rustled as if willing to convey otherwise undecipherable secrets.

"He knew a lot about plants and also about healing, they say."

Marfa looked up at him with real terror in her eyes.

"So...," Vasiliev decided to try out one of his bold guesses. He had always been an admirer of the American philosopher, Charles Peirce, whose theories on guessing he found congenial. He had met Peirce in London and they had compared notes on observing, guessing and detecting. Of course, guessing had to be guided. They agreed that this could only be done by a sort of intuitive method, knowledge acquired almost subconsciously but which could be brought to the surface by training the mind.

"I believe, Marfa, that Ivan Fedorovich had something to do with healing your boy. What was it, I wonder, rickets?"

He bent over and picked up a ripe tomato which had fallen off the vine. He held it up as if admiring its rich red color, trying every trick he knew to avoid the appearance of intimidating her. He sat down at the edge of the bench and kept turning the tomato in his hand. After a minute of silence he looked at her. She was obviously struggling to find the right words. At least, Vasiliev thought, she will not deny it; but would she tell him everything? He was willing to wait.

She began her story slowly, haltingly. The boy had begun to show symptoms of a serious illness in the winter of 1873 when he was two years old. They had just come to the village. It had been a hard winter; the sun seemed to hide behind layers of thick grey clouds; the cows had fallen ill and there was not enough milk for the children. They had prayed hard but the boy grew worse. One day their neighbor, Evdokia Vasilevna, told her that the lonely exile, Ivan Fedorovich, had cured her sick cow when all else had failed. The elder had told her about him. But she had to bring the cow to him; he would not come to the village to get it. She hinted that he had performed some strange rites which she refused to describe for fear of the wrath of God. She had told him about the sickness of children in the village. He asked her to have one of them brought to him. Marfa had secretly visited him with Sasha, their boy. He had led them into the grove; he wrapped Sasha in a great fur pelisse and ordered her to stay in his cabin. She heard a drum beating. Later, Sasha said that he was frightened at first but then the fear went away. Ivan Fedorovich had given her a small bottle. It contained a liquid that smelled of fish and told her to give some to Sasha every morning. He advised her to buy more milk from Evdokia Vasilevna. He said that when the sun came out, no matter how cold it was, Sasha must learn to play outside. Marfa was afraid he was a pagan sun worshipper. But she obeyed. In February the weather broke and Sasha was outside every day. Slowly he grew stronger. It was only the limp that remained. After that, she went back for more fish oil, but he insisted she bring Sasha for the rites. Sasha liked to go there. He liked to play with the dog. Ivan Fedorovich began to tell her how to plan a garden, what to grow, and supplied her with seeds.

"Father Iosifei, has fought paganism and heresy all his life," she ended her story, "and I was afraid he would forbid us to go...,"She broke off and lapsed into silence again. Vasiliev understood what her confession must have cost her.

"And others followed," Vasiliev said knowing how the gossip would travel.

She nodded. At that moment the cabin door swung open and Sasha came running out.

"Mama, mama," he cried, "Why do I need to stay inside. I need to be in the sun." Marfa held out her arms. Vasiliev stood up and thanked her. He caught a glance of Sasha's sunburned face as the boy limped past him.

As Vasiliev guided his horse down the muddy lane he saw Evdokia Vasilevna with a switch in her hand beating the flank of a razor backed sow in a vain effort to drive it through her gate. He rode up and told her to hold the gate open. He maneuvered his horse behind the pig and let loose a whoop that startled the animal that whirled to face him. The sight of the horseman bearing down on it encouraged the sow to seek safety in the yard and it trotted past Evdokia Vasilevna who heaped curses on its head. She nodded her thanks to Vasiliev. He leaned over in the saddle and asked her where the fire house was. She looked at him sharply, then pointed and said, "second cabin from the end."

There he found what he had expected. The ladder and the axes were missing from their proper places on the iron hooks driven into the wall of the fire hut.

Good God, he thought, the entire village or at least the female half must have been involved in disposing of the body! He wondered how these peasant women had learned about the shamanic platform burial. He had thought it was rare in any case. Perhaps Ivan Fedorovich had instructed them what to do in the event of his death? A strange man! That still did not answer the question of why two funerals. Nor did it answer the question of who had killed Ivan Fedorovich.

When Father Iosifei returned from the wedding, his mood had changed. Marfa had only seen him like this once before, and the sight of him made her tremble. It wasn't the payment for the service, she knew, for he had been given a gold ruble, which was unusual, even extraordinary. Was it the visit of the Inspector, or had he heard something about her visits to Ivan Fedorovich? She quietly warned Sasha to be silent and read his books in the corner under the window. Father Iosifei ate his meal without saying a word. Then he rose and walked down the street toward the small wooden church. When he came back an hour later, he said simply: "I must leave for a while. It will be a long trip, but when I come back things will be different." He asked her to prepare a travelling bag. He pocketed the gold ruble, kissed her on the forehead and solemnly blessed her and Sasha. Then he left. She heard a cart stopping outside their cabin and listened at the door until she could no longer hear the wheels turning in the distance.

Chapter Ten

Vasiliev forced himself to spend the next few days in Ivan Fedorovich's cabin. He half-anticipated half-feared a repetition of
the experience that continued to disturb him. But the sky remained
empty and the gentle breeze passing over the larches and birches
conveyed nothing more than the rustling of leaves. Vasiliev passed
the time looking through Ivan Fedorovich's books, sitting in the
garden and imagining the life of a lonely exile. At least Irina was
not alone. Curiously, he felt no jealousy toward Letchik, her comrade and companion, a young man who had sacrificed his passionate desire to become a doctor for some vague utopian goal. There
was something about the camaraderie among nihilists of both sexes
that enabled them, or at least some of them, to suspend, it seemed,
the normal sexual impulse. He could not say he understood this.

The last day before Serov returned, he was walking at dusk toward the far end of the garden where he had not been before; there
had been nothing to draw him there, no plantings just a pile of
stones. As he approached the fence he noticed for the first time that
the stones had been arranged in an orderly way to cover a small
mound of earth that appeared to have been recently dug up. The
mound reminded him of a grave site, perhaps – could it be – of a
child? He would have to ask the elder. As he stood examining it
the sun dipped toward the horizon and its rays struck the glass
windows at an acute angle sending out a flash of light. Until then
he had not noticed that the wind had picked up and the rustling of
the trees had grown louder. Vasiliev felt himself grow tense. He
automatically glanced at the sky, cloudless except for a few cotton

puffs that were moving rapidly now in his direction. He grasped the edge of the fence and gritted his teeth.

"I will not flinch," he growled. "I will master this." He fixed his eyes on the approaching clouds. They passed overhead and the wind died. The inner turbulence died with it. He relaxed his hold on the fence and without looking down again at the mound he walked slowly toward the cabin. He closed the door behind him and dropped the bar in place. He wiped the sweat from his brow, lay down on the bed, fully clothed and fell into a deep sleep.

In the morning he finished the last of Daria's rolls and was waiting in the garden when he saw a small figure approaching from the east. He recognized Serov's loping gait. This time he was determined to say nothing of what he had felt the previous day. He remembered Serov's words about things he did not understand and did not want to understand. So let it be, he thought. There was nothing supernatural about a pile of stones, a piercing ray of light, rustling leaves and scurrying clouds. No visions, no unearthly murmurs. It was entirely possible that a combination of natural forces could produce a supernatural effect on an imaginative mind. He thought how Ivan Fedorovich must have been exposed to these same effects, and had they convinced *him* that they had some deeper meaning? He saw the figure raise an arm in salute. It was always good to have Serov return from a mission.

"I believe that Daria had taken a liking to you, my friend. Now without committing yourself irrevocably, you might ask her about Ivan Fedorovich. I have the feeling that she might reveal more than her papa. After all he is an official of His Majesty's Postal Service. And will not say anything that might create problems for him. But perhaps I am wrong. In any case, I leave it up to you."

Serov winced at the word "irrevocably" not because it was unknown to him but because it conjured up marriage, a form of bondage in his eyes. Born into serfdom he had no desire to return to that status. Or so he repeatedly said. Vasiliev knew better. Over the years he learned from hints and a few experiences to respect Serov's image of the ideal woman. It came very close to resembling Irina except, of course, for the matter of her noble birth.

"And where would you be off too, Vasili Vasilievich, if I'd dare ask?"

"To seek salvation among the skoptsy," Vasiliev laughed.

"Yes," said Serov screwing up his eyes, "just don't commit yourself irrevocably-like."

Vasiliev had to admit it was a distinctive touch.

"I'll need to drop down a few steps in the social ladder. How about an old soldier, retired and wandering Holy Russia, begging his way in Christ's name? Perhaps you could ride over and borrow or buy some old clothes from the elder; make up an excuse. I'll be applying Foma's skills. By the time you're back, I'll be unrecognizable."

Every time Vasiliev donned a disguise he thought back to his childhood and the training old Foma, one of his father's former serfs, had given him. He had already noticed a few plants in Ivan Fedorovich's garden that might help him dye his skin and hair a darker color. The key to a disguise, as Foma had endlessly repeated, was to change the pattern of speech. Best to adopt a regional accent from a distant province, perhaps from the south, along the Black Sea Coast, a port city where a man would be likely to have picked up some foreignisms. Foma had once worked as a stevedore in Odessa and had learned the jargon which he taught to Vasiliev. Next, Foma instructed, it was important to adopt a few mannerisms, rubbing an arm as if tending to an old wound, holding the head a certain way as if thinking how to find the right word. Hands were a dead giveaway. Vasiliev's weren't callused, but he had been in enough fistfights to have acquired the knuckles of a boxer. A bit of dirt under the fingernails and rubbed into the seams of his palms would do for the time being. He just had to remember not to wash. He could draw on the great fund of folk adages and superstitions he had learned from the peasants in his mother's village where he had spent so many hours of his boyhood. He had thought of sending Serov, a real peasant, or even having both of them going together. But they could accomplish more separately. Besides, Vasiliev preferred to take the more dangerous assignment, ever since Serov had ended up in the hospital during the case of the murdered rabbi in Kiev. A pity he didn't have more time to grow his hair. But he always kept it longer than police regulations stipulated just in case he needed to look less like an inspector. Luckily he had a heavy beard. By the time he showed up among the skoptsy he would look scruffy enough.

* * *

The village where the skoptsy lived looked no different to Vasiliev than the other Siberian villages they had passed through. But the elder had said there was no mistaking the skoptsy cabin, and he was right. A high wooden fence surrounded the place and the windows were heavily shuttered. When Vasiliev pushed open the gate he was greeted by fierce barking from inside the cabin. As soon as he reached the porch, the door flew open revealing a short, thin man with a withered, yellow face wearing a worn soiled shirt and canvas trousers tied with a plaited rope. The barking reached a crescendo until the man turned and harshly ordered silence.

"Greetings, brother, why have you come?" The man peered at Vasiliev suspiciously, half blocking the doorway.

"I've come as a seeker," said Vasiliev screwing up his eyes and looking into the sky, which, he reflected, was getting to be a bad habit. "But I could do with a crust if you could spare it in Christ's name."

"We've more than a crust for a seeker. Come in and tell us your story."

Vasiliev exaggerated a limp as he crossed the threshold, ducking his head to enter. When he straightened up he was surprised again. The interior was sparsely furnished, but everything appeared to be neat and carefully arranged, giving an impression that an orderly mind had been at work. The man ordered the two snarling Siberian huskies to retreat to a corner where they slumped down and glared at the visitor. The *skopets* introduced himself simply as Kondraty. Vasiliev gave his own name, Vasili. He had read enough about the skoptsy in his study of the sectarians to know that they addressed one another simply by their given name.

Kondraty placed a bowl of *shchi,* cabbage soup, and a plate of *pelmeni*, Siberian dumplings, before him. Vasiliev noticed his soft, plump hands which seemed at odds with his withered face.

"So, a seeker," said Kondraty when Vasiliev had finished eating.

Vasiliev had his story ready. A soldier invalided out of the army after the Turkish War, a man who has seen too much killing and too many priests blessing the killers, even though the victims were *basurmany*, infidels. He had asked himself why men took pleasure in killing. He had no answers, but had heard that there were Christians who believed that man could be prevented from feeling the need to kill. He was searching for such men. He had been told about a great healer in these parts, but had not yet found him. Perhaps Kondraty could help him.

Kondraty listened intensely, his eyes fixed on Vasiliev whose gaze never wavered.

"A healer? So they say. Though his grace was pure, his flesh was insidious."

"Did you know this false prophet, then?"

"We met once many years ago. He told me he had come from the East. And had suffered much. That is true. But he had lost a chance for salvation." Kondraty's voice wavered as he spoke. "For this chance I would have given many years of my life."

"Had he met a true prophet, then?"

"He had met our Redeemer."

Vasiliev was not prepared for this. He cast his eyes down. "The Lord be merciful," he intoned. "And who might that be?"

"Ah, the question of a man who has not been initiated."

Vasiliev could see in his mind's eye the skopets sharpening his knife. He cast a glance at the huskies; they seemed eager to see what was coming next.

"Yes, well I seek guidance," Vasiliev said raising his eyes.

"He is known to the uninitiated as Kondraty Selivanov. You know his story?"

Vasiliev acknowledged that he had heard the name.

"A man who suffered much for his faith. Tortured and exiled to the Irkutsk region under Empress Ekaterina, the whore."

Well, thought Vasiliev, that could get you five years there yourself. But he was not here to protect the reputation of the imperial family, he reminded himself.

The skopets got up and went to the icon corner. Vasiliev watched him carefully, but he saw no knife. The man returned holding a small glass phial reverentially in his hand.

My greatest treasure," he said. "A few strands from the holy head of our Redeemer given by him during the years of his incarceration in the Evfimovsky monastery in Suzdal."

Vasiliev was not sure how he was supposed to act, but he crossed himself with two fingers like a good sectarian in hopes this would pass muster.

The skopets smiled and nodded his approval. He went on to tell Vasiliev how Selivanov had tried to convert Emperor Paul. The tsar had heard rumors that Selivanov might really be his father, Peter III, who had survived the plot to assassinate him by Ekaterina the whore and her lovers the Orlov brothers. Paul had asked him "are you my father?" Selivanov answered "I am not the father of sin, but if you accept my way then I will recognize you as my son."

Vasilliev had not heard all the details of the story but he recalled that Paul's response had been to send Selivanov to a madhouse. Paul's son, Alexander I, who took a peculiarly tolerant attitude toward holy men, freed him. When Selivanov began to "convert" junior Guards officers, Alexander confined him to the Evfimovsky monastery. The skopets had some unkind things to say of His Imperial Majesties, but quickly passed on to relate the extraordinary climax to his story. Selivanov had not died as was alleged in 1832 but escaped to Siberia where he continued to wander. That is when Ivan Fedorovich had met him.

Vasiliev sat silently for a few moments. He couldn't help wondering how Mr. George Kennan would react to all of this. Let's see, thought Vasiliev. How would I put it to him? Empress Ekaterina, known in the West as Catherine the Great had planned to assassinate her husband Peter III. But, hold your breath Mr. Kennan. The plot has miscarried and Peter has escaped to Siberia where he metamorphoses into Kondraty Selivanov, who also claims to be the Redeemer. So a double pretender, claiming to be the rightful tsar and the Saviour. He is arrested, tortured and exiled for his high crimes of political imposture and sacrilege. Somehow he gets back to St. Petersburg where he has a personal audience with the reigning emperor Paul, the alleged son of Peter III and Catherine. But, he would remind Kennan, there were rumors that his father was someone else. So Paul comes to hate his mother. Selivanov takes advantage of the rumor that he is Paul's true father and preaches castration to the tsar. For this he ends up in a madhouse from which he is rescued by Paul's son, tsar Alexander, who allows him to preach his bizarre faith until it threatens to undercut the army; pardon the pun, Mr. Kennan. He is then sent off to a monastery where he continues to receive the true believers. He allegedly dies. But instead he wafts off to Siberia where he meets the murdered man, a former Decembrist exiled for plotting against Alexander I. Now, Mr. Kennan, if you are still paying attention, just stretch your imagination a bit more. Not possible? Sure it is. Suppose our poor Ivan Fedorovich not only meets Selivanov posing as Peter III — who by the way would then be over hundred years old —but also another holy man, Ivan Kuzmich, also no spring chicken, who claims that he is really Alexander I. Poor Ivan Fedorovich now has to deal with two former tsars or pretenders, one of who claims to be the grandson of the other. No wonder he turned to shamanism.

The skopets was waiting for a response.

"These are strange tales," Vasiliev began. "Tell me, what did this false prophet, what was his name…?

"Ivan Fedorovich."

"…yes, Ivan Fedorovich, what did he learn from…the Redeemer?"

"He took away nothing to save his soul. What else is important?"

"True, but the encounter marked him, did it not? Or else he would not have mentioned it to you."

The skopets frowned and looked at Vasiliev suspiciously.

"Why would that interest you?"

"I was hoping he might have said something that would have at least planted the seed of faith in his stony heart."

The skopets shrugged. "There was nothing of that. He just enjoyed baiting me, like a trained bear."

"The devil! And how was that possible with your great faith?"

"Nonetheless, he tried in his clumsy way."

Vasiliev knew there was something important that the skopets did not want to reveal.

"May I?" he reached out for the phial.

The skopets hesitated then then handed it over.

"A sign of great favor," muttered Vasiliev. "No wonder idle teasing made no impression on you."

"Yes, idle teasing. He wanted me to believe that the Redeemer had confided some secrets. Stupid man. What secrets? "

"Surely nothing to do with the purity of faith." Vasiliev kept his eyes riveted on the phial.

"Of course not. Secular matters. I don't even remember. So insignificant. Something about the succession."

"As you say, nothing significant." Vasiliev asked more questions about the ceremony of induction and promised to return for further instruction.

As he left the two huskies rose from their places. They seemed disappointed at the outcome. As Vasiliev left he wondered what the skoptsy did with the "seals" they removed in the name of attaining salvation.

The skopets limply shook hands with Vasiliev on the threshold of his cabin

"Looks like another storm is coming up. You'll be drenched if you have far to walk."

"I'll be going back to the village."

"Then I advise you to take a short cut through the forest. Keep close to the stream and when it runs to the west, keep going straight ahead. That'll let you out just north of the village."

Vasiliev thanked him and walked slowly down the center of the street making sure to limp until he was out of sight. He had heard about the winter storms sweeping down from the Arctic Ocean, but these rain squalls seemed just as fierce. There seemed to be no way to predict them, although the elder had said something about Ivan Fedorovich's uncanny way of knowing when they would come.

The thick forest began abruptly at the edge of the cultivated fields, densely packed pines towered into the darkening sky like sentinels guarding— what? Vasiliev shook his head again. Pretty soon I'll be hallucinating about them too, moving along beside and behind me. The thought prompted him to turn and look back to the village, but at that angle the cabin of the skopets was hidden from view.

He followed the stream which meandered until it dropped off sharply, then, spilling over the rocks, it straightened out. Vasiliev bent over and scooped up a handfull of water. It was clean and cold. He stood for a moment and listened to the sounds of the forest. Some of the bird cries were not familiar to him, but the odor of resin and pine needles brought back vividly his memories of the hunts with Borka in the Urals. His missed his old companion on the annual bear hunt. So they never had brought down the great bear, Burya, 'the storm' they nicknamed him. Well, he was a Siberian bear so perhaps I'll meet up with him on his home ground. Vasiliev laughed to himself. That's a coincidence not even a novelist would tolerate. The only "storm" I'll meet is the one about to break over my head, he thought, and trudged ahead.

The light was fading fast. The stream no longer gleamed, but had turned almost black in color. A sudden sadness overcame him. He'd never found out who killed Borka, but he knew that the Gendarmes were responsible. Would he ever get rid of their dark shadow in his life? He felt that they would be standing in his way when he tried to free Irina. They had taken her away from him once. He would not let it happen again.

Suddenly, he caught sight of a movement in the brush and then a white blur flashed past him not more than a few meters away. He automatically ducked, fell to one knee and tugged at the revolver strapped to his leg. The white flash had vanished but in the same instant he felt a rush of air above his head and heard a dull thud as something struck the pine tree behind him. He turned and stared in astonishment at the handle of an ax, its blade buried deep into the trunk at the spot where his head had been. He fired rapidly into the darkness across the stream but there was nothing to be seen. He heard someone or something crashing through the undergrowth. He started in the direction of the sound just as a brilliant diagonal of lighting crossed the sky, illuminating the steam for an instant, followed by a terrific burst of thunder and a torrential downpour. A violent wind broke the protective cover of the pines, dumping cascades of water on his head.

Senseless to go after him—it — whatever. Vasiliev stopped in his tracks and retraced his steps. With some effort, he wrested the ax from the trunk of the pine. Nothing special about it, except perhaps the extremely keen edge of the blade. Not a woodsman's ax for sure. He was tempted to go back to the skopets and find out if he had set him up, wring the truth out of him if necessary. But what proof did he have? The man could have attacked him more easily in his cabin: two dogs, a sudden move. And was this the skopets way? But who else knew he was coming this way? Or was it a chance meeting? If so, then the attacker was either a maniac or was fearful of being discovered. Vasiliev hunkered down under a thick canopy of pine branches which gave him some protection once the gusts of wind had died down. The storm passed as quickly as it had come up. It was only then that Vasiliev remembered the white flash. What was it? If he hadn't ducked down…The rain had obliterated all signs; even his own footprints had been washed away.

For a moment he hesitated. Should he go back to get Serov? Impulsively he decided not. He thrashed about in the undergrowth until he found what he was looking for; no footprints in the muddy soil, but a few low hanging branches had been broken off. If he was lucky there would be more of them farther on. It proved easy enough to find them; his attacker had unwittingly blazed a trail for him to follow.

Chapter Eleven

The trail of broken branches ended abruptly. It was as if whoever had made it had vanished into thin air. Vasiliev was annoyed with himself for giving way to such thoughts. Darkness was closing in; he heard the sounds of the night starting up. He was about to give up when he spotted a thin plume of smoke rising just ahead of him. He moved toward it silently through the underbrush, taking care not to step on dry twigs, until he came to the edge of a small clearing where a rude lean-to backed up against a towering pine. He squatted on his heels and waited. In a while a shaggy figure came out of the woods, carrying an armful of branches. Vasiliev was relieved to see it was a man, after all, wild as he looked. What was wrong with his head that he could have conceived of anything else? The man glanced up at the sky as if he too were reading signs invisible to Vasiliev. He knelt down and began to feed the fire. Then he disappeared for a moment under the roof of the lean-to and re-emerged holding a long stick with what looked like a chunk of meat on the end. Vasiliev pondered his next move.

The man sat by the fire, turning the improvised spit. Vasiliev cursed his grumbling stomach as the aroma of roasted flesh drifted over to him. He smiled to himself. Nothing like the expectation of a good meal to distract a man. This was the best chance to take him by surprise. He circled around to the rear of the lean–to and edged along the side until he was within a few feet of the seated man. He had drawn his revolver, hoping he wouldn't have to use it. An idea suddenly occurred to him. Stupid not to have thought of it before.

Vasiliev knelt down and held his revolver at arms length.

"Father Porfiry," he said in a soft voice. "Do not turn around. A revolver is pointed at your head. I will use it."

The man let out a cry and dropped the stick with the half-eaten meat into the fire. It sizzled and the flame flared up for an instant. He leaped to his feet.

Vasiliev fired a warning shot into the fire. "Not another move. Or else you're a dead man."

The man groaned, pulling on his matted hair, and tottered as if he were about to fall.

"Down on your knees, Father, as if to pray."

The man fell to the ground, lowering his head and clasping his hands together in the posture of a penitent. By the light of the fire his glistening skin emitted a strange, yet somehow familiar odor

"Listen carefully! You tried to kill me in the forest. Perhaps you made a mistake. I'll forget it, if you tell me the truth about Ivan Fedorovich."

Vasiliev spoke rapidly. He had noticed that the fire was burning low; he worried that they might soon be plunged into darkness.

The man bent his head, pressing his faced against his tightly entwined fingers.

"I hope you are praying for forgiveness," said Vasiliev.

Father Porfiry raised his head. Vasiliev found himself staring into the eyes of a madman.

"Who are you?"

"It doesn't matter. Let's say a messenger from God."

"No, police."

So he wasn't that mad, thought Vasiliev.

"Ivan Fedorovich. Did you kill him?"

"He was a heretic."

"Who told you to do it?"

"The heavenly voices."

"In corporeal form. Tell me about the corporeal form."

"They came to me at night. I heard them whisper to me from the forest."

"What did they say?"

"Ivan Fedorovich had led my flock astray into the fires of damnation."

"Why did you violate your sacred vows and the commandments?"

"They said I was to be the instrument of divine vengeance."

"And you already hated Ivan Fedorovich, didn't you." It was not a question but an accusation. Father Porfiry was silent.

"After you carried out your mission, did you entered the devil's den?"

"No, no!"

"The voice told you only to destroy the tempter. Nothing else."

"Nothing else."

So, thought Vasiliev, someone else had searched the cabin and burned the papers.

Night was fast closing in, as if to hide the horror of the priest's confession. The outline of the figure on his knees merged with the gathering gloom. He was hardly visible when Vasiliev moved closer. He picked up a few branches the man had collected and tossed them on the dying embers. Suddenly, Father Porfiry leaped to his feet and uttered a piecing scream. Brushing past Vasiliev, he hurled himself on the fire, scorching his rags. Before Vasiliev could react, he was back on his feet, running toward the woods. Vasiliev leveled his revolver, aiming low at the figure glowing eerily in the dark. He shouted a warning and tightened his finger on the trigger. Before he could fire, Father Porfiry burst into flames, as if a heavenly fire had enveloped him. For an instant Vasiliev stood transfigured with horror at the sight. In the few seconds it took Vasiliev to reach him, Father Porfiry's body had been consumed by the blaze and turned into a smoldering, blackened corpse. Vasilliev recoiled, recalling what Father Iosifei had told him. My God, he thought, the man had been ignited by the stolen sacramental oil which he must have smeared all over his body.

Sickened, Vasiliev stumbled back along the trail to the post station. His thoughts were a jumble. He cursed himself for having failed to subdue the man. Another mutilated body! But this one was his responsibility. How could he have missed the odor of the oil? He tried to reassure himself. No one could have anticipated the act of self-immolation. But wait! What about the Old Believers who had burned themselves to death rather than accept arrest. That was two hundred years ago! Was it possible that in Siberia time did not have the same meaning as elsewhere in Russia? He shook his head; these are crazy ideas.

"Return to the real world, Vasiliev," he muttered half aloud, feeling the hatchet gripped tightly in his sweating hand. I have to notify the elder. Father Iosifei might give him a Christian burial. As he hurried through the woods, the stench of the burning corpse still in his nostrils, Vasiliev pondered Porfy's confession. If he had murdered Ivan Fedorovich darker mysteries remained unsolved. Had an unknown man or men speaking in 'heavenly voices' incited the half-mad priest to commit murder? Or did his inner voices finally drive him over the edge? There was still another alternative, thought Vasiliev ruefully. Could Father Porfiry have imagined the crime or been led to imagine it? What explained the mutilation? And who burned the papers? Vasiliev shook his head. By the time he reached Ivan Fedorovich's cabin, he had concluded that nothing was certain about this crime.

Chapter Twelve

The next morning Vasiliev woke up vaguely aware of disturbing dreams of fires and white flashes. Serov was sitting outside on a log bench, whittling as if he were bored and indifferent to his surroundings. Vasiliev knew better. Serov was good at containing his excitement whenever he had obtained valuable information, but little signs betrayed him. Vasiliev automatically catalogued them: head held inclined to the left and bobbing almost imperceptibly; a pose of complete absorption in a trivial task; a faint smile as he looked up to greet Vasiliev; in a word a game of exquisite deception designed to enhance the surprise he was about to spring. Vasiliev never considered exposing them for he had his own strategems for surprising Serov. Did his boyhood friend see through him just as clearly? Vasiliev never doubted it.

"Whittling is the past-time of an idle man. I hope you haven't been idle, Sergeant."

Serov moved to one side of the bench inviting Vasiliev to sit next to him.

"I'd be bettin' that you had an adventure, Vasili Vasilievich, while I was twiddlin' my thumbs here."

"I got more than I bargained for, that's for sure. The skopets was mild stuff. An unexpected encounter proved more exciting." Vasiliev related his adventure, as Serov insisted on calling it with the skopets and Father Porfiry.

"The skopets treated me to a lot of mumbo-jumbo, some of it I recognized as having been lifted from a *bylina*, a folk epos. Like 'Place a sword in my hand and I shall sever the serpent's head.'

Then he spouted a lot of talk about 'the small seal' and the 'big seal', giving me a chance to decide whether I wanted to cut off my balls and become an angel or the whole works and become an archangel. I assumed they have acquired the habit of speaking in metaphors to avoiding being denounced and persecuted. Not that the language is particularly hard to understand. One thing did horrify him: the idea of castrating a dead man. Seems that wouldn't count toward the 144,000 necessary souls to redeem the world. I think I believed him. But he might have been dissimulating.

"I learned that Ivan Fedorovich might have been privy to some secrets concerning the imperial succession. I couldn't get the man to say more. I wonder whether the secrets died with Ivan Fedorovich?" Vasiliev rubbed his chin.

"You can never be absolutely sure with these people. In the end, I made my excuses, exited as gracefully as I could, and promised to return for more instruction."

Then he quickly related the attack in the forest, without mentioning the white flash that saved his life. Why pile another mystery on all the others? But he solemnly related the immolation of Father Profiry. Serov shook his head in dismay.

"There are several possibilities, Sergeant. Right now, I'm tempted to think Father Porfiry was incited to kill Ivan Fedorovich by one or more men who then performed castration to throw suspicion on the skoptsy. What was their real purpose? Did the burned papers in the oven have something to do with it? Whatever their purpose it looks like some sharp people were involved."

Serov gave a full orchestral accompaniment, as was his custom, of whistles, snorts, tongue clucking and finger snapping. Vasiliev produced his crooked smile in appreciation.

"Now, tell me about your idle hours."

Serov was often disappointed when he thought to surprise Vasiliev and found that his friend had been there before or ahead of him. Once again, he thought, his story's a good 'un. But still I've got a good 'un too.

"You was right about Daria. I felt a bit uneasy about playin' up to her, but I did nothin' wrong. She just seems lonely here. Well, to be short," Serov coughed apologetically," it seems that our Ivan Fedorovich had what you might call a lively correspondence. But not so you'd notice. It gets a bit mysterious here, as it should right-fully be. You see the elder used to come visitin' on Thursday to Ivan Fedorovich like he says. And he picks up some letters and brings them over here. They're all addressed to stores and a few to what you might call centers of learnin'. That's how he gets his books and medicines. All above board. Now here's the interestin' part."

Vasiliev had been listening carefully while at the same time watching a figure riding in from the east. Serov too had noticed and paused as the man drew closer. They could tell by his headgear that he was a Cossack and he was coming at a full gallop, whipping his mount as if pursued by the devil. They both stood up. The station master, hearing the thunder of hooves, came out onto the veranda. Daria peered through the window.

"Not a courier," muttered the station master. "A Cossack and not sparing his horse either," he shook his head disapprovingly.

The rider reigned in enveloped in a cloud of dust. He swung out of the saddle and waved a paper at the station master. Then he saw the uniforms, saluted and turned to Vasiliev.

"You Honor, it's God's grace that brings you here. I thought I'd have to ride on. But now…"

The station master had seized the horse's bridle and was leading it into the barn.

"Igor, wash her down. She's had a hard ride," he cried out. The Cossack was very young, no more than twenty, thought Vasiliev. Yet he seems very self-confident, if breathless.

The Cossack handed the paper to Vasiliev.

"What's happened, trooper?" he asked.

"Courier's been killed," the Cossack gasped, wiping the dust from his face. "It's a letter from the Marshall of Nobility. They didn't know an officer was here. You'd better take a look."

"All right, go inside and get a drink. We'll talk then."

The man saluted. "Thank you Your Honor."

"Just as you were getting to the interesting part, Serov," Vasiliev opened the envelope and unfolded the paper. The handwriting was agitated. Vasiliev read it out loud. "Courier Karpov found dead. Terrible wounds. Saddle pack missing. Request immediate as-sistance of police officer." The signature was illegible. The words "terrible wounds" alarmed him. Could this be another ax killing, he wondered. Serov had glanced sharply at him. Clearly, he was thinking the same thing.

"Perhaps the trooper can tell us more," said Vasiliev as he headed toward the station master's house. Serov followed him. When they came through the ante room they heard the sounds of weeping. The Cossack was standing by the table, his fur cap in hand, looking helplessly at Daria. He had extended one hand toward her. The girl was slumped against the stove, her apron pressed to her face as she shook with grief.

"I...I just told her," the young man stuttered.

"What exactly did you tell her?" asked Vasiliev.

"Just that Courier Karpov had been killed."

Vasiliev went up to Daria and took her hands in his and lowered them.

"Daria," he spoke to her gently, "you must not grieve. Tell me, did you know him?"

"Yes," she gasped and shook her head as if to drive off the sadness that was consuming her. "Yes, he was a good man." Then she broke into sobs and freeing herself from Vasiliev's hands she ran into her room.

"So, an affair of the heart?" muttered Serov.

"You shouldn't have said anything," the voice of the station master sounded angrily behind them. The Cossack stood bewildered by what he had done.

"Let's try to figure out what's happening here," said Vasiliev. He turned to the station master. "The man needs some tea. He's been riding hard. He had no way of knowing how the news would affect Daria."

The station master glared at the trooper and than shouted harshly, "Daria, get us the samovar." But there was no response from the girl's room.

Serov stepped forward, "I'm just as able to prepare a samovar." The astonished station master watched him take down the samovar from its place and set about to make tea.

"Please sit down both of you," said Vasiliev. "Now, my young friend, Tell us what you know about this," Vasiliev flourished the paper.

The Cossack struggled to recover his poise. "It's as the message says, Your Honor. The Courier Karpov was found by the side of the road several versts outside the village. His head had been badly smashed up, Looked like the work of a heavy saber or an ax. But that wasn't the worst of it. His trousers," the Trooper swallowed hard, "his trousers had been ripped open and they had cut off his genitals."

The station master groaned. "You didn't tell Daria...?"

"No, no. I swear it," he gasped.

Serov put a glass of tea down in front of him, and he gulped down half of it, scalding his throat.

"The message says his saddle bags were missing. This means all the documents and letters he was carrying have disappeared. What happened to his mount? Who discovered the body? Was a thorough search made of the surrounding fields?" Vasiliev felt his anger rising as he impatiently shot off his questions. Not like him, thought Serov.

"Some local peasants found him. The horse was grazing a bit farther off. The saddle bags had been cut off. "

"Were the peasants questioned? Did anyone see another rider in the vicinity?"

The Cossack shook his head. "They sent me off for the police. They were all afraid to do anything else."

"Of course," Vasiliev muttered. He knew what the peasants were thinking. They would be the first to be blamed. Better not to get involved. He was surprised they had even sent for the police. Perhaps an elder had been with them and taken charge or else they sent first for the landowner, the Marshall of Nobility.

"And why you?"

"I was visiting my parents in the village. I had the only horse that wasn't in the fields, and you know how they are. A uniform..." his voice trailed off.

Vasiliev was drumming his fingers on the table. He was ready to leave, but something held him back.

"You'll need to ride on to the county seat and organize the transfer of the body. We'll go on ahead." He nodded to the station master who understood and went off to saddle the horses.

Vasiliev motioned to Serov and they left the cabin.

"So, how are the two crimes linked?" Vasiliev seemed to be

talking to himself, but Serov knew that he was sharing his thoughts with him. No need to answer just yet.

"Now, quick, what is the interesting part of your story?"

Chapter Thirteen

"Well, Vasili Vasilievich, as I was sayin', there's the elder bringin' over these letters on Thursday. You know, as I said, letters askin' for this and that. Daria tells me that the past few times he's been bringin' somethin' else. She tells me it's like a bundle of papers wrapped up in oil skin. That's interestin' all by itself. But what makes it more interestin' you'll soon see. It seems the same kind of packages have been showin' up before this. But they've been brought by someone else. This someone else, Daria tells me, is a servant of a certain Sofia Vadimovna."

"And who is this certain Sofia Vadimovna?" Vasiliev asked, knowing that Serov enjoyed having these questions asked as if secrets had to be pried from him.

"That's it, Vasili Vasilievich. No one is quite sure. The servant likes a glass of tea but gives little back by way of reward as you might say. He keeps his mouth shut pretty tight. But he lets it be known that Sofia Vadimovna is a kindly mistress, not much help there; that she lives alone, not much more to go on. But it seems that once the servant let slip she is an old friend of our good and lately dead Ivan Fedorovich." Serov spread his arms as if to emphasize that this was the extent of his knowledge but wasn't it worth waiting to hear it?

Vasiliev thought again of the chared pieces of paper in the stove of Ivan Fedorovich. The murderer must have suspected that Ivan Fedorovich was writing something that was so incriminating that he had to be stopped at all costs. No, more than suspected; he must have been sure. After Father Porfiry had killed Ivan Fedorovich the conspirators must have burned the papers they found. Had something told them this was only part of a larger manuscript? Where was the rest? The conspirators had searched the house carefully, making only the one mistake of misfiling the book on herbs. He must have concluded that Ivan Fedorovich had been sending the rest of the manuscript to an accomplice. Could they be sure how much of it might already have arrived at its destination? There were at least three perhaps four people who might have revealed the address of the accomplice: the elder, Dmitri Ivanovich, Sofia Vadimovna, her servant and Daria. Vasiliev doubted that anyone of them would have betrayed Ivan Fedorovich. A veteran of conspiracies and a survivor of years in the wilds of Siberia, Ivan Fedorovich would be careful in choosing whom to trust. If anyone had betrayed Ivan Fedorovich, the conspirators would not have had to attack the courier. It had all the appearance of a desperate move. The death of an Imperial courier was bound to cause a serious investigation.

They must have been certain that Karpov was carrying part of the manuscript. What might have led him to that conclusion? Had they been watching Ivan Fedorovich's cabin? Difficult. No easy concealment and the villagers would have noticed a stranger hanging about. Probably some note or reference in the material the killer had found and burned had revealed the method and date of the mailing. Then his only recourse was to intercept the courier, seize the package and read the address before probably destroying it. From the Cossack's description, the killer had then mutilated the body, trying again to throw suspicion on the skoptsy. More evidence of desperation, thought Vasiliev. What did that tell him about the conspirators? Time to stop guessing. He realized how fine and fragile a web he had woven. Well, he would test it at every point. First thing was to examine the body of the courier and go over the ground.

Serov stood silently by, recognizing that Vasiliev was sifting through the information he had given him. He thought it would be amusing to have a small window into Vasiliev's brain. Would he see a machine turning in at high speed? He laughed at himself. What did he know about the workings of the human mind? He was just the son of a serf.

"Well done, Serov. I think you've found the link between the two murders. We still don't know what was so important about these papers that a man would kill for them."

"We'd best be lookin' to Sofia Vadimovna to find that out. But Daria might not know where she lives."

"But the elder must."

"My very thoughts, beg ..." Serov bit his tongue.

"Ah Sergeant I have come to realize how unfair it was of me to deprive you of your natural way of expressing yourself. You have my official apology and permission to restore 'begging your pardon' to your repertoire."

Serov beamed. "Thank you Vasili Vasilievich. I'll promise not to abuse the privilege." Serov finished with a good imitation of a nobleman's bow.

Vasiliev couldn't help laughing. "So there's an end to the only shadow over our long friendship."

The Cossack was dousing his head with water from the pump in the yard when the station master brought out the three horses.

Vasiliev turned to the station master. "How fast did the courier normally ride, would you say, a steady canter, a fast gallop? Just give me your best estimate."

The station master rubbed his chin. "We'll, I can tell you, he started off at a good clip but as I watched him he settled into a steady canter. Nothing leisurely about it, if you get my meaning."

"And when did he leave here?"

"Early morning, it was. Maybe six o'clock."

"I need a more precise hour. You see, if we set off at the same pace and time how long it takes to get to the body we should know exactly when he was killed."

Serov already had his foot in the stirrup when Vasiliev took him by the arm and half-whispered to him. Serov looked startled but then nodded and walked back to the station house. He returned in a few minutes.

"She says six-thirty, a bit later than usual. They'd been talkin'."

Vasiliev glanced at his watch. "Let's go now."

It was early afternoon when they came to a slight rise on the road and saw the three men standing at the summit. As they rode up Vasiliev looked at his watch again. "So it happened at nine-thirty or thereabouts." Vasiliev took a closer look at the three men. One was a peasant, probably the elder of the nearest village. The second man was obviously a nobleman, judging by the fine looking bay mare he held by the bridle, the expensive leather tooled saddle, the soft leather hunting jacket he had thrown casually over his shoulders and jodhpurs, of all things, looking every bit like an English country gentleman. The third man was wearing the uniform of a Uhlan officer. He was still sitting astride his coal black stallion, leaning slight over the saddle in a deferential pose, as if hanging on every word the nobleman was addressing to him.

Vasiliev quickly ascertained that the nobleman was the Marshall of the Nobility and owned the property on both sides of the post road. The peasants had notified him first. He had been the one who sent the message by the Cossack trooper. Vasiliev exchanged a few pleasantries with him. The Marshall invited Vasiliev to dine that evening but Vasiliev made his excuses. He hated to visit manor houses of the nobility with Serov in tow; they always sent him off to the kitchen. Vasiliev couldn't stand it, though Serov never seemed to mind. The Marshall rode off.

The third man was of greater interest to Vasiliev. He said he had come upon the body shortly after the peasants found it and stayed to make certain that the area around the dead man would not be disturbed. He admitted he had examined the body and was shocked by the brutality of the killing. Vasiliev wondered whether he had observed anything of interest in the vicinity of the corpse. The officer, who had introduced himself with a smart salute as "Captain Bark, Andrei Filipovich," said no. Serov was surprised that Vasiliev peppered him with a barrage of questions; again, not his usual style. Serov wondered whether he had missed something.

Vasiliev had dismounted and was examining the ground as he tossed out his questions.

"So you came up from the east, Andrei Filipovich, and no one passed you." Vasiliev seemed to be talking to himself as he looked down the post road stretching to the horizon. Serov could tell that Vasiliev was sorting out the signs he had read in the ground.

"And when did you arrive on the scene? You see, I'm trying to understand where the killer could have come from and where he went. You'll have to admit there are no places to hide here on the steppe. You were behind him and we at the station were in front of him. So he would have had to have ridden over the fields where there was every chance the peasants might have seen him."

Vasiliev turned to the elder. "None of your people saw a lone rider crossing the fields today?" It was more of a statement than a question. The elder shook his head. He appeared eager to leave.

"Did any of your people examine the body?"

The elder shook his head again. "They knew he was dead. A fearsome death."

Vasiliev nodded and told him to take the courier's horse back to the village, feed and stable it until the post service came to retrieve it.

"Well, thank you, Andrei Filipovich. Serov and I will take our time poking about, doing what detectives are supposed to do," Vasiliev smiled his crooked smile. "Your regiment is stationed nearby, I take it, and so if we need to take some written statement from you we can reach you easily enough?"

Bark stared at Vasiliev for a moment. "I fear I haven't been of much help," he said shortly.

"On the contrary you've helped me narrow the field, as it were, a great deal."

Bark saluted smartly, wheeled his horse and rode back the way he had come. Vasiliev watched him for a long time.

Chapter Fourteen

By the time Vasiliev and Serov approached the station master's cabin it was already dusk. The air was still warm and absolutely still. Vasiliev wondered if the leaves were motionless in Ivan Fedorovich's garden. He caught himself visualizing the dead man's body suspended in the branches of the birch. On the ride back he had discussed the second funeral of Ivan Fedorovich. Serov had thought it was a pagan tradition that some Orthodox believers had made part of their faith. It reminded Vasiliev of Viking rituals. Could it have come to old Rus' with the Norsemen in the early centuries? Nothing ever seemed lost or forgotten in the countryside. Just more layers on layers.

Vasiliev was relieved to see a light burning in the window of the cabin. He began to worry that more killings were in the offing. Someone was trying to eliminate all traces of Ivan Fedorovich's writing; letters perhaps or some kind of treatise. But why were the ramblings of an old exile who had been tried for treason more than half a century earlier become so important?

As they dismounted Vasiliev spoke quietly to Serov. "We need to find out more from Daria. I think she still has things to tell us. Now that her lover, or whatever he was, is dead, she may be more willing."

"Or else more frightened," said Serov.

"Try talking to her in the kitchen while I keep the station master company."

Vasiliev found the elder seated at the station master's table. He rose and bowed, twisting his cap in his hands. Vasiliev quickly told him about the death of Father Porfiry and instructed him to inform Father Iosifei. The elder crossed himself and shook his head

"He was a good man before his mind went wanderin'," he muttered. "Will there be no end to these misfortunes? Years of peace and then..." his voice trailed off. "As for Father Iosifei, he seems to have gone off somewhere. I'll get the deacon to bury him."

Daria served them without speaking a word. Her eyes were red from weeping and her hands trembled as she set down the dishes. The station master seemed preoccupied and the meal passed in almost complete silence. Once Daria had brought out the samovar, Vasiliev began asking the station master about the relay system. Serov managed to spill some tea on his uniform and, excusing himself, went into the kitchen to remove the spots. He was gone for some time, but the station master took no notice of his absence. Later Serov reported that Daria hadn't much to say. "She kept rubbin' her eyes. What could I do? But there's a couple of things she said might help. She told me how to get to Sofia Vadimovna's. It seems the servant let somethin' slip. It's a short ride north along the stream. It'll be easy to find. Then there's the address in Omsk, the one where Ivan Fedorovich was sending these packages."

"Well done, Serov. Now we need to split up again. I want you to send another telegram, this time to the Governor-General's office in Omsk. We have to warn them about a possible attack on the person living at that address. I'm requesting a guard. If the courier was carrying a packet this time the conspirators will know the address and we'll have another butchery on our hands. I'm off to pay a visit to Sofia Vadimovna. She's got to know more about all of this."

They were standing by the overnight hut for travelers. Vasiliev looked up at the full moon. He was tempted to send Serov off at once. But he hesitated. He still wasn't sure that whether the conspirators still had a man in the vicinity. Best to wait until morning.

They rode off at dawn in opposite directions. After less than an hour, Vasiliev caught sight of a low building made of planed wood with a tin roof and a veranda. A picket fence enclosed a garden with a profusion of flowers. He was reassured by the smoke coming from the chimney and, he smiled grimly to himself, the absence of larch trees planted in a pattern. Only a few silver birches grew close to the house.

The old man who answered his knock peered at him with rheumy eyes through old fashioned spectacles that threatened to fall off his long pointed nose. Vasiliev wondered if this was the messenger. If so it was clear why the packages might have stopped coming. He looked as though he could hardly make it across the entry way as he led Vasiliev into the parlor. He was mumbling something about Sofia Vadimovna's not being well. Did he say rheumatism? He announced Vasiliev in a loud voice.

Sofia Vadimovna was indeed not well. She was seated in an overstuffed arm chair, bundled up in some kind of heavy cloth that looked more like a horse blanket than a comforter. A lace cap perched uneasily on her head. She wore a pair of matching lace gloves. Vasiliev noticed how cramped and misshapen her fingers were before she tucked them under the cloth. But her eyes were clear and bright, pale blue and wide with astonishment which, as it turned out, was their normal expression.

Vasiliev introduced himself. For some reason, intuition again he later reflected, he mentioned that he was a retired major in the army as well as an inspector of Police.

"Welcome, welcome. I've expected you ever since I learned of the tragedy that befell my old friend Ivan Fedorovich."

Of course, thought Vasiliev, the elder must have told her. He was surprised at how calm she was and she immediately detected this.

"Ah don't condemn me as hard-hearted; I've done my grieving already. Not many tears left in this old woman. I've seen too much. Well, more of that later. I'm actually glad to see you Major. I prefer the old army rank if you don't mind. The police, well meaning as they might be, make me nervous. What was your regiment, Major?" A curious question from an old woman, he thought.

"I was attached to the Life Guard Grenadiers but..."

"How extraordinary, how simply extraordinary! Well, I wonder what else we have in common. But you said your name is Vasiliev. I don't know it."

Another surprise.

"My father was Count Vorontsov, but I was born on the left side."

"My dear boy! Extraordinary is hardly sufficient. Miraculous is more appropriate. Your being here might even cure me of my ancient skepticism. You see I'm a child of the Enlightenment, like your father. But of course, more than that connects us. Ah, you must be wondering about all of these explosions of sentiment. We'll get to it all soon enough. But you've not come here to help me recover my past. Please, how can I help you, Major?"

It seemed to Vasiliev that she lingered over his rank as if...as if what? There were too many possibilities.

"I'm from Moscow, Sofia Vadimovna, but for various reasons I've been put in charge of investigating the murder of Ivan Fedorovich."

"Ah! 'Various reasons.' How often I've heard that expression to cover a multitude of sins. Some of omission, others of commission."

Vasiliev crooked smile was genuine enough. He knew what she meant. He usually avoided these bureaucratic clichés.

"You might be interested in the 'various reasons.' But like you, I'll save some things for later."

"*Touché*, Major. We both have something to look forward to. But I am forgetting my manners. I have so few visitors these days. Would you please ring that little silver bell on the table? Sometimes it just slips from my fingers. Then I am stuck here until Mitya remembers he has a mistress. Poor fellow, I rely on him too much. But then...Oh, how I rattle on. Please ring, Major."

Vasiliev held his breath while Mitya struggled to prepare tea from the samovar. Once the suspense was over, Vasiliev told Sophia Vadimovna what he had learned and asked her help.

"So, you want to know about the packages. A long story." She looked down where her hands were folded under the blanket. Then she met his gaze and held it unblinking.

"You know after the amnesty of '56, Ivan decided to stay in Siberia. There was nothing left for him back home. His wife had gone off to France after selling his estate. He had no children. His relatives disowned him after the trial. So what was left? Nothing. But he had gotten interested in the customs of the Mongols. And he began to collect artifacts, catalogued them and even corresponded with the Ethnographic Section of the Academy of Sciences. One day—he used to say it came on him suddenly— he had a spiritual experience. After he had fallen ill with some mysterious ailment, a local Mongol shaman managed to cure him. Well, so he said. And in return the shaman made him promise he would help others, you know, become a shaman himself. I don't know. Perhaps, and perhaps he was only half-convinced. There was the rational side of him, you see. Why didn't he stay on there? You might ask. I don't know. But he began to wander and somewhere in the south— my geography is not too firm— he had taken to living with a girl from a nomadic tribe. So many confusing names. I think she was a Mongol of some sort but converted to Orthodoxy. She died shortly after giving birth to a second child. You might think that would have ended it, I mean living there."

Sophia Vadimovna, paused and swallowed hard several times, pressing her lips together.

"We can take this more slowly," said Vasiliev.

She smiled faintly. "Just a moment, please. A shortness of breath. It comes over me, from time to time. I'll be all right in a moment."

"Perhaps it's my turn, then," Vasiliev smiled back. "Let me explain the 'various reasons' that brought me here."

He told her about his mission to accompany Kennan and the orders from Omsk. He was not ready yet to tell anyone about Irina and his plan to rescue her, although he sensed he would have a sympathetic audience in Sophia Vadimovna.

"There was something else too," she resumed her story.

"Ivan never repented. Russia was beginning to reform in the sixties. The serfs were freed. But he thought it was too late and too little. And then a new generation of exiles began to arrive. The 'so-called nihilists' as he referred to them. They seemed so young and naïve. But he felt a strong affection for them; their ideals attracted him. He used to tell me, 'Sophia Vadimovna!' He used to cry out like that when he was deeply moved. 'Sophia Vadimovna! Listen! If we had succeeded – well, you know he didn't' have to tell me what he meant – if we had succeeded, these youngsters would be finishing their studies. They would be our future doctors and teachers in a free society. Think of it! Instead, they are going to waste away like we did. What talents they were!' And then he'd go on, down the list of names of his friends. It was sad to hear him. Sad because my Nikolka was among them."

90

The angle of the sun had brought the shadows of the birch trees into the room. When Sophia Vadimovna paused, it was very quiet. Mitya must have been dozing off somewhere. Then a slight creaking sound could be heard as if the old house was sighing.

"You accompanied him, your husband was he? Into exile?"

"Yes. You guessed that didn't you. My Nikolka Panov was twenty-two when he went into the Senate Square that cold December day to bring down the autocrat, our late unlamented tsar whose name he shared – Nikolai Pavlovich. He was an ensign in the Life Guards Grenadiers. So you see you came from the same regiment. They let wives, those who wanted, accompany their husbands into exile. But you know that surely. Your father must have told you about the wives of the Decembrists, or read to you Pushkin's poem about us. Your father was one of the few who knew about the conspiracy but never denounced the plotters. He even wrote to some of us, to Murav'ev and Volkonskii I think. A risk. But he was a man of honor. So you and Nikolka, fellow Guardsmen. Imagine!"

Vasiliev thought it was better to spoil the symmetry. He had told her the truth; he had been attached to the Life Guard Grenadiers. It was during the Russo-Turkish War of '77-'78 when he was on a special mission; but he was never commissioned as a regular Guards officer. In fact, he had resisted joining the Guards after graduation from the Lycée. No one could understand his decision. He would always remember his father's reaction; a hard cold look, no reproach but deep disappointment. And then to sign up with the regular police! It seemed like a bizarre decision to everyone except Irina. Even then as a school girl she thought the Guards were glittering playboys – and her father was a Colonel! That was long before she became completely alienated from him. Vasiliev never knew the whole story. He often wondered whether it was something about her father that had driven her into the ranks of the underground Land and Liberty Party. Well, they were both rebels of a sort, she and he, and soon his rebellion would match hers.

The shadows were deepening and the samovar had grown cold. Sophia Vadimovna gave a slight shudder.

"I think we need a fire. The old house holds on to the winter cold all throughout the summer months," she smiled apologetically. "Would you ring for Mitya, again, please?"

"Let's not disturb him, Sophie Vadimovna. I build a fine fire. Let me do it." Vasiliev had already risen from his chair and moved toward the hearth. In a few minutes he had a respectable blaze going.

"Just like Nikolka. He learned to make a good fire and to do many other things with his hands out here. He was strong. Never sick. But he worried about me after I lost the child. Then one day he went out hunting and did not come back. It seems he was drowned trying to rescue a comrade who had fallen through the ice. Yes, Major, plenty to grieve over. And now Ivan Fedorovich. Well, you did not come here for to hear my life's story. How can I help you?"

Chapter Fifteen

Listening to Sophia Vadimovna, Vasiliev felt the familiar sadness come over him. The Decembrists, cream of the Russian nobility, veterans of the victory over Bonaparte, educated and patriotic men coming back from the wars in high hopes that the "Angelic tsar", Alexander I, would set Russia firmly on the path of Enlightenment. But he had turned aside and embraced mysticism. And his brother had embraced the absolutist tradition, also western, the despotic part of enlightened despotism, repressive and brutal. Somehow it did not seem necessary to say these things aloud to Sophia Vadimovna. She had lived through it all. Now it was a matter of finding a murderer, a very small act of justice. Who would notice things like this when the history of these times were written? Vasiliev sighed inwardly and heard an echo in the boards of the old house.

"Why should anyone wish to kill a man like Ivan Fedorovich? That is my problem. I don't think the skoptsy had anything to do with it despite the mutilation."

Sophia Vadimovna shook her head in agreement.

"We've just learned that a courier was also killed, probably by the same person or persons."

Sophia Vadimovna gave a start. Vasiliev immediately reproached himself for not having prepared her.

"When did this happen?" she half whispered.

"Probably yesterday after mid-day."

She sucked in her breath. Again Vasiliev feared she might have an attack, but she quickly recovered.

"Was anything…" she paused, "taken?"

"The saddle bags with all the mail."

"Then they got the latest installment."

"What do you mean?"

"Oh my dear Vasili Vasilievich! You remember I told you Ivan was unrepentant? He was writing all about it. Oh, my!" she gasped. "I'm sorry I am not making things clear. Where to begin?" She drew her blanket closer around her.

"It was about the exiles," she blurted out. "He left the steppe to come here, to the beginning of the Great Siberian Road. He wanted to tell the world about the exile system from where it began. Oh, he knew about the others, Kuropatkin and Stepniak. But he started writing before they published in the West. Over the years he had organized a network of informers inside the system. They furnished him with information. The notes and letters to me by mail. Mitya would pick them up at the station and deliver them to Ivan Fedorovich. He wanted to testify, yes that was the word he used. But in great detail so that on one could refute what he was saying. If he'd only known about your Mr. Kennan and his friend."

Vasiliev remembered the ashes in the oven of Ivan Fedorovich. Could this have been part of his record of the exile system? And then other chapters in the missing saddle bags of the courier.

"So he brought his writing to you. Why?"

"Well, you must see why. He was afraid that if he sent out the mail under his own name it would be intercepted. He was very suspicious. Experience had taught him that. "

"To whom was it being sent?"

"An old comrade, another Decembrist, a close friend of my husband, Aleksei Pestov, who lived in Omsk. You see he too was young in '25 like my Nikolka. We could trust him. Perhaps there were others writing too. And Aleksei was going to get the material sent abroad. To London I think. They did not tell me everything. Too dangerous they said. Ach! What could the Gendarmes do to me?"

"So you sent the packages of papers under your name to Omsk. And no one was the wiser. Then what happened? Was Mitya no longer able to ride?"

"Yes, you've guessed right again."

"And then you persuaded the elder, Dmitri Ivanovich, to carry them for you."

"Yes, yes, that's just what we did."

"Sophia Vadimovna. I have to ask you a difficult question now. I'm sorry. But can you trust Dmitri Ivanovich?"

"Why on earth not? "

"Well, think about it for a moment. Soon after he begins to pick up the package from you and takes it to the station master, Ivan Fedorovich is attacked and killed. Was this a coincidence?"

"Oh my God, I never thought…No, it's impossible! He loved Ivan Fedorovich. They all did in the village. He helped them in so many ways. Sometimes he told me about it, Ivan Fedorovich that is. How he would subscribe to the newest science. I don't know what to think about that shamanist stuff. To me it was superstitious nonsense. But with the peasants, who knows? It might have made it easier to convince them that the medicine had magic properties. Can we ever understand them?"

"Can you tell me what the latest installment was about?"

"Yes, I always read his notes. He wanted me to smooth out his prose. 'Too rocky' he used to say. Well, he was direct and sometimes, abrupt. I tried my best to make it more readable, you know for a Western audience. I'd been well educated as a girl. My tutors were excellent. I haven't forgotten."

Vasiliev tried to imagine her as the young wife of a Decembrist plotter, leaving the easy, even luxurious life of a daughter of the nobility for the wasteland of Siberia, the long trek, two thousand miles, at best by private cart and perhaps part of the way by foot to arrive in a remote, isolated village among the nomadic tribesmen and then to lose her only child. And this brought his thoughts back to Irina. It was his turn to feel a shudder pass through him.

"And the subject of the last installment?" he persisted.

"The Tiumen Forwarding Camp. It's where the system really began. You see, he was working backward and…Why what's wrong Vasili Vasilievich? You've turned quite pale!"

Vasiliev could barely control himself. He stood up, seized by an impulse to start off immediately for Tiumen. Then he checked himself and sat down abruptly. His thoughts were rushing ahead.

"That was Mr. Kennan's first destination," he said quietly. But that was not what shook him to the core. The questions came to him with frightening rapidity. What had Ivan Fedorovich known about Tiumen and how much of what he knew did he write into the manuscript? And did what he knew and wrote place Irina in danger? Was she part of the network of his informers about conditions in the system? Then, suddenly another thought seemed to explode in his head. What about the danger to Kennan and Frost? If someone was determined to stop an exposé of the exile system, wouldn't Kennan become an obvious target? And here he was, Inspector Vasiliev, who had been assigned to accompany him, implicitly to protect him, separated from his charge, not even knowing precisely where he was. Did the killer know? And was he stalking Kennan at this very moment?

He quickly made his apologies to Sophia Vadimovna, bent over to kiss her gnarled fingers and left the house without arousing Mitya. She caught a glimpse of him through the window and wondered what she had said to speed him on his way. Oh to be young again and ride with him! She liked him, but she had hesitated to tell him about the letters. They really didn't have anything to do with Ivan Fedorovich's treatise or it would seem with his death. Besides, she thought, there were some secrets you did not share with the police no matter how nice they were.

The next morning Sophia Vadimovna awakened early, frightened by a shortness of breath. Recently, this had often happened to her. This time the attack seemed more severe. She thought of ringing for Mitya. Why bother? If this was the end, she would accept it. She had never believed in the afterlife. She had heard of last minute conversions, but she was not going to deceive herself. When Nikolka had disappeared, she knew she had lost him forever. There would be no meeting in heaven or hell. Suddenly, she remembered her dream. Nikolka and Ivan Fedorovich were saddling up their Siberian ponies. How young and handsome they looked! They mounted and then she noticed that they had saddled a third pony; Nikolka was holding its bridle. A dog was barking. They were waiting for someone. She could tell they were waiting a long time. The clouds scudded across the sky as if driven by a relentless hand; the grass turned brown and then green again. Leaves swirled around them. Then she knew they were waiting for her. But the stern look on their faces held her back. Why did they not welcome her? Had she done something they disapproved of? Of had she somehow failed in her duty?

She dozed and when she opened her eyes again she felt the sharp pain in her chest. Suddenly, everything became clear. The letters! They were waiting for her to pass on the letters as they had passed them on to her. She could not break the chain. She reached out to the bell. The pain shot down her arm and she could hardly grasp it in her fingers. She rang frantically. Mitya appeared. She could hardly see him. She pointed to the iron box on top of the wardrobe. Mitya stared at her, terrified by the dead white color of her face. She could not speak. Why was he hesitating? The key! Of course, the key! She knew he would not take it from her neck. With a final burst of energy she tore off the ribbon. The key fell beside her. She could no longer move; she struggled to stare him into obedience.

Mitya was trembling so hard he could scarcely lift down the box. His fingers seemed to crawl along the bedclothes until they reached the key. Sophia Vadimovna willed herself to stay alive until he had fumbled open the lock. As he threw back the cover of the iron box he heard the death rattle behind him. He turned and watched incredulously as Sophia Vadimovna's features relaxed into a beatific smile. His tears half blinded him as he peered into the box and saw a small packet of letters wrapped in oilskin covered with a sheet of her notepaper instructing him how to dispose of them.

Chapter Sixteen

Boris Ippolitovich Krasin, the chief police officer of the Tiumen district, sat staring at the half-eaten remains of his dinner. He reached for an almost empty carafe, emptied the rest of its contents into his glass and tossed it back. He sighed deeply, reflecting on the cruel fate that had not only sent him over a thousand exiles but provided him with a wretched cook as well. He held the empty glass up to the light. Vodka, the only salvageable part of the meal. He ran a small silver bell and his servant appeared immediately. Krasin waved his hand dismissively over his plate as if consigning it to the garbage pail.

"Your Excellency?"

"Abominable. You can tell the cook that if you wish."

Krasin wondered what kind of concoction the cook would serve up as a sweet. It was times like these he regretted being a bachelor. But what woman in her right mind would wish to marry the man responsible running such an abomination as the Tiumen Forwarding Prison.

"Damn it," he exclaimed out loud. The servant peered around the corner of the kitchen door. Reassuring himself that the chief was engaged in some private quarrel having nothing to do with the meal, he withdrew and conveyed his feelings to the cook with a shrug of the shoulders.

"Damn it to hell," Krasin muttered, as if to express that his unhappiness was growing by the minute. It had been two months and fifteen days since he had suffered his greatest loss since his favorite prostitute had joined up with a free exile and left town for an honest life, as she put it. No, he thought, that was a minor loss compared to this new catastrophe. But what could he have done to prevent it? Nothing. The order had come from the Governor-General in Omsk, signed by the great man himself, although he probably hadn't read a word of it. Anyway what would the Governor-General know about conditions in the forwarding prison? He glanced unhappily at the empty carafe. For the moment he was tempted. He clenched his fist. No! That was the way to perdition. He recalled the fate of his predecessor who had drunk himself into a stupor every night for a year and then shot himself while sitting at this very table. He shuddered.

The servant entered on tiptoes as quietly as he could. And set down another plate in front of him. Krasin took one look at the apple turnover and stood up abruptly. He threw down his napkin and stormed off to his study. It even looked indigestible, he thought.

He took out a cheroot, snipped off the tip with his pocket knife and sank down on the worn leather divan. Yes, he reflected a devastating loss, not only for him but for the poor devils crowded in that hateful prison. He recalled the exact wording of that cursed telegram. It had ordered him to send the prisoners Irina Borisovna Davydova and Ivan Ivanovich Letchik to Omsk to assume duties as trustees in the prison hospital. And why not? Who else could have performed such medical miracles under such miserable conditions as the two of them?

Krasin pulled down a large record folder from the bookcase behind the divan. He knew the figures by heart, but he took a perverse pleasure in re-reading them for the hundredth time. What did the Germans call it? *Schadenfreude*. But didn't that mean to take pleasure from someone else's grief? Maybe even the Germans had no word for what he felt ever time he ran his eyes down the column of figures. There it was; the statistics didn't lie, not in this case. He was a stickler for accuracy. When Davydova and Letchek arrived, the number of deaths was running at an annual rate of over 300. Within a year after they had been assigned to the hospital ward, the figure had dropped to two hundred; after another six months, to one seventy five. "Still too high," the young man would say, and she would plead the case for more medicine. "Ask the local merchants to contribute," she pleaded with him. "Appeal to their better feelings. Aren't there some Tolstoyans around?" she persisted.

And he, the chief of police no less, would meekly raise the question with the first guild merchants, and then be surprised at their generous response. "So, Russian capitalists have their uses," she would say and laugh. How could anyone resist her? They set the prisoners to scrubbing the barracks and washing their clothes regularly. They seemed gradually to take over the warden body and soul. He also did their bidding as he began to observe what was happening. It was a depressing business to run a prison, but somehow those two managed to turn it into, well not a pleasurable activity, but a useful one. They were all working together to save lives. Some of those lives, Krasin knew, were not worth very much. But he too was becoming infected by the change in the prisoners' attitudes. It could not be denied, he kept telling himself, that it was a less depressing place in which to work. And then the bombshell! And it had all been his fault. He should have held his tongue. But no, he had to boast at a dinner given by the Governor-General about the remarkable turnaround in the prison. Yes, to boast and what was more, to the pretty young wife of the governor's assistant. No doubt she had blabbed about her charming dinner companion and his humanitarian work. Fat lot of good a pretty woman's look of admiration had meant compared to the disaster of losing Davydova and Letchik.

Then steeling himself, as he always did, he ran his eyes down the figures for the year they left. The deaths had shot up to over 300 again. And it was not just the raw data, but the percentages that kept haunting him. And now this American was on the verge of paying a visit. Why not last year? And the governor had given this Mr. Kennan him carte blanche. What could he have been thinking? That he, Krasin, could continue the work of Davydova and Letchik? Was he supposed to run around the hospital, bandage up the injured, give medicine to the sick, help organize the cleaning of the barracks, wash their damned rags! He was tempted again to ring for another carafe. Well, the American would see what he would see. There was nothing to do about it. Except maybe to complain about inadequate resources and overcrowding. He shuddered when he thought of the 'family cell' with men, women and children squashed together.

The family cell at Tiumen

He could not tell the true story. That would be too humiliating. He stormed off to bed.

Krasin woke up in the middle of the night drenched in sweat. He sat bolt upright and stared into the darkest corner of the room. Only a dream, he kept assuring himself. Yet, he thought…no it was too fantastic. He wasn't accustomed to entertaining visions. Later, in the light of day, he still had his doubts. She could not have appeared in his room. So, it was only a dream. She had been standing at the foot of his bed, dressed as a grand lady, as she must have looked in her father's house. But he had never seen her there or dressed like that. She had extended both hands in supplication. 'Tell the truth' she had said, 'tell the truth.' That was all. It had lasted a few seconds. But the image had burned itself into his consciousness.

In the morning, he brushed his hair carefully, put on a freshly pressed uniform and applied a dash of eau de cologne. He sent his equerry out to meet Kennan's coach and to deliver an invitation to lunch.

Krasin was determined to charm his guests. He hired a cook from the Grand Hotel in Tiumen. It was not so grand, but at least the food would be edible. Lunch turned out to be a pleasant occasion. Kennan spoke excellent Russian and Frost was content to listen to his friend's occasional translations while he devoured the rabbit stew and *pelmeni*. Krasin could imagine the kind of fare they had to endure on the Great Siberian Road.

Kennan seemed a bit surprised when Krasin agreed to let him visit the prison.

"The place is greatly overcrowded and in bad sanitary condition," Krasin had said. He was only telling the truth. He promised to accompany them, but had already decided he would let Ignat'ev do the honors. He was a member of the prison committee and knew his business. It was one thing to 'tell the truth' and another to have to stare it in the face. He would beg off, a diplomatic sickness.

The following day he did not get out of his dressing gown but spent the day lying on the couch in his study. He might as well play the game right. Who knows what his servant or the cook night blurt out if he did not appear to be ill? He closed his eyes and dozed. Irina's image came back to him, silent and more faintly this time. What do you want? I've told the truth, for God's sake. And Kennan will see it with his own eyes. Krasin turned on his side. A shaft of light from the window fell on the folder of statistics lying on the table where he had left it.

Not that too! Always pleading with me for one more thing. And now this. Well, I won't do it.

A fierce storm descended on the town in the evening, sweeping in from the Arctic Ocean. Kennan was surprised to hear a knock on his door. Who would be abroad this wild night? A man who identified himself as Krasin's servant, Ilia, handed him a large folder wrapped in seal skin.

"His Excellency, Boris Ippolitovich Krasin, sends his compliments. He hopes that this will help you in your investigation. He only asks that you return it tomorrow. I shall come at ten o'clock to pick it up. Good night, sir."

Kennan copied the statistics until early in the morning. Frost was up early to hand the package back to the servant.

Chapter Seventeen

Krasin hated to wake up early. The day was long enough, he always said, without prolonging it. But there it was. What was worse he had a headache. Not the splitting kind, but the dull throbbing variation. He shaved and dressed quickly, sloshing extra eau de cologne on his face. This did not improve his spirits. He could hardly expect salvation from breakfast. He really had to do something about the cook. The trouble was she was a widow with three children. What would she do if he freed her from mangling his meals? He feared the effect of turning her loose on the public. But there it was. Another sign of the sentimentality that stood in the way of his promotion to a higher rank. He rubbed the back of his neck as he reluctantly made his way into the dining room.

The mail pouch was already waiting for him. He groaned inwardly. What horrors were lurking there? He rang. Tea was brought in with fresh rolls and *blini*. At the first bite, he started as if overcome by an unfamiliar sensual pleasure. Not possible he thought. He took a second bite. Marvelous! He rapidly consumed the *blini* fearing that the savory taste would vanish. He rang and for the first time looked up from his plate. A young girl appeared dressed in an embroidered Ukrainian blouse and a pleated skirt.

"Who are you?" he bellowed.

She curtsied but did not appear intimidated.

"Anna Bogdanovna, Your Excellency."

He stared at her for a moment. "And what are you doing in my house?"

He regretted making such a stupid remark as soon as the words were out of his mouth. It was too late to retract them.

"Cooking and serving Your Excellency."

"You prepared the *blini*?"

She curtsied again.

Well, he thought, she isn't very talkative. But that may be all to the good.

"And where are the others?" He couldn't quite recall their names, the cook and the servant; it was the headache that did that to him.

"My mother's sick and your man's missing." So she didn't remember his name either, or else she was the soul of discretion. He opted for the latter explanation.

"I'm sorry to hear that," which, of course, he wasn't. He dismissed her with a few words of praise. No sense overdoing it. Then suddenly the terrible truth of what she had told him banished the delicious taste of *blini* as he feared would happen, but not in this way. Missing? What did that mean? And the folder of statistics?

The body of Krasin's servant was found later that morning behind an abandoned hut in the outskirts of town, stuffed under a hay rick. His throat had been cut. The police found no weapon or, when Krasin questioned them, a folder of statistics. When the constables left him, he felt a wave of despair strike him with the power of a physical force. His headache jumped from the level of dull to splitting. He staggered into his study and collapsed on the sofa, struggling to get hold of himself. Anna Bogdanovna peeked in through the half open door and returned a few moments later with towels and a bowl of steaming water laced with vinegar. She made a compress, motioned for him to turn over, and applied it precisely where the pain was the greatest. He uttered a muffled blessing upon her. She kept applying the towels until he felt able to sit up. Then he grasped her hand and kissed it.

"Your Excellency!" she exclaimed but did not withdraw her hand. He noticed how prettily she blushed. The thought crossed his mind that if he could recover the statistics his future might turn out to be tolerable; perhaps even more than that.

With uncharacteristic vigor, he dispatched a message to Kennan explaining only that the folder had been misplaced and he needed to have the copies returned as soon as possible. Then he instructed two of his detectives to begin investigating the murder.

"It looks like a murder for profit. The killer probably thought the folder contained money. You know what to do." He dismissed them, hoping they did know what to do for he did not. He thought of himself as a man whose job it was to administer prisons not to catch the criminals who filled them. He was beginning to look forward to lunch. But first he decided while the energy lasted to look at the mail. He quickly regretted his decision.

Among the crop of useless papers that went the rounds of the offices, there were two letters that caused him concern. The first was from the bishop of Omsk who informed him of information about illegal pagan practices in some village he had never heard of, that required immediate investigation.

And where am I to find the men for that, now that my servant's been murdered, he thought. The second letter might have provided the answer but he only thought of the complications it might involve. A certain Inspector Vasiliev was on his way, shortly to be expected. He was on the trail of something or other and trying to catch up with someone or other. The message was written by a half-literate, it seemed, and did not make a great deal of sense. What it meant for Krasin was another headache, quite possibly worse than any he had yet experienced. Well, there was always lunch and then more hot compresses. Did life always have to swing from one extreme to another, he wondered?

Chapter Eighteen

Krasin was looking forward to meeting Inspector Vasiliev with a mixture of relief and trepidation. His detectives had not turned up a thing. He thought they had blundered around a lot, offended people and gone off in the wrong direction. He wasn't sure about the right direction, but Vasiliev might. An impressive reputation, although he understood that the Gendarmes didn't much care for him. Was that so bad? So, it might be a stroke of luck that Vasiliev had arrived just when he had. What was worrisome was that the Inspector might not agree with how he had dealt with Kennan. Had he been too accommodating, too frank? What else could he have done? Still, the authorities in Omsk might not take kindly to having conditions in Tiumen exposed, as Kennan might well do. Well, damn it; it was their own fault. Or at least the fault of the Ministry. They had authorized the visit. Yes, another small voice in his head spoke up, but they might have been relying on your discretion to put a better face on things. And that matter of handing over the statistics! Krasin called for Anna Bogdanovna and compresses.

When they first caught sight of the Tiumen Forwarding Prison, Serov felt Vasiliev tense up. He had long ago given up thinking about what he would say at this moment. He knew there was nothing he could say to make it easier. Vasiliev reined in and sat stiffly in the saddle gazing at the brick walls, the guard posts and the small groups of women, either young girls or old women gathered in front of the prison. As they drew closer they saw that the women were selling bread, cold meat, boiled eggs and meat pies, presumably to the prisoners who could afford them. They dismounted and

Vasiliev handed the armed sentry at the prison gate his letter of permission with his and Serov's papers. The guard saluted then called for the officer of the day, "*Starshe!*" drawing out the last syllable in a ringing voice. An officer appeared, took the letter, and requested them to wait. Vasiliev glanced at the walls, which he estimated were about four or five meters high. How ridiculous even to think of scaling them! The few minutes they had to wait was torture for him. Then the gate swung open and the officer conducted them to Krasin's office. The warden had dressed that morning with special care and doused himself with eau de cologne. If he was going to have to enter the stinking ward, he would make sure first to envelope himself in a cloud of protective scent. He greeted Vasiliev effusively.

"I regret that I was not able to accompany Mr. Kennan and his friend Mr, ahh…"

"Frost," muttered Vasiliev between his teeth as they walked through the prison yard. Separate groups of exiles and convicts were walking about or sitting on the ground. Most of them wore leg irons. They were all dressed in gray from their homespun linen blouses and trousers to their shapeless caps.

"Captain Krasin—" Vasiliev began.

"Please, Boris Ippolitovich!"

"Very well, Boris Ippolitovich, I am not here to inspect the prison, but to inquire about two recent inmates, politicals, who may be important witnesses in a trial that is being organized in Moscow. I have to confirm their whereabouts, you see. My information is that they were assigned to the prison hospital. May we examine the place?"

"Yes, of course," stammered Krasin. He felt a sinking feeling in the pit of his stomach. What could this mean? Were they going to crucify him over Davydova and Letchik? Would Omsk protect him? Not against Petersburg they wouldn't. No, they couldn't reproach him. True, he had taken an initiative. But wasn't it for everyone's good?

"This way; it's on the third floor. You must understand the ward is terribly overcrowded, and we suffered a great loss when prisoners Davydova and Letchik left us," Vasiliev started; what did 'left us' mean?

Krasin swung open the door to the women's ward and a fetid odor struck them like a Siberian storm. Vasiliev pressed a handkerchief to his face; Serov covered his mouth with his hand. At a prearranged signal from Vasiliev, Serov spun on his heel and left the ward.

"My Sergeant has a weak stomach," said Vasiliev, feeling queasy himself. God spare us, he thought, how could she survive working here?

About a dozen iron bedsteads were ranged against the walls. The sick lay on thin mattresses and were covered with gray blankets or ragged quilts. Vasiliev noted that over every bed there was a blackboard with a crude scrawl naming the prisoner's disease. Vasiliev read "typhus," "scurvy," "rheumatism," and "syphilis." There was no ventilation in the ward; the odors were unspeakable, the atmosphere suffocating. Krasin sensed that his eau de cologne was evaporating fast.

"You see they are no longer here!" he exclaimed.

"Come below. We need to soak you in carbolic acid. Some of these diseases are highly infectious."

Properly disinfected but badly shaken, Vasiliev followed Krasin to his office.

"Please Inspector, some refreshment?" Krasin ran a bell and Anna immediately appeared. "The samovar and brandy," he ordered.

"Boris Ippolitovich, the ward...it was appalling."

"Of course, of course! I know this only too well! I have complained endlessly, endlessly to Omsk. Things have changed so. It was so much better six months ago. You have no idea." This was not the way he wanted to explain things. But Vasiliev looked stricken. God. They'll crucify me! It was all Krasin could think of.

"Boris Ippolitovich! What did you mean when you said the prisoners Davydova and Letch had left you?"

Anna wheeled in the samovar, her eyes lowered, not daring to look this visitor from Petersburg in the face. She feared she would betray herself. Vasiliev hardly noticed her. She rushed out.

"I must tell you, a sad story. That is, sad for the prisoners."

Krasin looked around for Anna. Why hadn't she prepared the tea? He rang again. She peered around the door.

"Please, Anna, prepare tea for the Inspector!" he sounded harsher than he wanted and Anna blushed from her neck to her forehead. She busied herself at the samovar. The two men sat silently watching her. She almost dropped Vasiliev's glass. Then she turned and fled the room again.

"A new girl. Please excuse her clumsiness."

"How did they leave you, Boris Ippolitovich?"

"Yes, left or to more precise were called away."

"Is this some euphemism? Did they die?" Vasiliev gripped his glass tightly.

"Die? Oh my goodness, no! They were summoned to Omsk. Orders of the Governor-General. You see, Inspector, they were angels. Ha! Ha! Not a word to be used in official correspondence. They changed the conditions here, put the sick wards in proper shape. Got funds from the local merchants to buy medicine. Oh, I can't tell you all they did. And how they kept healthy through it all I don't know. Well, of course, I did my best. You must understand, inspector, I did my best! The death rate was declining, the prisoner morale improved, even the guards felt better—all the result of their good works. So, I took the liberty of giving them separate quarters. They each had a room with decent air and so forth. Was this wrong?" Krasin's face had grown almost as red as Anna's. Vasiliev felt a wave of affection for this man.

"Boris Ippolitovich, I commend you. Your humanity does you credit."

Krasin grasped Vasiliev's hand. "Thank you my dear sir. I must confess, I was concerned you might…well, not approve."

"So they were called away; a message from the Governor-General. Impressive."

Well, to be more accurate, a message from the Deputy Governor-General, brought to me by special courier, a Uhlan officer." Krasin poured two glasses of brandy.

When he handed Vasiliev a glass he was startled again to see the look of alarm on the face of his guest. What had he done now? Just as he was about to ask Vasiliev about the murder of his servant.

Vasiliev sipped his brandy. He had to get hold of himself.

"Excellent stuff!" he said forcing a smile. Krasin noticed his crooked teeth. Somehow this comforted him.

"Well, now a Uhlan officer, no less. And did he by chance tell you his name?"

"Yes , but these names fly out of my mind so easily. Let's see," Krasin raised his eyes to the ceiling. "Ummm. You know I always try to remember names by association. Where did I read about that? No matter. His name had something to do with the sea, a ship?"

"Perhaps a barque? Was his name Bark? Andrei Filipovich?"

"My goodness, yes! How extraordinary that you should guess... ah but you didn't guess, did you? You know him?"

"Slightly. Did he have a written order?"

"Of course. I wouldn't have let them go without an official paper."

"Do you still have it? I'd like to see it."

Krasin became worried again. Should he produce it or not? There really was no choice.

He reached for the little bell and then hesitated. His servant would not answer. He was lying dead in the city hospital.

"Inspector Vasiliev, Vasili Vasilievich, my servant..." this was not the way he hoped to broach the subject.

"Well?"

"In a moment, I'll get the document. But first, I have to confess, there is something else I must talk to you about. You see there's been a murder...my servant for ten years, God save his soul. Well, it's complicated. You see while Mr. Kennan was here he requested some statistics. I sent my servant over to his hotel with the papers. He made copies and then returned the papers. But my servant was killed on the way back. The papers disappeared. Mr. Kennan made fresh copies for me. He saved me from embarrassment. But I have not been able to discover the murderer. My detectives...you know how it is in the provinces. The best men go to the capital." Krasin bit his lip. He realized that he had just condemned himself. Too late. Still, this Vasiliev seemed like a decent sort. He had to trust him.

"I'd hoped you might spare a day or two to investigate. I'll provide the best horses for your trip to Omsk."

"And if I don't help you I won't get the horses?" Vasiliev smiled again.

"No! No! Nothing of the sort. Oh, my! I've been clumsy. Please forgive me. But I do need your help."

   "A day or two, Boris Ippolitovich, to discover a murderer? You flatter me. But I'll do my best." All he could think of was the recurrent disappearance of the papers. Three sets now. There had to be a connection.

Chapter Nineteen

When Vasiliev came down to the prison yard, he spotted Serov in a corner talking to an old man with a bushy head of white hair and long white beard. A closer look revealed a scar that ran the length of the man's face, where no hair grew, from his chin to his left ear which, at some point, had been half torn off. There were no guards in sight. Vasiliev went to the office of the officer of the day and chatted him up until Serov appeared. They left the prison without exchanging a word, mounted their horses and rode silently to their hotel. They ordered tea in their rooms and sat together in worn overstuffed armchairs at the window overlooking the vast expanse of the Ob River. Beneath them was the steam ship landing where a convict barge was loading. All along the flimsy wooden bridge that zig-zagged down the high bank to the landing stage, a throng of exiles guarded by soldiers with fixed bayonets were trudging aboard.

Vasiliev recounted his meeting with Krasin. "And what did you turn up, Sergeant? Did the old man know Irina and Letchik?"

"It seems every soul in that hell hole knew them. I'd asked a guard who was the longest server. He pointed out Osip; they call him 'Sokrat'. A Greek philosopher wasn't he? Osip was a lifer. Killed an estate manager in a quarrel over a girl, they said. In prison, a fighter. But also a learned man. Self-taught. He used to have long talks with Letchik. I gave him some tobacco, but I think he was willin' to talk without the smokes. Lots to tell. But the main thing is this. Irina Nikolaevna and Letchik were collectin' information all the time when they wasn't healin'. Conversin' with each new group of exiles, sortin' out the politicals. Wrote up their notes at night. Osip helped as much as he was able. Then they gave the notes, sown up in coats and trousers, to exiles goin' on to Omsk and Semipalatinsk. Osip saw what they was up to. 'Forgin' links' he said. What you might call a network. They was aimin' to get to Omsk. Seems there's a man there who pulls it all together."

"That'll be Aleksei Pestov."

"Always a step ahead, eh Vasili Vasilievich?"

"No, Serov, just the terminal point. Without you taking the intermediate steps I couldn't get where I want to go."

Serov chuckled. "That's a pretty way of puttin' it. Makes me feel better."

Vasiliev tapped him on the shoulder.

"My turn to fill in more steps. Ready for this?" Vasiliev was staring out the window at the party of exiles. The stream of convicts boarding the barge seemed endless.

"I'll go at this backwards, so to speak. Kennan arrives, gets some statistics from Krasin on the Tiumen Prison. Presumably, they expose the terrible conditions. But also they reveal the good works of Irina and Letchik. The servant is killed on the way back from retrieving the documents from Kennan. Six months ago Irina and Letchik are summoned to Omsk by order of the deputy governor-general. Meanwhile they've been collecting information on the conditions of exile and creating or tapping into a network of informants. Does someone in authority find this out? Is that why they are transferred? To break the links?

"Then we have the killing of the courier and theft of his saddle bags. We know he's also carrying documents collected by Ivan Fedorovich who's writing about the exiles he meets on the Great Highway. Ivan Fedorovich is also killed. An attempt is made to put the blame for the murders of the courier Karpov and Ivan Fedorovich on the skoptsy. The deception might have worked with provincial officials, eager to 'solve' the crimes. But we're more skeptical. Even the attack on me in the forest might not be connected with these murders. So who do we have as a suspect? We arrive at the murder scene to find three men there. The peasant elder, the Marshall of the Nobility and the Uhlan officer, Bark. Is there any reason to suspect the first two? None at all. And I couldn't think of any good reason to suspect Bark until now. Yet, remember, there was no evidence of any fourth person at the scene.

"Now it turns out that Bark is the same man who delivered the message to Krasin ordering Irina and Letchik to Omsk. A connection? Tenuous, of course, but worth pursuing. We need to find out more about our Uhlan friend. But first we've got to go over the killing ground. Our usual procedure. We go into the district where the body was found and see what we can find out. Not as officers, of course. So prepare yourself, my friend for a deep disguise in the best tradition of Foma."

Vasiliev's monologue had lasted about an hour. The last of the exiles was now being hustled aboard the prison barge. They were packed in the long cage that occupied most of the deck, the "chicken-coop" the exiles called it. Vasiliev watched as a crowd of peddlers like those who were camped outside the prison, came down to the wharf to sell food to the prisoners. The trading was brisk. The guards seemed to have no problem with helping out by passing money and even opening the sliding doors so large items could be handed in. Vasiliev later learned that Kennan had witnessed the same scene and recorded it in his notes. What would Americans think of this?

As they were about to leave their rooms there was a knock at the door. Standing in the hallway was a man who introduced himself in strongly accented Russian as Mr. Jacob R. Wardropper, a Scottish businessman. He said he had a private communication from Mr. George Kennan who had been his guest for many days during his stay in Tiumen. Vasiliev invited him to sit down, but Mr. Wardropper pleaded pressing business and merely handed Vasiliev a sealed envelope.

"Mr. Kennan asked me to stay while you read his message and answer any questions if his meaning was not clear." Vasiliev scanned the bold handwriting and smiling, thanked Mr. Wardropper who bowed in return and left.

"Kennan writes that he and Frost have decided to change their itinerary. Instead of going directly east to Tomsk by steamer or overland on the Great Siberian Road, they intended to take a detour to the south through Omsk heading for Semipalatinsk. He asks us 'in the name of friendship' to keep the information confidential so that he could enjoy greater freedom of movement. But he hopes we can re-join him soon. Splendid, Serov! That relieves my mind. Anyone pursuing him will be thrown off the trail for a while at least. That gives us more time!"

Vasiliev and Serov spent the next few hours purchasing an odd assortment of herbs at a pharmacy and collecting an equally odd assortment of fruit and clothing at the local bazaar. By the time they walked back to the river bank, the barge had been attached to a steamer which was about to cast off. They paused and watched. The exiles were pressed against the cage, hands grasping the wire network as if by a great collective effort they could tear it down.

"A long way to Tomsk," said Serov.

Every time Vasiliev donned a disguise he thought of his teacher in the art, Foma, the former serf of his father, Count Voronstov. The lessons had lasted years, building from the simple application of herbs and berries to darken the skin, to more elaborate techniques, perfecting mannerisms and speech of various classes and ethnic groups of Russia's exotic population from Tatars and Finnish tribes along the Volga to mountain men of the Caucasus, and nomads of the steppe. Vasiliev had noticed a few nomadic tribesmen in the town which meant that it would be dangerous to try to imitate them since he did not speak their language. He had fooled the skopets as a Black Sea seaman, so chances were it would work again. He was getting used to the role. Serov preferred to assume the disguise of a meat pie peddler.

"I'll not be goin' hungry at least," was his verdict. It was clear from the preliminary investigation of Krasin's two detectives that the servant had been killed elsewhere and his body dumped in the outskirts. There had been no traces of blood at the crime scene although the victim's throat had been cut.

"So, Sergeant, no ax and no slicing off the genitals. Nice to see that our killer is not stuck in a rut. For the moment, at least, I have to assume that same man or men have been at work in all these killings. Here's what we'll do, then. I'll start at what must have been the beginning of the poor devil's death day and you'll finish up at the end. I'll try to find out what happened to him after he left Kennan's rooms at the Grand Hotel. Did someone follow him or abduct him in a carriage? You'll try to find out whether anyone saw the body being dumped, or spotted any individuals in the neighborhood who didn't belong there at the time. We'll meet later tonight."

Chapter Twenty

Irina woke with a start in pitched darkness. She sensed it was still early and she was tempted to sink back into that delicious oblivion where the cries of the sick and the odors of decay could not reach her. But then she remembered the importance of the day and felt a surge of excitement.

She dressed quickly and met Letchik at the guard house. He had the two passes clutched in his hand. They had been authorized to pick up some supplies from an apothecary who was sympathetic to exiles and once a month provided them with quinine and other medicines without charge. He once whispered to Irina that he was the son of a Decembrist exiled in 1826. It seemed they were everywhere in Siberia.

The guard winked at them as he opened the gate; "Don't tarry," he leered, convinced that they were lovers and used their errand to spend an hour or two in a local rooming house. Letchik winked back. The prison authorities had given up assigning them an escort after the first few months. There was no chance of their escaping. Where would they go? Irina and Letchik then were able to make their first contact with the network of politicals in Omsk and pass on the messages they had collected in the Tiumen Forwarding Prison. This was the day they were to meet a different man, the 'spiritual center' of the movement; that was what they called him.

Irina and Letchik always felt conspicuous since most of the men in the street were in uniform of one sort or another. "A real haven for *chinovniks*," they had been warned already in Tiumen. They walked rapidly past the police station which was, the exiles joked, appropriately the most picturesque building in the town with its high fire tower dominating the landscape. They picked up their supplies, exchanging a few friendly words with the apothecary and hurried on past the house of the Governor-General. They always avoiding the flat ground where the stockade that had held Dostoevsky during his many years of penal servitude once stood. Shortly after they arrived in Omsk, they met an exile who recalled how he had shared a cell with the writer and witnessed the terrible flogging he had received for complaining about the filth in their soup. "Took him to the hospital, just where you're working," he added. "We thought he was dead; lay there for six weeks. Afterwards we called him *pokoinik*, the dead man." He coughed into his handkerchief which was stained red. "If you can live through that, telling about it must have been easy." Irina remembered attending the reading by Dostoevsky in St. Petersburg with Vasiliev. A brief moment of happiness. She felt the terrible welling up of emotion that always follows such memories. She knew they would never again sit together in the gilded halls of the capital.

They made their way down a narrow, muddy lane and turned into a yard overgrown with weeds. A tall pine leaned protectively over the cabin. The wattling fence was broken in two places, threatening to collapse. The side of the cabin facing them sagged as if it were tired of holding up its end. The Siberian glass in the window gave off its characteristic iridescent glow. There were no flowers to relieve the dilapidated appearance of the place. They knocked and were admitted by a wizened old man with an enormous thatch of white hair and a large goiter on his neck. He bowed ceremoniously, kissed Irina's hand and waved them inside.

There appeared to be only two rooms in the hut. The walls were covered with whitewash which had worn thin over time. The floor was made of rough, mismatched planks. Books were stacked in piles along the walls as though they were re-enforcing them. Through an open door they could see the edge of a wooden bedstead, crudely hammered together and covered in a grey, but clean sheet. A small table stood at the side of the bed covered by another precariously balanced pile of books. They sat down facing their host in two of the three wooden straight back chairs in the room.

"My friends tell me you haven't much time, so I'll come quickly to the point. Recently, I came into possession of letters written more than eighty years ago by a member of the imperial family. There is no question about their authenticity. I have had them examined by people who were close to the writer, but who for reasons you know all too well, are now my colleagues in exile." The man paused as if to measure the effect of his words.

"These letters prove beyond a shadow of a doubt that Emperor Paul I was not the legitimate son of Catherine, miscalled 'the Great.' They bear out the suspicion that the father was in fact Count Saltykov, or as he was known in those circles, 'le beau Sergey.' So, the Romanov line appeared to have come to an end with the strangulation of Emperor Peter III in 1762 at the hands of Aleksei Orlov, a brother of one of Catherine's lovers, Gregory Orlov. The murder was covered up by a story put out for European consumption that Peter had died of colic. There were suspicions but until now, no written evidence exited to contradict the story, you understand? So our beloved 'little mother' as the Orlovs liked to call her was not only a whore but an accessory to murder after the fact; one assumes after and not before, but who knows about the timing of her knowledge? There is more to come! Remember! I said the Romanov line appeared to have come to an end with the death of Peter III. But my tale does not end with the proof in these letters."

Suddenly, the man jumped to his feet and ran to the door which he threw open. He stood for a moment looking rapidly from left to right. Then he returned to his seat shaking his head.

"Sorry, sorry," he muttered. "Old habits die hard." He passed his hand gently over his goiter.

"Listen friends, my comrades and I are getting old. We have lost touch with the outer world. But you are still young and vigorous. Yes, yes, I know, you are exiles, but you do not live under a life sentence. One day you shall be free and you will spread these stinking secrets to the world. And then the world will learn that we who came out on the Senate Square fifty-five years ago were righteous and noble in our cause, to end the illegitimate tyranny of the usurpers."

The man's voice cracked. He lowered his head.

"You must forgive me for ranting like this. It's been so long since I saw the faces of young Russia, you who carry on the spirit."

"Please, we will do anything to help you," Irina began, "but we have already overstayed our prison leave. The guards will wonder. They may send to find us. We cannot expose you. Let us come back. We can manage perhaps in a week."

Letchik stood up. "Irina is right. We must hurry even now to get back in time to avoid suspicion. You know how they are."

The man looked dazed. Irina took his hands in hers and pressed them hard. "We will come back. We give you our solemn word."

"Of course." His voice was hoarse, "of course. I understand. Go and remember that if by chance, which comes in many forms these days, you do not find me here then you must consult the 'Prince.'" He worked his lips into a bitter smile.

Chapter
Twenty-One

Vasili Vasilievich had often reflected on the fact that official investigations did not manage to get very far in Russia. People in the streets and teahouses who might have seen something unusual were not eager to share their information with the police. It wasn't even easy to get the ordinary citizen to serve on the newly created juries, fearful as they were of bringing in a verdict of not guilty that could be interpreted as a lack of trust in the authorities. These thoughts ran through his mind again as he sipped tea in an establishment across the street from Kennan's hotel. The place was half empty and it was a simple matter to strike up a conversation with one of the waiters.

"Dull town, this Tiumen," he finally said.

"You think so? And where is it lively?"

"Why Odessa, where I come from."

"Ah, you southern types are always bragging. Well, we have our murders too. Maybe not so many as you, but there you are."

Vasiliev ordered another tea, and the waiter leaned over wiping the table for the third or fourth time. He cast a glance back toward the rear of the teahouse.

"The boss don't like us to gossip. But I can tell you that I saw something that day."

"And what day was that?"

"Why the day they found the body of the warden's servant."

"So, you knew him, did you?"

"How did you guess?"

"I'm a great guesser. You might call it a pastime of mine."

"Next thing you'll be telling me that you read tea leaves."

"Been known to do that too."

The waiter laughed and wiped the table again.

"Yessir! I was throwing out some slops when old Ilia comes out early in the morning from that hotel across the way. Seemed strange to me, his being there that early, or, come to think of it, of being there at all."

"Not the kind of guest they entertain," said Vasiliev, showing his crooked teeth.

The waiter laughed again, but was called away to serve another customer. He came back shortly and, glancing around, made a show of wiping the table again.

"That's not the strangest part."

"Sounds like you've got a mystery in hand."

"Right you are. A smart little trap pulls up and the driver asks old Ilia if he can give him a lift. So it seemed, at least. And Ilia jumps in and off they go."

"What's so strange about all that?"

"Why the driver was an officer!" the waiter said triumphantly, as if he knew how to end a good story.

"Can't be," muttered Vasiliev.

"So there Mr. Odessa, can you top that?"

Vasiliev admitted he couldn't and before the waiter had a chance to wipe the table again he tossed down a few coins and left.

By the time they met later that evening Serov had sold off all his pies and made a small profit which he invested in a bottle of vodka and slices of smoked fish. He had arranged these on a table in their modest quarters near the Tiumen Prison. Vasiliev had spent the rest of the day fruitlessly trying to trace the route of the small trap with the officer and Ilia. But no one else seemed to have seen them. Vasiliev could tell from the twinkle in Serov's eyes, that he had had better luck.

Serov ceremoniously uncorked the bottle, produced two *riumochki* and filled them to the brim. They tossed them back and took a bite of the smoked fish.

"Now that the preliminaries are over, what have you got?" asked Vasiliev.

"Why do I have to go first? Jus' so you can tell me you knew it all the time, beggin' your pardon," Serov gazed fondly at the bottle."Well, maybe this time, I've somethin' to surprise you." Serov filled their glasses again and held his up to the light, then put it down on the table.

"Buyin' pies brings out the best in people," he began. Vasiliev knew he had to wait while Serov spun out his adventures of the morning.

Serov coughed. "This tale tellin' is increasin' my thirst." They quaffed off the second glass. "I runs into this old woman. Them's always the best source, you know. And she tells me that she was draggin' her goat across the yard when this trap passes her..."

"Driven by an officer," Vasiliev broke in.

Serov shook his head and reached for the bottle again, but then thought better about it and let his hand drop. He looked sharply at Vasiliev, but then chuckled.

"Yes, Vasili Vasilievich, and it damn near ran down her goat. But what kind of an officer?"

So it had always been, thought Vasiliev, ever since they were boys together in his father's village. Their game was all about who knew more and how he would reveal it. In this way he knew they would never entirely surrender their youth.

"No, I don't know."

"You might even guess," teased Serov.

"But I might guess wrong and then you'd lose faith in my powers."

Serov had to laugh at this. "I'll end it now. A Uhlan. He was, and I *guess* it was our old friend Captain Bark from how the old woman described him."

"Where did she see him? Was there anyone else in the trap?"

"Two streets down from the dump where the servant was found and the officer, she said, was all by himself."

"Damn it! I might have arrested Bark on the highway. I felt the impulse as we were standing over the body of the courier. The signs were clear. You remember I took a good look at the ground. There were only two sets of hoof prints besides those of the courier's mount. One glance at the Marshall of the Nobility told me he could not have been the killer. Did you see the difficulty he had in raising his right arm? An old war wound I expect. No, it had to be Bark. I should have demanded to examine Bark's saber. Yet I couldn't be absolutely sure. There were two or three other possible explanations of the absence of a third set of hoof prints."

Serov was tempted to ask what those might be. But he held his peace. He knew when it was important not to interrupt Vasiliev's train of logic.

"There was something else too that made me hesitate. I couldn't imagine Bark acting alone. Who was behind him? A man like Bark was not going to break down and tell me in an interrogation. And I didn't know whether the Marshall of the Nobility might have been somehow involved. There is another part of the puzzle. The killing of Ivan Fedorovich and the courier showed some similar features: the single blow to the head and the obvious mutilation. But, notice, Serov, that the murder weapon in the two cases were different. Ah! That surprises you! Good! Ivan Fedorovich had obviously been killed by an axe. The skull was smashed in. This was the work of Father Porfiry. The courier's head wound was clean cut and could only have been cause by a saber stroke. A clean saber stroke, it seems to me, which could only have been delivered by a trained swordsman. This must have been the work of Bark. But now we have the puzzle of a third murder and a third murder weapon. Krasin's servant had his throat cut. An officer was seen at the spot. True, a Uhlan. But there is a regiment of them in town. Was this Bark or are we looking for an accomplice? It could be, of course, that a clever killer, the same one, might have used different weapons just to cause confusion. Our mad priest says he was incited by 'heavenly voices' to kill Ivan Fedorovich. Were these voices imaginary? I think not. Let's suppose they were also the work of Bark. Just how he was able to perform this trick, I don't yet know. A ventriloquist? "

Serov raised an eyebrow.

"A man who can throw his voice. My old village teacher, Foma, learned how to do it when he was in the circus. It's one thing he never taught me. But I heard him do it. Amazing! Well, Bark may be a man of many parts. Did he also mutilate the body? Why would he do this? To cast suspicion on the skoptsy? Why castrate the courier as well? It would seem this was a clumsy attempt to link the two murders to the sectarians.

"So what does my grand scenario look like now? Bark incites Porfiry to kill Ivan Fedorovich, mutilates the body in order to implicate the skoptsy and then steals the mysterious papers. He then intercepts the courier, in order presumably to get hold of the rest of the papers or a different set and mutilates him as well, to mask the real motive. But the murder of Krasin's servant does not fit into the grand scenario. Unless we assume that the papers he was delivering to Kennan are related in some way to the other two sets coming from Ivan Fedorovich. If all this speculation of mine is correct, it still leaves us with the question of the missing papers, what they contained and why they were important. It also leaves unexplained the connection between all three murders. The papers, especially the last set carried by Krasin's servant, would not seem to have any value for a man like Bark.

"From what Sophia Vadimovna has told me, I would guess that all the papers are connected with an exposé of the exile system. If important people want to cover up the rot, we could be facing a wide conspiracy. Another political crime? Just what I'm always afraid of. Here we go again, Serov! First, the plot to assassinate the Tsar; then the pogroms concealing the murder of the rabbi in Kiev. Now this? I hate political crimes; they leave too many loose threads. We've got to try to tie them up. The first thing is to find out who Bark is working for."

Vasiliev got up from the table and started to pace the room. Serov looked wistfully at the bottle but knew there would be no more drinking that night. Reluctantly, he inserted the cork.

"Krasin must know more about him," murmured Vasiliev. "Or would it be best just to go right to Omsk?" It was no Rome, he thought, but all roads seemed to lead there.

Chapter
Twenty-Two

Captain Bark made his way slowly back to his room in an old building on the outskirts of Omsk. He felt restless, though he had played well again and won a considerable sum. Poor Rykov had lost heavily; he was a fine fellow but hopeless with cards. Bark had staked him again. Was it a mistake to encourage his wild playing? Bark thought not. Some day it would prove useful to have Rykov in his debt. After collecting his winnings, Bark had ordered champagne, as he always did. They expected it of him. It was a gesture he could afford, and it kept him popular in the regiment.

He stopped short of the low wooden structure where he was quartered and glanced at the sky. A faint light in the east was beginning to wash out the stars on the horizon. He was reminded of another dawn when the curse of winning had first fallen on him. The same feeling overcame him every time he left the others drinking his champagne and discussing whether to attribute his winning to skill or luck. That kind of talk made him nervous. His thoughts carried him back to the time when he was a young lieutenant, already a good player but indifferent to the feelings of the losers. He could still see the faces of the other players that fateful night, especially Zenkov's ridiculous bushy moustache rising and falling like a furry animal when he spat out the ugly words."You're cheating, Bark!" There was nothing to do but challenge him. Dueling was illegal but it still happened, and his fellow officers were not going to stop it.

Bark intended to wait for Zenkov's first shot— he could tell the man was too excited to aim carefully— and then fire in the air once Zenkov had missed. Later he realized what a foolish risk he was taking, but when one is twenty two, he reflected, it is easy to gamble with one's life. Zenkov's shot came closer than he expected. He felt the rush of air against his cheek. Then he was enraged by the sight of that bushy moustache, as if it were taunting him again, his coarse voice snarling: "You're cheating, Bark." Bark took careful aim and shot Zenkov right through his mouth.

It was impossible to hush up the incident. His colonel was sympathetic, but Zenkov's family was influential. Bark had been stripped of his commission and sent down as a common soldier to a Caucasian line regiment. The Murid uprising rebellion had just been repressed and Shamil taken captive. Men no longer died of saber wounds but of typhus or more rarely from playing Russian roulette induced by boredom. It was there Bark had learned to win moderately, to lose occasionally and to order champagne after the last hand. He was determined to win back his officer rank. He volunteered for every dangerous assignment, for there were still bandits among the mountaineers who had been in Shamil's service. He earned a reputation as a daredevil, and a crack shot to boot. He had finally been promoted for gallantry. When General Grigoriev passed through on a tour of inspection, he was impressed by Bark's record and made him an aide-de-camp. At the time, Bark didn't realize at the time what impressed him most. His fellow officers were surprised and envious. Bark realized that Grigoriev had saved him from a slow death in the Caucasus. But he failed to anticipate the price of his liberation. He only gradually learned what was in store for him.

Grigoriev was not only ambitious but a born intriguer and a reactionary as well. Bark was no liberal but he felt uneasy listening to Grigoriev rant about the dangers of the subversion. As if the monarchy could be toppled by a handful of crazy students. Of course, the assassination of Alexander II had shaken Bark. But he blamed the security arrangements. If he had been in charge of the tsar's bodyguard, he kept saying to himself, it would never have happened.

He entered his room and sat down on the bed. His servant had long since gone to sleep. No sense rousing him; he could take off his own boots. That much he had learned in the Caucasus, he laughed bitterly to himself. He never thought he would look back on his days in the mountains with regret but, recalling his Dante, he knew he had moved deeper from the first circle of hell to another nearer the center.

Damn Grigoriev! Why did he have to pick me out for his dirty work? A rhetorical question, he knew, if there ever was one. He sank back on his pillow, still fully dressed, and stared at the ceiling, as if he were still searching for the fading stars. It was one thing to kill man in a fair fight, a duel or a skirmish; another to cut down an unarmed man who had done you no harm. That made him a common criminal. As for the rest, he shuddered and cast the revolting image out of his mind. He had been skeptical from the first that Grigoriev's elaborate deception would work. Then Vasiliev, of all people, had to show up! What the hell was he doing on the Great Siberian Road? The last time Bark had heard about him, he was in the south; Kiev wasn't it? Something to do with the pogroms. He recalled what else he knew about the detective. Nothing that could reassure him. Their paths had never crossed in the Caucasus, though Bark knew he had been there on a mission during the war. There were plenty of stories about Vasiliev's exploits, how he had solved the murder of a senior officer during the siege of Plevna and restored morale in the army on the Danube. Perhaps Grigoriev could fill him in. Bark could tell from the way Vasiliev looked at him that he was already under suspicion.

He groaned and rolled on his side. A few coins fell out of his pocket. He fingered them thoughtfully. Perhaps it was time to quit. He had been saving his winnings for the right moment. No one would have suspected how much, still less why. Champagne for everyone! Loans to Rykov! Loyal, even obsequious to his lord and master, General Alexander Alexeevich Grigoriev! He was confident *his* deceptions had worked. Tomorrow he would count his little hoard, though he was already certain that he had amassed enough to make his way to Europe. Desertion? What the hell did he care! Once there he would take his chances as a professional gambler, making the rounds of the watering spas. Why not? Hadn't he outwitted the best players in the Russian Army? He had planned it carefully. Just the one more sordid job, a necessary one, to cover his escape.

There was much to plan but he needed to sleep. He forced his mind to dwell on more pleasurable things. He rubbed his crotch and conjured up Anna's ravishing body. Such an easy conquest! He couldn't believe a virgin could be that good in bed. Besides, she was such a valuable inside source. Of course, a little money helped along the passionate side of their relationship. He owed her the information about Kennan's visit and that idiot Krasin's criminal behavior in passing along state secrets. He didn't need Grigoriev's instructions to do what had to be done. He reached under the bed to reassure himself that the statistical reports were still safely packed in his strong box.

Too bad the servant had been so stubborn. Bark felt he had given him a fair chance to live. A few gold rubles and the story about a robbery gone wrong. But the man resisted. Bark had no choice. He wondered how Anna would react. Then he thought about how he would comfort her. His somber mood evaporated. He undressed hurriedly and fell into bed. He slept soundly and in the morning could not remember any dreams.

Chapter Twenty-Three

Anna Bogdanovna curtsied low when Vasiliev and Serov appeared the following morning at the door of Warden Krasin. Serov couldn't help admiring the effect produced by this simple gesture. His opinion of Krasin moved up a notch. Vasiliev noticed that the warden appeared to have recovered from the loss of his man servant, Ilia. Greeting Vasiliev his face assumed a mournful expression, but not so quickly that Vasiliev failed to catch a glimpse of a different emotion. A sense of satisfaction? Contentment? Something stronger?

Krasin invited them into his study and called to Anna to prepare a samovar. Vasiliev asked him about Bark. Krasin was happy to oblige, but he could not restrain himself from stealing glances at Anna who was taking her time in preparing the samovar. She bustled about with a hint of a proprietary air. When she left the room the door remained slightly ajar.

"You see, Vasili Vasilievich, I made some inquiries among my fellow officers. Captain Bark enjoys a certain notoriety as a gambler. The story is that he once killed a man in a duel over cards. He wins a great deal more often than he loses, but always treats his comrades to champagne at the end of an evening of cards. So he is popular, yet he seems to lack any close friends. He has carried out a number of missions for the deputy Governor-General, Grigoriev. So he enjoys a reputation for loyalty. Yet, there is something about him that does not inspire trust. Does this make sense?"

Vasiliev nodded as a sign of encouragement.

"He comes and goes a lot. To Omsk I mean. He has no fixed schedule or duties, as far as I can judge."

"And Grigoriev, what kind of a man is he?"

Krasin rose from his seat and began to pace the room. As he passed the slightly open door, he mechanically closed it and then stopped, cocking his head. Vasiliev heard it too, a slight shuffling sound outside in the corridor. Krasin's hand close around the door handle. He hesitated, then shrugged and continued to pace.

When he began speaking again his face had grown hard. "General Grigoriev is an ambitious man. Oh, ambition is common enough among our *sanovniki*, our high officials. But," he whirled in his tracks and fixed Vasiliev with a sharp glance, "some kinds of ambition pass beyond the limits of good taste, if you know what I mean. Yes, Grigoriev's ambition knows no bounds. There are also tales, no more than rumors *as yet*. Well, you didn't ask me for gossip so..." his voice trailed off.

Vasiliev did not believe he could press Krasin any further. The man had already probably said more than he should have about his superior. After all, why should he confide in a man he hardly knew? Vasiliev thought it was time to give him a reason. He proceeded to tell Krasin what he had found out about the murders of the courier and Ilia.

"If I am right, then, Bark must have been acting on instructions from Grigoriev. A lieutenant in the Uhlans would have no use for statistics about the Tiumen Forwarding Prison. But presumably, Grigoriev might see an advantage in preventing them from falling into the hands of a foreigner, the American Kennan, who would certainly publish them abroad. At the very least the statistics would damage the reputation of the government, and surely ruin Grigoriev's career. If as you say, Grigoriev is ambitious and Bark is unscrupulous, they make a good team. What they did not count on was your quick decision to lend the documents to Kennan. The question is do they know about this? If so then Kennan and his friend, Frost, may be in mortal danger. This is why we must get to Omsk as quickly as possible. It Bark has killed twice, at least, he will not hesitate to kill again."

Krasin held out both hands to Vasiliev. "You are a wonder, Vasili Vasilievich! You have already solved the murder of my dear

Ilia. I promised you the best horses for your trip to Omsk. I shall personally see to it that you get them immediately."

Krasin accompanied them to the stables and ordered two Siberian ponies to be saddled. "They're not much to look at, but they are tough and fast. You can push them as hard as you want."

On returning to his house, Krasin rang for Anna, but she did not answer. He went to look for her and found her in the kitchen bent over the table writing. He had approached quietly and she looked up startled. His first reaction was to be surprised. He did not imagine that she was literate. Then he registered the look of terror on her face as she covered the paper with a towel.

"Anna. What is this? What are you writing?" He pushed her rudely aside and snatched up the paper.

He read it out loud: "My darling Andriusha. They know about you. You must flee. I will leave too. We shall meet in Semipalatinsk as we..."

He lowered the paper and stared wildly at her. He remembered the door left ajar, the sound in the corridor.

"You're nothing but a spy! Who is this?" he shook the paper. "Bark! Of course! And did you tell him about Ilia? My God!"

Anna sank to her knees and grasped his hand, kissing it wildly.

"No! No! Boris Ippolitovich; you have it wrong! I can explain this. It's not Bark." She whimpered.

He looked down on her feelings of pity, rage and desire swept over him.

"Anna, Anna! What a fool you are. Now I have no choice but to arrest you. We could have..." he cut himself short, wrenched his hand loose and turned away from her. He crumpled the unfinished letter, tossed it aside and turned on his heel, leaving her kneeling behind him. Anna bent her forehead to the floor. Images of the women in the Tiumen Prison flashed through her mind. Ten years in prison would destroy her. She had seen them, the women whose beauty quickly faded quickly and whose strong bodies wasted away. A wave of horror swept over her. She leaped to her feet and, trembling in every part of her body, she cried out, "No!"

Krasin ignored her. Her head was in a whirl; she was blinded by tears. She could no longer see him, only hear his boots pounding on the parquet floor as he strode out of the room. She seized a carving knife from the board and rushed after him. He half turned as she plunged the blade into his side. Krasin cried out and fell to his knees. Groaning, he began to creep on all fours along the corridor toward the entry door. Anna stood paralyzed with fear and the horror of what she had done. Now he was calling for help. His voice was weak but if he made it to the door he would raise the alarm. She fought down her nausea and stepped back into the kitchen, reaching behind her for support. Her hand grasped the handle of a heavy iron skillet on the table. She wrapped her fingers around it, squeezing with all her might. Then she staggered back into the corridor where she saw the trail of blood and, for an instant, hesitated. He had reached the door and was reaching up for the handle now. She rushed up to him, raised the skillet high in the air, shut her eyes and with a cry of rage brought it down on his head with all her strength. At the crunching sound of the impact, she fainted.

Outside the police stables, Vasiliev and Serov had mounted their ponies and turning north cantered down the road to Omsk.

Chapter
Twenty-Four

Vasiliev and Serov started their journey to Omsk in a leisurely fashion until they learned at the first few post stations that Kennan and Frost had been pressing hard. Well, thought Vasiliev, the Americans are tough, just like the novels of Fennimore Cooper described them. A *tarantas* passing over these roads at such a speed, they must have been willing to endure a great deal of discomfort. There was no chance of catching up with them, but Vasiliev was worried about their getting too far ahead. No telling what Bark had in mind. They stepped up the pace. For the first two days they hardly rested, but they seemed to be falling behind.

"Kennan and Frost must be made of iron. They seemed to have mastered the art of sleeping in a *tarantas* that bounces around like a skiff in the Baltic. I think at the next station we'll have to follow their example. It's either that or stop more frequently to rest."

"I don't know, Vasili Vasilievich. I'd rather ride hard, change the horses more often. Then we could flop down for a few hours and get some real sleep."

The countryside was monotonous. A great marshy plain stretched out in all directions, dotted with large, shallow pools of water interspersed with clumps of stunted pines and small birch trees. At one village they heard that two foreigners had ordered fresh horses but not before paying a visit to the local *barin*, a gentleman of some means. Vasiliev decided they might find out something from him about the Americans' state of mind. Did they think they were being pursued?

At the threshold of a large two story wooden house, they were greeted by a robust and cheerful man, Valerie Sergeevich Kolmakov, a merchant industrialist whose success in life was amply displayed in the most exotic garden Vasiliev had seen since he had been on military service in the Balkans. Several winding walks led through flower beds and plantings of current and raspberry bushes to a conservatory filled with all manner of tropical fruits. In the center of the garden stood a huge greenhouse sheltering a grove of banana and palm trees. Kolmakov invited them to dine with him. Over roast pheasant and caviar he shared his vision of Siberia as storehouse of treasures which properly exploited would lift Russia out of its impoverished condition to the level of the United States.

"This is what I told to Mr. Kennan, but I don't believe I convinced him," he chuckled as he poured more wine. "Of course, we need more men who are willing to take risks, not more government bureaucrats. We'll be getting more free peasant colonists now that the period of temporary obligation is over. But they will need guidance. Let me tell you, as I told Mr. Kennan, who at least agreed with me on this matter, that we could use these political exiles to better use. There are men and women of great talent among them. Some of them have already achieved local fame, if you catch my meaning. Take for example, the young medical couple who recently transformed sanitary conditions at the Tiumen Forwarding Prison and are now doing such splendid work in Omsk. Yes, their fame has spread even to remote corners like mine."

Vasiliev wanted more, but held back. Later perhaps others would come to visit Kolmakov inquiring pleasantly about the views of Inspector Vasiliev. He turned the conversation to Kennan's views on road conditions, and asked, incidently, whether others had recently passed this way. Kolmakov had to admit that Kennan's travel experiences had cast doubt on the prospects of a Siberian paradise. And yes, it was peculiar that another visitor had showed up a few days later. "For months no one from the outer world and then, a crowd," he chuckled, pouring more wine. "But this was a bird of different plumage, if you get my meaning. These army officers can get under your skin with their arrogant ways. What do they produce? I ask you. He too was in a great hurry, but Mr. Kennan and his friend were polite in their haste, if you catch my meaning."

Kolmakov pressed them to spend the night. When Vasiliev declined, Kolmakov rubbed his chin, shook his head and otherwise expressed his dismay.

"I'm beginning to wonder, Inspector, whether there is something missing in my hospitality. It seems as though you are all involved in some mad race. But what could be the prize at the end?"

The road to Ishim did not improve, yet they found out that Kennan and Frost had made more than 200 miles in a day and a half. Vasiliev wondered whether even Bark could keep up the pace. And Kolmakov seems to have thrown him off the track. The wily merchant had played dumb when Bark demanded information about the two Americans. "It was all a matter of how people treated you," he had grinned, pouring more wine.

"I wonder if Kennan and Frost are typical Americans?" Vasiliev mused as they rode into Ishim. "They don't seem to pay much attention to class or rank."

"Or to what thoughts you might be havin'," said Serov as they dismounted.

But not everyone appeared happy about the Americans.

"Seems they're out to ruin our post horses," grumbled one station master. "They hardly stopped for the coming home of the 'Mother of God.'" Vasiliev looked puzzled.

"The pilgrims, Vasili Vasilievich, the pilgrims. They're greetin' the icon's returnin' to Ishim from its wanderin's," said Serov. "They're comin' from all over."

Vasiliev's eyebrows shot up. "My, my Sergeant, you have unplumbed depths."

Serov smiled. It wasn't often he could surprise Vasiliev and it always gave him pleasure to do so.

"Village wisdom," he muttered.

They rode hard the next day until they came to a neatly painted signpost by the gate of a long fence that enclosed the pasture land of the commune.

'Village of Krutaya

Distance from St. Petersburg 2992 *versts*.

Distance from Moscow 2526 *versts*.

Houses 42. Male souls 97.'

Cossack gate keeper

The gatekeeper, an old Cossack, had a tale to tell. The Americans had come "whizzing through like the devil was after them," he chuckled. "But they had to wait around while fresh horses were called in from the pasture. No one knew where America was except for a young feller had been to Omsk. He thought the Americans 'were the wisest people God had created.' Not all of 'em saw it the same way." The gatekeeper gave a gruff laugh. "An argument broke out.The Americans were enjoying it."

The gatekeeper paused and squinted his eyes.

"Your Americans are naïve ain't they?"

"What do you mean?"

"Well, it seems they thinks all exiles are innocent victims. Nothin' of the sort! They've not seen a *bunt'*, I'll bet you that."

Vasiliev said nothing but thought of Pushkin's words:'terrible is the Russian revolt.'

"Yes, a real *bunt'*. Why I'll wager there isn't a good word for it in English, eh, Vasili Vasilievich?"

Vasiliev shrugged. No sense interrupting the man's monologue. He would go on to the end no matter what. How many times had he told his story? Vasiliev was certain that a story was coming. He knew all the symptoms. The old Cossack put down his pipe and leaned forward on his stool. So, thought Vasiliev, I'll be a good audience, and keep my mouth shut.

"Yes, a real *bunt'*. I've seen one or two in my time. The first one was in 'sixty-four, it was. A God forsaken village in Orenburg province. Some peasants got pissed all because of a little thing. God know what. They starts cutting timber, you know how it is, and hauling it away. God knows what for. Firewood? More likely to fix up some hut that was falling apart."

The man spat to the side and wiped his mouth. He glanced at his pipe but rejected the idea. Instead he coughed, his chest heaving. Vasiliev sat quietly waiting.

"Eh, beg pardon. My last gasp!" he croaked and shook his head as if that would give him a little more time to finish what he had to say.

"Yeah, it all started with the cutting. The estate steward gets wind of it and has the bright idea of riding out to get them to stop. Imagine! All by himself! A stupid German, no doubt about it. And they knocks him off his horse and gives him a beating. That gets them riled up. So they decides to take it out on the barn, burns it down and marches on to the manor house. Now, it's a lucky thing the house is a few versts away. Otherwise they'd of sacked it for sure. But they wastes time getting organized and rounding up some of the young village hot bloods. By the time they gets ready, the stable boy is wondering what happened to the steward. He finds out quickly enough and rides off to get help. Lucky for him he knew where we was billeted. Thirty of us, Cossacks of the Ural Host. We rode like hell and got there in the nick o' time. We pass the smoking barn, the roof all fallen in. No reason to stop. The peasants had driven out the cattle. Hey! They sees us coming; we're raising a hell of a dust cloud, though it's gettin' dark. And then— can you imagine what happens next, eh?"

The old Cossack leaned forward, his eyes glistening as if they were about to burst into tears. He paused, waiting for Vasiliev to say something. Then he grunted and went on.

"Well, they sees us coming; I said that didn't I? Yeah, and they turns to face us. I could see the flash of the pitchforks and axes in the light of the torches, you know. We're in for a fight, I thinks. But no—can you imagine it?" He waited again for Vasiliev's reaction.

"No, I can't," said Vasiliev grudgingly.

That pleased the old Cossack. " 'course not, and your American friends couldn't neither." He spat again.

"They sees us and they're going down on their knees! The pitch-forks and axes are falling from their hands like someone snatched them away. We rides up and makes a circle around them. They're on their knees, you understand, and they whip out their crucifixes, as if someone gives them an order. And they hold them high. God Almightly! I thinks; they're praying for mercy.

"Our Sergeant jumps down, quick as you please. He's a big man, you know. He takes hold of the first old guy he can get his hands on, pulls him up and spins him round. He lifts him up and shakes him like a rag doll and shouts at them that's kneeling down. 'Listen you sons of bitches,' he says, 'I could round you up and send you off. You'd get a tenner for sure. Half of you'd never come back. But God as my witness, I'm a forgiving man.'

"Well, Vasili Vasilievich, I'm amazed at this little speech. But I was new to the unit; the rest, they'd been around a while. They're leanin' on their saddles, taking it all in like they'd heard it all before. The Sergeant isn't finished. 'You poor bastards, you don't deserve anything better, but I'm going to give you a chance. So hand over your ringleaders, and we'll flay their asses off. Then you'll take the timber and re-build the barn. I'll settle things with the *barin*. Then we'll be quits. What do you say?'

"He sets the peasant down on his feet. The old guy is trembling, but he spits it out; 'Brothers, we've met a merciful man. We've sinned and we'll take what's comin' to us.' He calls out a few names and half a dozen men steps forward, heads bowed. The old man begins to strip to the waist and they does the same. The Sergeant gives an order and three troopers dismount, each one holding his *knut* and they beat until the blood flows. The Sergeant calls a halt and the troopers mount up again. The Sergeant rides on to the manor house with his corporal. The rest of us wait for him. The peasants have lifted up the beaten men. They puts their arms around them and lead them off. The last thing I sees is the line of them trudgin' back to the village."

The old Cossack took up his pipe which had gone out. He took a few minutes to light it. Then he looked up again.

"So, Inspector, how is that for a story to tell your American friends, eh?'

"I liked your tale," said Vasiliev. He handed the gate keeper a few rubles. "And then another stranger came by, didn't he?"

The gatekeeper screwed up his eyes.

"Yes," he said, 'nother one."

"You're not of these parts, are you? Why if I didn't know better," Vasiliev drawled in imitation of a man of the south, "I'd say you hailed from Odessa or thereabouts. It's the way you tell a tale. And if that's the case, I wouldn't be surprised, given your honorable age that you might even have served in the Turkish War; maybe even in the siege of Sevastopol in '54. "

The gatekeeper's eyes widened.

"Your Honor looks deep into a man."

"Let's see if I can guess some more. It's a game with me you see. The way you spoke about 'nother man, I'd say you didn't much care for him. Army wasn't he? You navy fellows did all the fighting during the siege, right? And your limp tells me you've got some nasty memories. So this army man comes waltzing through and right away start pumping you. And you don't like it. You know, there's something about this country, Siberia I mean. People don't like to be pushed around. You learned that when you came here. And humble as your place may be, you've been a Cossack trooper; you've got your dignity. Right?"

During Vasiliev's monologue the gatekeeper kept his eyes fixed on him, and began to nod.

"So what did you tell this high and mighty officer? Nothing, I'll wager, Nothing about what he wanted to know."

The gatekeeper broke into a grin that revealed a set of rotten teeth. He said nothing but touched his fur cap and swung wide the gate.

"Bark doesn't seem to have learned much about Siberia, Serov. Some day I'm going to tell Kennan how we tracked him through merchants and gatekeepers. He'll laugh for sure. Still, the first thing to do in Omsk is to make sure the Americans are safe and then to find Irina."

Chapter
Twenty-Five

Captain Bark strode briskly out of the Omsk Police Station when he spotted Vasiliev and Serov riding into town. Cursing to himself, he quickly moved back out of sight and watched as they stopped in front of the Imperial Hotel where, as he had just learned, the Americans were staying. Now he would have to change his plans. He stood by the window for a few minutes, trying to sort out his thoughts, when he heard a voice behind him that made him start.

"Can I give assistance to Your Honor?"

It was one of Grigoriev's flunkies. He brushed him off but realized that he was drawing attention to himself. A mistake. He would have to avoid looking as if he were snooping around. He quickly left, taking a back way to his quarters.

Kennan and Frost were happy to see Vasiliev and Serov. As they sat down to tea in the Hotel's dingy dining room, Vasiliev asked Kennan if he was training to get a job with the Pony Express when he returned home. "It seems you Americans are always in a hurry."

Kennan smiled. "In the States the pony express is a thing of the past. It's all railroads now. Even the cowboys are beginning to fade from the scene. A pity, really, but such is the engine of progress."

"Ah, yes, railroads. We're well behind you there. I met an interesting gentleman in Kiev last year, a certain Sergius Witte, who dreams about building a Trans-Siberian railroad like your Trans-Continental. So it is we who should be in a hurry. But that does not seem to be part of the Russian character. Serov is closer to the ground on this one. What do you think, Sergeant?"

Serov seemed not to be paying attention. Then he looked around at all three men. "Beggin' your pardon, but Russians are in a hurry when it counts."

"And when is that?" asked Frost.

"Well, when the crops ripen, you know, the wheat and oats, you've got to bring them in fast. If you let the rain get to them first, they're sure to rot. So you work fast. Up before dawn, work 'til the sun sets. A crust of bread to keep you goin'. Why I've even seen harvestin' by the light of the moon. But when it's all over, there's little to do. And when the snow comes, you settle in."

"So, it's a different rhythm of life" said Kennan. "But in the States the farmer is always busy in winter, repairing his gear, caring for the stock, plenty to do."

Serov shrugged. He knew nothing about a farmer's life in America. He couldn't imagine anything different from the Russian village. But he did notice that an officer who came in after them had quietly shifted his table to be nearer to them. He signaled Vasiliev with a quick glance that something worth seeing was happening behind his back.

"Been there long?" asked Vasiliev

Kennan and Frost looked puzzled.

"Long enough to hear," Serov muttered noisily sipping his tea.

Vasiliev proposed continuing the conversation in Kennan's rooms. On the way he explained that surveillance of foreigners increased the closer they got to the center of power, even in a provincial capital.

"Not very subtle," remarked Kennan as he closed the door behind them.

"Some are, some aren't. It would be a mistake to underestimate the Gendarmes, for instance. They are better trained at such things."

"Well," Kennan continued, "the Governor-General certainly couldn't be one of them."

"You've already met, have you?"

"He deigned to give us an interview. Grigoriev by name. A coarse man in every way. He managed to be abrupt and suspicious at the same time. He barely glanced at our documents from the Ministry of Interior. I'll always remember what he said. 'God's in His heaven and Petersburg's far away. Such is the saying of our

Police station and fire tower in Omsk

peasants.' He said he couldn't encourage us to visit the prison. 'Under repair; it would give you a misleading impression. You'd best look elsewhere,' is what he said. There was nothing to do but leave."

"I did get to sketch the police station," said Frost. "It's the most impressive building in town. Now I'm surprised they let me do it. They might have thought I was a spy," he chuckled.

"Ten years, Mr. Frost, if you're lucky," Vasiliev laughed showing his crooked teeth. But then his smile faded.

"Listen, gentlemen, you are in some real danger. There are men in positions of power who are frightened by the fact that you now have in your possession statistics about the Tiumen Forwarding Prison that reveal the system as inhuman and corrupt."

"But the director, a Mr. Krasin, freely gave us these statistics. He was very cooperative and friendly. I had the impression he wanted to help reform the system by making these terrible conditions public."

"Perhaps he did," said Vasiliev. "There are decent men in official positions scattered all over Russia. But they are scattered. There are no reforming societies as in England or your country. Any such organization would be considered subversive. Some of us do our best to correct injustices. But we act pretty much alone. The people who organize do it secretly. They are, as you know, determined to overthrow the government not reform it. Well, I don't want to give a speech. But I guess I am giving one." This time his lips barely cracked a smile. "You probably know that the present tsar doesn't favor the reformers in his own government; he doesn't agree with what his father, Alexander II, had in mind before he was assassinated. No consultative assembly! The tsar's advisers don't want the outside world to know anything about the conditions in the Siberian exile system."

As Vasiliev spoke, Serov had wandered over to the window. "He's outside now, across the street. The same man."

"To come to the point, then. I think there will be an attempt to relieve you of the statistics," said Vasiliev

"You mean threats, intimidation? They'll get nowhere that way."

"I'm sure they wouldn't; they know you well enough not to try it. Perhaps I'm wrong. But I fear they will try something more violent."

"Robbery, assault?"

"Not to be excluded." Vasiliev did not add that there had already been two men murdered.

Chapter Twenty-Six

Vasiliev's request for an interview with the Governor-General, Grigoriev, was answered promptly, setting a time early the next morning. He steeled himself for what he expected would be an unpleasant meeting. He already suspected a link between the Governor-General and Bark, but would a man in Grigoriev's position take the risk of commissioning a murder? It seemed unlikely, but there were other ways of accomplishing the same ends. The plea of Henry II rang in his ears: "will no one rid me of this troublesome priest?" As Vasiliev had learned to his chagrin, in the matter of political crimes there were always shadowy figures standing in a row, one behind the other. There was no telling where the line ended, how high in the hierarchy of power brokers the ultimate arbiter sat, impervious to the investigations of a lowly police inspector. He would have to be careful too, he thought, how he raised the question of arranging an interview with Irina. He despised these moments when he was forced to act the part of an obsequious courtier.

He had gone over in his mind many times how he would react at his first meeting with Irina. He had to admit to himself that his feelings were confused. This annoyed him. His love for her had in no way diminished. If anything it had become more intense, the need to be with her more urgent. But he was also fearful that what she had suffered since they last met in Moscow must have left a scar on her spirit, perhaps even blunting her earlier true feelings for him. He found himself struggling to dismiss his gloomiest thoughts. He recalled the faces of the women in the yard of the Tiumen Prison, faces marked by great suffering, hopelessness and despair. Irina was made of stronger stuff, but it might take her some time to restore her natural emotional life, perhaps, he thought with a sickening feeling, if ever. And what of her relationship with Letchik? He was her constant companion; she could not have survived without him. Krasin had made that clear to him. They were already comrades in the movement before they had been thrown together in circumstances so desperate that he could only imagine them. As they fought sickness and disease, the bond between them must have grown stronger. Had the comradeship of revolutionaries become something more?

He remembered his own moment of weakness in her absence when he had been attracted to Ruth, the beautiful daughter of Rabbi Meyer in Kiev, and how he carried within him the pain of responsibility for her death. How could he expect Irina to have remained absolutely steadfast in her love for him? Did it really matter? He refused to believe he might have lost her. He wouldn't be like Orpheus, he promised himself; he would not look back. They'd come out of the darkness together. The main thing was how to organize their escape. For he had become convinced, he couldn't remember exactly when, that they couldn't make a life together in Russia.

Perhaps the idea had been growing since the assassination of Alexander II, when he first realized that there was no longer much hope of changing Russia. The new tsar, Alexander III, was a man of limited vision, a hopeless reactionary surrounded by like-thinking creatures. But what was the alternative?

For all their idealism, the revolutionaries did not offer a path to freedom. They lacked any political experience or, what was more serious in his mind, any real understanding of the peasantry. He was half peasant himself, yet he was often bewildered by them. How could it be otherwise? The other half of his self, nourished by foreign nannies and tutors in the house of an aristocrat, educated in the Page Corps, left him suspended, as his mother often reminded him, between two world, at home in neither. So, he knew what the peasants said they wanted, but in their way they were as utopian as the revolutionaries: divide the land, leave us alone, we'll take care of our own affairs. They seemed to swing from lethargy and fatalism to wild outbursts, as if they had been storing up their rage until they could no longer contain it. And then, the pogroms in the south, the killings in Kiev, Christians turning against Jews; but weren't they all fellow sufferers and subjects of the same tsar? They had lived together peacefully for a century ever since the partitions of Poland had brought hundreds of thousands of Jews into the Empire. What had happened since then? And what hope now was there that the fear and hatred unleashed by the mobs could be put to rest? The government still refused to emancipate the Jews, leaving the youth little alternative but to emigrate, rebel or submit to a humiliating life.

On top of that, he thought, counting up his moments of disillusion, he had been exposed to the exile system, not just to the knowledge it existed, to the impersonal lists of statistics, but to the cruel reality and injustice of the system. Yes, he reminded himself, there were always a few good men standing out against the tide, his friend Ivan, the Iron colonel fighting a rear guard action in St. Petersburg, the Kiev Chief of Police trying to manage fairly a city roiling with ethnic tensions, and Krasin, the head of the Tiumen Prison, sadly aware of the hopelessness of his position, mourning the loss of two exiles who had improved conditions where the government had failed. The odds against them were too great.

Chapter
Twenty-Seven

Some men's faces mirror the state of their soul, thought Vasiliev, as he entered the office of the Governor-General. Seeing Grigoriev for the first time, made his heart sink. The Governor-General was seated at a massive, ornate desk, the legs of which were carved in the shape of acanthus leaves as if announcing the presence of a Byzantine Emperor. Grigoriev was a large man, with a broad chest fashioned, thought Vasiliev, to accommodate his many medals and orders. An unnecessary and vain display for a day time reception. His coarse features were masked by a heavy black beard with faint traces of gray and a matching tangle of hair that seemed to spurt from the middle of his forehead, leaving very little of his puffy flesh exposed to the curiosity of his visitors. Stiff tufts of hair even protruded from his ears and nostrils like mountain brambles. He growled a greeting and gestured Vasiliev to a plain wooden chair at some distance from the desk. Vasiliev wondered how such a savage looking creature could have risen to the rank of actual state councilor. Of course, there was his reputation as an efficient if brutal administrator. Then he remembered that Grigoriev had married a Gagarin, freeing him from monetary worries and the temptations of corruption, at least in the form of bribery. But power was an even more potent aphrodisiac. A single folio had been placed in front of him, in the exact center of the desk. His first words were spoken as if he were reluctant to part with them.

"So Major Vasiliev, your reputation precedes you." He deliberately spread his large hands on the folio, which Vasiliev assumed was his service record, giving the impression of bringing it under his control. "I understand you have been assigned to accompany the Americans. Is this to protect them from our barbarian *inorodtsy*, the native tribes, or perhaps from escaping convicts? I can assure you, the tribes have been domesticated and convicts who try to escape are soon hunted down; few even reach the shelter of the woods along the Great Siberian Road. But what does Petersburg know of our security arrangements?"

Vasiliev was determined not to be drawn. He addressed Grigoriev in the measured tones he reserved for *sanovniki*, high ranking bureaucrats with exaggerated opinions of their own importance. He explained his mission by quoting the letter of instructions issued by the Minister of Interior.

"Yes, yes, I know what the Ministry wants to get out of all this. But since you have been dancing in attendance on the Americans, tell me how much poking around have they really done?" Grigoriev kept his hands pressed down tightly on the folio.

Vasiliev confined himself to a few bland remarks about the trip, omitting any negative impressions that had struck Kennan and Frost so powerfully.

"They were here, you know, in my office, babbling away, trying to convince me that nothing was further from their minds except to give the world an honest account of our exile system. Why do we need foreigners meddling in our affairs, which they do not understand? Let me tell you something about them. I know about their camps, yes their camps! During the Civil War, not so long ago, there was an abominable place called Andersonville, where Union prisoners of war died like flies. And these were not criminals, Major! Our exiles live in comfort by comparison. Oh, I do not speak of the prisons; everywhere prisons are the same, overcrowded, dirty with the filth the lower orders produce wherever they live. Is this not so? Think of the civilized English with their Bedlam, a byword for miserable incarceration! Haven't we all read Dickens? The Americans might be surprised to find out what we have. People in the slums of London live worse than our exiles in the fresh Siberian air. They laugh when I say that. To them Siberia is nothing but an ice box. Have they seen the beauties of the flowering steppe in summer? No! Our political exiles, who represent a real danger to the state, live in their own cottages and not in miserable hovels, prey to the criminals and prostitutes of Whitechapel! And do we send Russian investigators into the London slums to tell the world of the misery they find there?"

Vasiliev wanted to reply that the there was no need. The English produced their own official reports on conditions in the slums, and journalists wrote freely about them. But he was not going to go down that road with Grigoriev. He was content to nod his head and look solemn until Grigoriev had finished his tirade.

Grigoriev lifted his hands and folded his arms on his chest. "So what do you want from me?" he said after a brief pause.

"Your Excellency, I request permission to interrogate two of your politicals in connection with the murder of Ivan Fedorovich Golitsyn in the village of Dubno."

"Who might they be?"

Vasiliev produced a paper from his jacket and handed it to Grigoriev; he did not trust his voice to pronounce Irina's name.

Grigoriev held the paper at some distance and snorted.

"Ah, yes, the medical people. Came up from Tiumen. I must say they've been efficient enough. But what's their connection to this murder? Ivan Fedorovich Golitsyn, you say. The old Decembrist who went mad; or did he just go native?"

"Yes, a Decembrist." Vasiliev did not intend to offer his opinion on Ivan Fedorovich's psychological state. He had his story ready. Information had come to him that an old rival of Ivan Fedorovich from his days in Eastern Siberia, had passed through the village on his return from exile and learning of his enemy's presence had taken revenge, making it appear like a sectarian outrage. Vasiliev said he had traced the murderer to his last stop in Siberia, the Tiumen Forwarding Prison. There with the help of Major Krasin he had discovered that the killer had been treated by two exile medics for some rare disease he had picked up while living among the nomads. They could identify him and might have information on his present whereabouts. Krasin had informed him the medics had already left for Omsk and since the Americans were also going there, Vasiliev concluded with a flourish, his visit would "fulfill two imperial missions." Grigoriev could hardly object.

The Governor-General listened impatiently at first, lifting and lowering his hands on Vasiliev's dossier. But half-way through

Vasiliev's account, he began to nod his head. Vasiliev breathed an inner sigh of relief. Grigoriev had taken the bait. Perhaps he was reassured that Bark was not mentioned. Grigoriev was almost smiling at the end, which is how Vasiliev interpreted what was happening to the lower part of his face.

"Well, good!" Grigoriev could not resist pounding the dossier one last time. "As they say, the master detective. Arrived just in time, too. The order has been given for the transfer of the two exiles—" Grigoriev glanced at the paper again to recall their names— "to Semipalatinsk. You see, while I value their services, they've have been in touch with some unsavory types in Omsk. Another old Decembrist." Grigoriev frowned as if something had occurred to him, but then he quickly continued. "You can never trust these revolutionaries; they have rebellion in the blood. You may see them, of course. I'm the last person to obstruct an official mission, as you put it. But in two days they leave in an armed convoy for the south."

Chapter
Twenty-Eight

Bark went over his plan carefully looking for weaknesses. The main thing was to distance himself from the assassination, yet make certain that it was carried out. The first step had been to recruit Rykov. The Governor-General had not raised any objection to his suggestion. He made it clear that he couldn't get the job done himself. So Rykov. Bark knew he had to bind Rykov irrevocably. Well, he wasn't asking him to do the deed—just to incriminate himself! Bark smiled. Poor Rykov! It had been easy enough to hook him. An evening of cards with a few trusty friends, plying Rykov with vodka. They let him win at first. He became over-confident and reckless. The bids mounted, so did his losses. By early morning he was hopelessly in debt. In desperation, he surprised even Bark by staking the small estate, the only property he owned, where his elderly parents still lived. He lost and collapsed in his chair.

Bark broke out the champagne for the winners. He had played cautiously and avoided winning big. He had let the others clean out Rykov. He chided Rykov, but then reassured him. He would personally see to it that Rykov got back his personal note. The next day he persuaded the officer holding the note to give it up in return for a few cases of Veuve Cliquot. What did he want with a miserable little estate, mortgaged to the hilt in the wilds of Olonets Province? Rykov broke into tears. Bark cut short his promises of eternal devotion. Just a small favor or two. Rykov jumped at the chance to be of service. Right now, thought Bark he would be searching the Tatar bazaar for the chosen instrument of Bark's little affair. Then he would send Rykov to nose around Pestov's house, make inquiries of the neighbors, just to make certain that he was seen in the vicinity. And *voilà!* Rykov would be the prime suspect. The Tatars would remember him; so would the neighbors. Having recovered his estate and secured his parents' welfare, he could hardly denounce Bark. Besides, the Governor-General would probably get him off with a light sentence and then pardon him. For the good of the state. Bark would have worked off his debt to Grigoriev. Then he might not have to get involved with the Americans. If he did Grigoriev could easily hang him out to dry, just as he was doing with Rykov. Bark thought about it. He might just follow them to the south and then make his break for freedom.

Chapter
Twenty-Nine

In his disguise as a trading peasant, Serov made sure to use the servants' entrance to the hotel when he returned from canvassing the town. He entered Vasiliev's room in a state of suppressed excitement. Vasiliev immediately recognized the symptoms. Serov usually took his time in reporting, savoring every moment as he spun out the story of his "little adventures," as he called them. This time, he got straight to the point. It had been easy to track down Bark who was living in the officers' quarters of the local Uhlan regiment. But there was more. The best news he had picked up in the bazaars, always his favorite source of information. Two exiles, a man and a woman were seen from time to time, it seemed once a week on Thursdays, picking up supplies at the pharmacy near the prison. They were not under guard. They had become familiar figures to the locals who described them in detail. No doubt about it; they were Irina and Letchik.

"It's Thursday, Vasili Vasilievich, just in case you'd not noticed!" Serov could hardly contain himself. "You might just catch 'em right now." Serov clapped his hands in a display of enthusiasm that Vasiliev had rarely witnessed.

Vasiliev seized Serov by the shoulders. He felt a surge of excitement.

"Where's the pharmacy?" Vasiliev demanded, pulling on his jacket. "You'll have to keep an eye on Kennan and Frost. How can we be in three places at once? Guard our American friends, keep tabs on Bark and make contact with Irina?" Vasiliev was muttering, but Serov understood. They would have to wait for Bark to make the first move, rather than anticipating what he intended to do. What Vasiliev did not say was that he was thinking of using Kennan and Frost as bait to lure Bark into showing his hand. A risky business. It would take time to prepare. But they hadn't much time. In two days Irina and Letchik would be on their way to Semi-palatinsk. So would Kennan and Frost. It would be difficult to protect them on the road and keep in touch with Irina. He desperately needed a plan, but nothing occurred to him. His mind was filled with the prospect of seeing her again.

Vasiliev's cab just pulled up on the street near the pharmacy when he saw her familiar figure together with Letchik coming out, carrying a few small parcels. Not many people on the street; no one who looked like a prison guard; only one officer coming toward him. He force himself to wait until the man passed by. He had already given the cabby instructions and a note. Irina and Letchik were walking slowly away from him when he jumped out of the cab and hurried down an unpaved side street lined with single story log huts. He was gambling on Irina's quick intelligence. He knew she would not fail him. He glanced behind him, worried that Grigoriev might have him followed. There was no one.

The cabby drew up beside Irina and Letchik.

"Madam, a message, please." He handed down a folded slip of paper. She glanced at Letchik who shrugged. He read her glance as a question: "Some kind of provocation?" She looked up at the cabby but he had already turned on his box and urged his nag forward. She slipped the paper into her sleeve and dropped a parcel. She and Letchik both bent over to retrieve it, each one glancing in a different direction up and down the street. They straitened up. A slight shake of the head. They walked on several steps and then Irina opened the message inside her sleeve, pulled it out for an instant and then replaced it. Letchik caught the rising color in her cheek. Her heart was pounding. She had recognized the signature. At the first cross street they turned left and headed for the Cathedral. Vasiliev had gotten there ahead of them and had lit a candle to St. Sergius. The mid day sun had given way to a thick blanket of grey clouds. The Church was dark and almost deserted at that time of day. Several old women were worshipping in a side nave. Vasiliev heard steps coming up behind him. For a moment he stiffened, then a pair of arms wrapped around him. He remembered the scent of her hair and felt her body press against him.

"Vasya, I thought you promised, 'no romantic gestures.'"

"No," he said turning to embrace her. "*You* said 'no romantic gestures.' I made no promises."

He kissed her forehead and stroked her cheeks which were wet. They said nothing more for several minutes until they heard a discreet cough.

"Yes," Vasiliev murmured, "Letchik is right to warn us. We are both under the pressure of time."

He whispered quickly, telling her as briefly as possible what had happened and how he planned an escape. He and Serov would accompany the Americans to Semipalatinsk, following behind the armed convoy. He would work out a way to keep in touch with her. Somehow he would have to take down Bark. He wasn't sure how. But he couldn't leave Kennan until he had eliminated all danger. Semipalatinsk was close to the border. They would cross into China. It all sounded too vague as he spoke. He felt himself groping in the dark. But she gripped his hands tightly. He could hardly see her features.

"Listen," she said. "My God! There is so much to say. The orders to move south fell like snow on our heads. We still have a contact to make. We planned it for tonight. We've bribed the guards. They think Letchik and I have some love affair going," she paused aware of a tightening grip on her hands. "We *do not*, Vasya. He's like a brother to me." Vasiliev took a deep breath.

"A contact?"

"An old Decembrist who has some documents..."

"Pestov."

Irina stepped back. "How did you know?"

"You forget, my dear, I'm a detective."

She shook her head. "All right, we'll share our Siberian secrets later."

He could tell she was smiling. If he could only see that smile!

"Do you know about the letters? We have promised to take them with us. I don't know what we will do with them. But they are powerful ammunition."

"I've no idea of what you are talking about. More Siberian secrets?"

"Pestov told us that he had just received a packet from Sophia Vadimovna. Her servant Mitya brought them. I never met her, but she must have been a great woman."

"You speak of her in the past tense."

"Mitya said she died suddenly, but forced him to promise to deliver the letters to Pestov. I don't know why she kept them so long. I've not seen them, but Pestov says they are political dynamite, if the word does not offend you!"

Another cough interrupted them.

"We must go or they'll send out a search party."

"Listen, I'm worried about tonight. Grigoriev told me you have been in touch with 'unsavory characters' in Omsk. He mentioned an old Decembrist. That must be Pestov. He could only know this if you were under surveillance."

"We took precautions."

"Of course. You know your business. But somehow they found out. It might be better if I make the contact."

"No, Pestov is very suspicious. He doesn't know you. Please believe me. We can do this."

Vasiliev saw no point in arguing. He would take his own precautions. He kissed her hurriedly. Letchik was waiting at the door, having made sure no one was lurking in the courtyard. As Vasiliev watched them go, he could not suppress a feeling of foreboding. He left the Church a few minutes later. As he walked back to the hotel he debated with himself whether to follow them discreetly later that night on what he considered a mad adventure. But there were risks. It wouldn't be easy. They were no strangers to conspiratorial activities. They would easily spot anyone they suspected of trailing them and shake him off. No matter how good his disguise, he wouldn't be able to get too close. They knew the streets of Omsk, the double entrances to courtyards, the dead ends. He was a stranger here. At night he would be blundering around. If Irina found out, she would be furious, as he would be if someone were to compromise one of his operations. The alternative was to arrive at Pestov's early and conceal himself just in case the unexpected happened. He hadn't a clue what that might be. But there were limits, he smiled to himself, even to his imagination.

Chapter
Chapter Thirty

Bark stayed in his rooms all day. At twilight Rykov arrived, brimming with confidence that he had carried out Bark's instructions to the letter. Bark sent him off with an avuncular warning to avoid the gaming table, knowing how quickly his advice would be ignored. He dismissed his orderly, locked the door and lay down full dressed waiting for the midnight bells to ring. He dozed fitfully, dreaming of riding a camel across the Gobi Desert.

He awoke with a start, automatically reaching for his service revolver which he kept by old habit under his pillow. Someone was fumbling at the door handle to his room. He sat up in the darkness and lowered his feet to the floor without making a sound, then stood up and moved silently toward the door. The rattling stopped as he approached, followed by a light tapping. Surely this wasn't Rykov; not his style and it was still too early for his return from the gaming tables. But he could not imagine who else would try breaking in on him and, failing that, timidly announce his presence as if fearing to arouse the barracks. Bark didn't like the smell of it.

He backed out of the line of fire.

"Yes," he whispered. "What is it?"

He was startled to hear a familiar voice whisper back.

"Andriusha, quick, let me in."

Bark drew the bolt and swung open the door, hardly having time to lower his revolver before a body crashed into him and a pair of arms wrapped round his neck.

Bewildered, he staggered back and almost lost his balance. His revolver clattered to the floor. He could not see her but he recognized the scent of her hair and the soft whimpering as she pressed her face against his chest. He pulled her quickly inside and kicked the door shut, holding her from collapsing completely as she babbled incoherently, mixing together the most extravagant endearments with sobs and appeals to save her. He couldn't make head or tails out of what she was saying. She was shivering under her heavy cloak which slipped from her shoulders as he tried to calm her. He stroked her hair and was suddenly overcome with a great desire for her. He pulled her down on the bed and rolled on top of her, pushing up her skirts.

"Yes, yes," she cried out, "you love me...love me."

Vaguely he heard the midnight bells, but time suddenly lost any meaning for him. He felt caught up in a frenzy of passion that he had never experienced before, driven by her sharp cries rising and falling in a wild cadence. Then, as she lay next to him he wanted to say something she had never heard before. He touched her cheeks and was surprised to find them wet. She had never cried before. Had this time been so exciting? For him it seemed so too. He murmured her name.

"So beautiful," she said, "after so much horror."

He was immediately on full alert. "Horror?"

She turned to him. "I tried to tell you, but feeling you, your strength, I couldn't." She paused.

"He tried to rape me so I hit him. I think he is dead."

"In God's Heaven, Anna who? What are you saying?" He jerked away from her.

She blurted out what had happened, forgetting half of the carefully thought out explanation she had rehearsed all the way to Omsk; of how she would accuse Krassin so that it would appear it was not her fault; how frightened she was that she would be arrested; how now only her lover could save her.

He stared at her in the darkness, letting her talk on, fiercely biting his lip to prevent himself from cursing her. He heard the bells strike one o'clock. His plan was ruined and now he was saddled with a fugitive murderess. They would never believe her even if she were telling the truth, which he doubted. She had not only run away but straight to the man whom she thought would help her, implicating him as well. He fought to contain his rage, to restrain himself from striking her. No, he steeled himself; this was a time for the greatest self-control. He had to think. But Anna was waiting for him to comfort her, he knew that. He made a great effort to keep his voice steady.

"How horrible for you, my darling." He could barely pronounce the words. Would she hear how false they sounded? Could anything be salvaged from this wreck? He wondered.

"Does anyone know you are here?"

"No, I just left without packing. I have nothing but the clothes I am..." she giggled, "was wearing." The giggle sent a chill down his spine.

"Good. Now listen." His thoughts were flying ahead. Perhaps he might gain a slight advantage from all this; however slight it was better than being accused of being an accomplice to murder.

"You must stay here with me tonight and perhaps even tomorrow. I have to go out now on a mission. I will lock you in. You must not answer the door no matter who demands to come in. I expect no one, except possibly an officer friend. Just stay quiet and have no fear. Tomorrow we will make out plans to escape together, but you must trust me no matter what happens."

She nodded eagerly.

You stupid bitch, he thought. Well, you might be my ticket to freedom after all.

He changed his trousers in the dark before he left, slipped the dagger in his belt and left the barracks without being seen. He quickly made his way to Pestov's house. He was determined not to make a mistake this time.

Chapter
Thirty-One

Vasiliev knew he had to find Mitya. He was the only one who could tell him where Pestov lived. He returned to the hotel and sent Serov out to search the rooming houses in the in the quarter where trading peasants and other visitors to the city could find cheap lodging. This gave him time to get out of uniform and disguise himself as an artisan, darkening his skin with an herbal preparation he always carried with him, applying a beard and thickening his eyebrows with false hair. He tucked his service revolver in his leg wrappings and pulled on his low boots.

Vasiliev trusted Serov's uncanny ability to blend into the local scene and elicit information from strangers without seeming to ask questions or appear inquisitive. But this kind of elaborate deception took time. Vasiliev fretted as the darkness fell on the city. He fought off the feeling that the Americans were as heavy and unlucky as two albatrosses around his neck. Having to watch over them cut his resources in half. The only moment of pleasure they gave him was when they failed to recognize him in the corridor of the hotel. But it was awkward always having to conceal himself in their rooms when maids came or servants brought food for their modest dinner. If only he and Serov could have been working the streets together!

Serov returned at eleven o'clock with the look of satisfaction Vasiliev immediately recognized. He drew a rough map showing where Mitya was staying, as he wolfed down the remains of the supper they had left for him.

It took Vasiliev about an hour to find the place, and even then he just caught Mitya as he was going out for his dinner. Mitya was startled to be accosted in the street and raised his hands to his face as if to conceal himself. Vasiliev wondered how the fragile old man had managed to make the arduous trip. He was trembling when Vasiliev told him who he was, gently took his arm and murmured a few words of condolence for the loss of Sophia Vadimovna. He guided Mitya to a near by *traktir*, ordered cutlets and two hundred grams of vodka. When Mitya had calmed down, he was able to tell Vasiliev about Sophia Vadimovna's last wish to have a packet of documents delivered to Pestov. No, he did not know their contents. But he was able to give Vasiliev instructions on how to reach Pestov's cottage. Vasiliev gave him a few rubles for another two hundred grams. He wondered on leaving him what would become of the poor man without his benevolent mistress. Had she provided for his old age? He remembered his father's instructions for the house servants. These people hold our lives together, he thought, and then what becomes of them?

Even following Mitya's instructions, Vasiliev got lost several times in the maze of muddy lanes without names and shacks without numbers before he recognized the few landmarks Mitya had remembered to tell him— the protective pine, the broken wattle fence—which set aside Pestov's cottage from the others. The outskirts of the city had the familiar look of an overgrown peasant village as if the countryside was growing into the city rather than the city expanding into the countryside. In the cloudless sky, the stars seemed to have crowded together more thickly than usual. There was no moon. A faint flickering light appeared in the window of Pestov's cabin. The other cabins were shrouded in darkness. As Vasiliev studied the shadows, looking for a place of concealment, he wondered whether he had come too late. The light in the cabin gave him hope. He stood hesitant in the lane for a few moments. Then he eased himself through the break in the wattle fence and took up his position in the darker shadow behind the pine. He thought of how Serov could stand for hours like a statue, *stolb*, the pillar, as his childhood playmates called him. He didn't have the patience. He would wait an hour. If Irina and Letchik hadn't shown by then, he would assume they could not come, and he would go in to uncover Pestov's Siberian secrets before Bark did.

He heard them coming before he saw them. They were very careful, passing the cabin before they turned back and entered the yard. Noiselessly, they mounted the wooden stairs and knocked softly on the door. He was surprised that Irina was using the same code as she had in Moscow when she was an activist in the Land and Liberty Party. Well, why not? Wasn't she still operating clandestinely?

They were in the cabin for only a few moments. Before they left again, the flickering light went out. They passed a few feet away from him. Letchik was clutching something in his right hand; it looked like a small packet. They turned down the lane in the direction from which they had come and were soon out of sight.

Vasiliev felt a wave of relief. He had to assume that they had retrieved the Siberian secrets, whatever they were, and that the danger was over. Just as he was about to leave his place of concealment, he heard another sound in the lane, as if someone had slipped in the mud and grunted in exasperation.

He stepped back into the shadows. A man's figure stopped in the lane across from the cabin. It was too dark to make out his features. He stealthily approached the cabin. As he mounted the stairs, just like Irina and Letchik he avoided stepping on the middle board, which Pestov had purposefully weakened to serve as a crude alarm system in case an unexpected visitor arrived. But Vasiliev failed to notice this; his eyes were glued to the package in the man's hand. The familiar signal of knocks, the code of Land and Liberty, rang out. Could Letchik have come back for some reason? To return the packet? Had there been some mistake? The door swung open and the figure disappeared inside followed by the sound of a wooden bar falling into place and muffled noise that could have been scuffling. Then a human cry that was unmistakable. Vasiliev rushed the cabin, pulling out his revolver and shouting "police, open up!" When the middle board broke under his weight he fell heavily, pain searing his knees, and his gun skittered off along the porch. He pulled himself up and threw himself against the door which hardly budged.

A light came on in the cabin and then flared into a flame. Vasiliev staggered to the side of the cabin and peered through the translucent glass which distorted the figure of a man sprawled on the floor. The flames were spreading with unnatural rapidly among the piles of books. Vasiliev realized they must have been soaked in some inflammable fluid—the packet! It was only then that he saw the small door in the rear of the cabin which stood wide open, another device of Pestov to provide an escape route. Damn it! Vasiliev swore, cursing himself for having failed to reconnoiter the whole place before blundering in. But he hadn't had any time, and Serov had been out hunting for Mitya. The old refrain hit him again: always too few men to handle the job. He was sick and tired of acting alone when the criminals were many and backed by evil men in high quarters

He hobbled back to the porch and threw his weight against the door until it splintered. He fell to the ground to avoid the blast of hot air and the cloud of smoke that billowed out from the interior of the cabin. He crawled toward the inert body of Pestov. He grabbed his ankles and pulled his smoldering body out of the cabin onto the ground. By the firelight he spotted his revolver, retrieved it and fired three shots into the air, crying out "fire, fire!"

The inhabitants tumbled out of their cabins and ran for the pumps in their yards. They filled buckets with water and then clambered up on their roofs, ready to extinguish the sparks that might ignite the thatching. No one came to help him as he pulled up a bucket from the well in Pestov's yard and doused the body. And how was he to order them to do otherwise? What could they see through the smoke? A man unknown to them, dressed like an artisan, armed with a revolver, frantically trying to douse the flames; steam was rising from a darkened corpse lying on the ground in the firelight. Vasiliev realized he couldn't do anything more here, and it was dangerous to stay until the Gendarmes arrived. He had no good explanation for why he was there. He gave Pestov's scorched body a rapid examination. His throat had been cut, the huge goiter now slack against his neck and a dagger had then been thrust into his heart. Why leave the murder weapon after the victim had been mortally wounded? He thought about taking the dagger, but then checked himself. No sense making things more complicated for the Gendarmes, if, of course, they cared to spend much time investigating the death of an old revolutionary. He shrugged, threw down the bucket and walked into the darkness.

Chapter
Thirty-Two

Irina drew the candle closer and began to examine the leather fo-lio, running her fingers over the smooth surface, feeling the soft calf skin. Judging by the quality and the workmanship, she imag-ined that it could only have been made in Italy, although it was stamped with the double eagle seal of the Romanov dynasty. She felt a strange quiver go right through her as she untied the leather thongs and recognized the knot as similar to that which held the eighteenth century folios in her father's library. It contained what appeared to be a great variety of old documents, mostly in French but some in Russian. She bent low over the folio and drew the candle closer, careful not to allow any wax to fall on the parchment. She had smuggled the folio under her skirt when they entered the barracks and she had persuaded Letchik to go to his room; other-wise, it would have been suspicious. His downcast look gave her a guilty feeling, but it passed quickly. She could not suppress the thought that this was her prize, surely to be shared with him, but not until she had uncovered its secrets, the Siberian secrets. Even Vasya would have to wait his turn. She recognized the selfish feel-ing, but the pleasure of discovery would be short lived and she had sacrificed much to enjoy it all by herself at least for the moment.

The first document was a letter written in French, dated April 10, 1881; it began with the salutation, "Mon cher Alyosha." So ad-dressed to Alexei Peskov, she assumed. She glanced at the last page; it was signed "je t'embrasse, Vania", the name being written in Cy-rillic letters. She assumed again that the writer must have been Ivan Fedorovich. The two men had been close friends, from boyhood, as

Peskov had told her, and fellow officers in the Guards. The spidery handwriting was bold and clear. As she read she felt a growing sense of excitement, so that her hand trembled as she turned over the first page. She re-read the passages that moved her deeply.

So you see, dear friend, our work has finally come to an end Remember how it began! We were young bloods, naïve enough to believe we could topple the dynasty by force of arms, end two centuries of tyranny by firing off a few volleys on the Senate Square. Instead, it has taken us fifty-seven years to gather a different kind of ammunition to blow away the tyrants. And all the time they thought we were reconciled to our fate! You and I, we shall have our victory as we did in the campaign of 1813 against the usurper, Bonaparte. The final piece came into my possession just recently. It passed through many other hands, unknown soldiers in the sacred cause. Hard to imagine what risks were run to smuggle it out of the Imperial Library where it was kept under strict guard. It is unlikely that the theft, if that is what it was, will be soon discovered. Among other treasures we have in our possession is a letter from our mysterious "angel", tsar Alexander Pavlovich, to his brother, Nicholas Pavlovich. It is dated Taganrog, October 15, 1824. I understand that Nicholas Pavlovich had given orders to destroy all his brother's personal correspondence; somehow this letter survived. Officially, it never existed! Alexander Pavlovich explains in detail his intention to falsify his death! He seeks to expiate his sins by exchanging his imperial regalia for a monk's simple habit. Very touching! But you realize the significance. It confirms my suspicions. I met this 'holy man' Fedor Kuzmich in Tomsk in 1860 and was convinced then of his true identity. Since then I have been collecting documents. But this one is the proverbial last nail in the coffin — or rather the last nail out of the coffin! Yes, the tsar lived on to 1864 as Fedor Kuzmich. Which means that all legislation since 1825 has no legal standing! Taken together with the other documents we have gathered, it will

destroy the legitimacy of the Romanov dynasty and will reveal to the entire world the corrupt and false nature of our
August Rulers!

The documents had been carefully sorted into smaller bundles
tied with faded rose colored ribbons. A sheet of foolscap of recent
origin was attached, identifying the contents. There was a memoir
of some sort by a man called Semyon Feofanovich Khramov, iden-
tifing himself as a merchant of the first guild. It declared that he
had given shelter to Fedor Kuzmich from 1859 to 1864. There were
a few letters from Nicholas I to Fedor Kuzmich, obliquely suggesting a fraternal tie. Then a letter, apparently never mailed, from the
court physician, Sir James Wylie, to a correspondent in England,
revealing his role in the plot to help Alexander I escape. A note ap-
pended to this document by an agent of the Gendarmes states that
when Wylie died in1854 he left an enormous fortune. "How was
this obtained?" the agent asked. There was no attempt to find out.
The last packet contained materials gathered by the Over Procura-
tor of the Holy Synod, Konstantin Pobedonostsev, authorized by
Alexander III to investigate the mystery.

The documents contained some names that were familiar to
Irina, others were completely unknown to her. It would take time
to sort it all out. She would need Vasiliev's help. But she was already convinced that she possessed what Ivan Fedorovich had
already hinted in his letter to Pestov. There was enough material
here to compromise the reigning dynasty and seriously damage its
reputation in Russia and throughout Europe. Perhaps not enough
to spark a revolution. But she recalled the scurrilous writing that
preceded the French Revolution of 1789. Who knows, she asked
herself, how much it takes to undermine the faith of the people in
the monarchy?

The candle was burning low and she was very tired. She looked
about her. Where could she hide this bulky package? In her cell-like
room there was no place to conceal it for long without running the
risk of discovery. Perhaps they should have left it with Pestov. But
she feared returning there. No, it would have to be somewhere in
the prison. The hospital? She thought about it for a long while as

she undressed and slipped the packet under her mattress. It could not remain there for long; they were leaving in two days. In the morning she would consult with Letchik. He knew every crack and cranny of the hospital. She had to smile to herself; he was the perfect fellow conspirator.

Chapter
Thirty-Three

It took Vasiliev longer than he expected to find his way back to the hotel. He had made so many false turns getting to Pestov's that he was unable to retrace his steps. A low bank of clouds obscured the stars. No lights shone in the huts. He had only a general sense of the direction of the hotel. Lost in Omsk! The idea almost amused him. It would have been easier to find his way in the forests of Viatka. And Bark was out there somewhere, although it seemed unlikely that he would run into him. Still, the possibility remained, however remote. It was time to turn another of Foma's's tricks; he kept his mind alert for odd noises and shifts in the currents of air that might presage a blow and at the same time he fixed his thoughts on the problem of how to free Irina—and Letchik as well—while protecting the Americans. He had long realized that freeing Irina meant ending the life he had chosen. From being a policeman he would become a criminal in the eyes of the law he had sworn to uphold. As a criminal it would be complicated if not make impossible to protect the Americans. Even if he was somehow able to repress his moral feelings, the dilemma seemed insoluble. From the purely selfish point of view he needed Kennan's help to get Irina out of Russia! And then there was Bark. How could he who had dedicated himself to bringing such vicious murderers to justice simply forget about him as if he had never existed? The picture of the dead courier flashed before his eyes. A barking dog interrupted his thoughts. A warning? He stopped and waited until the howling stopped.

He needed to talk to Serov. It was often the best way to work out the toughest problems. Not that Serov had the answers. No, it was how he listened. Those marvelously expressive grunts and low whistles, the way his eyes crinkled up and the eyebrows rose and fell, following a rhythm of their own. Serov, the mime, at his most eloquent! Vasiliev was convinced that after he had rehearsed all the possibilities out loud, things would become clearer. A one-sided dialogue, but it had always worked in the past.

Suddenly, the hotel loomed up in front of him. He approached cautiously, reason and instinct no longer divided. He waited, listening for the sound of breathing, watching for movement among the darker shadows. It would not do to underestimate Bark. He was no ordinary cavalry officer obsessed by women and horses, much as he might admire both. Here was a man who had somehow induced the mad priest, Porfiry, to kill Ivan Egorovich and then burned or stole documents from the dead man's cottage. Someone who had intercepted and murdered a courier, pilfering his saddle bags of important documents, and then pursued them all the way from Tiumen to Omsk; someone who clearly enjoyed the protection of a powerful patron..

Serov was waiting with the samovar. Nothing unusual had happened while Vasiliev had been "wanderin' about" as he put it. Kennan and Frost were preparing to leave in the morning. There was nothing to keep them in Omsk. They had hired a *tarantas* and would drive straight through to Semipalatinsk across the steppe. They said they expected to find more politicals there in the south close to the Chinese border.

Vasiliev told Serov about Bark's attack on Pestov. Sipping his hot tea, he began to try out the ideas forming in his mind and see how Serov reacted. They might split up, he said. "You'd go ahead with Kennan and Frost to make sure Bark doesn't intercept them. We don't know whether Bark will follow. He might get ahead of them and set up an ambush. I'm going to get myself attached to the convoy conveying Irina and Letchik. Even better, maybe I can convince the Governor-General to put me in charge of the prisoners. It's a long shot, but he wants to get rid of them quickly and keeps complaining about being short-handed. He might jump at the chance to saddle me with the responsibility. This way he could save his own men from making the long trip south and back. It all depends on what arrangements he's made for a full convoy."

Serov didn't much care for the idea of splitting up. They'd done it before, but this time he had a feeling that nothing good would come of it. But he didn't have anything better to suggest. And he could tell by Vasiliev's voice that there was no sense arguing; anyway, that was against his nature. There was nothing to do but nod his agreement. Vasiliev knew Serov well enough to notice his reluctance. But he had he had thought it out carefully. This seemed the best course of action.

Early the next morning, Kennan and Frost set off in the *telega*, with Serov riding along side, doing his best to appear carefree. He even joked with Frost about the lack of good subject matter for his sketches in Omsk. The supply of horses was the one practical matter that worried him. He knew that the Americans wouldn't wait for him if there wasn't an extra mount available at one of the post stations. They were always in a hurry. He heard that this was an American trait. They thought the Russians were too slow moving. It might be true, mused Serov, but that was not always such a bad thing. As for protecting them...well, that was all very well and good, but he didn't have Vasiliev's authority. He couldn't tell the Americans what they should or shouldn't do. They seemed to like him well enough; they didn't treat him differently because of his rank or class. But he could only warn them of immediate danger. Then it might be too late. Besides they were traveling through country about which he knew little or nothing. He had only heard that the the local tribesmen, whom some people called Kirghiz and others with the less flattering epithet of Tungus, had once been known as fierce nomadic tribesmen, but had long ago calmed down. He wished he knew whether it was more or less dangerous to ride through Indian country in the American West. He would have to ask the Americans about it. And then there were the Tatars to be considered. Less predictable, as rumor had it. No, he didn't like the prospect at all.

Vasiliev watched them leave and then strolled over to the Governor-General's office where he handed in his written request to accompany the convoy of prisoners to Semipalatinsk. He was kept waiting for an hour before the deputy governor received him.

"His Excellency is not available but he authorized me to inform you that there has been a change in plans. The convoy has been postponed. It won't be leaving for a week. If you wish to interrogate the prisoners and catch up with the Americans, then he recommends that you take responsibility for conveying the prisoners to Semipalatinsk. We can provide a driver but no armed guard. The deputy governor broke into a broad and insincere smile. "If you do not consider the prisoners dangerous, the arrangement might suit you perfectly. The procedure is unorthodox. But the Governor-General prides himself on his administrative flexibility."

The deputy governor handed Vasiliev two sheets of paper. One was an authorization to convey the prisoners Davydova and 'Letchik' to the prison at Semipalatinsk, and the other a release form binding the prisoners over to Inspector Vasili Vaslievich Vasiliev of the Moscow Police. The order required his signature. Vasiliev scratched down his name aware that his signature spelled the end of his career. But he was so pleased at the outcome that he failed to suspect what should have been obvious— and what he only realized later— that the arrangement, as the deputy governor put it, had been made to suit Governor-General Grigoriev and not him.

Chapter
Thirty-Four

Governor-General Grigoriev had good reason to make himself unavailable to Vasiliev. He sat at his enormous desk pondering the Gendarmes' report on the badly burned body of Pestov, the evidence of Lieutenant Rykov's involvement, which he doubted, and the disappearance of Bark which worried him. He had planned it so carefully that Bark would be arrested, sentenced to administrative exile and banished for life to the mines of Eastern Siberia. His first reaction had been outrage, but he had trained himself not to remain outraged about anything for very long. It impaired his ability to reason which he prized highly.

He closed his eyes and reviewed the events of the past few days. Gradually, he persuaded himself that everything had worked out for the best. The nosy Americans were out of his hair. They had seen nothing that might have embarrassed him. Pestov, whom he had long suspected of being the center of all manner of conspiracies, was dead. If Bark had done the deed, which seemed highly probable, then his disappearance was the next best thing to his arrest. He would give order to hunt him down. Rykov would give enough evidence to put him away for good. And he had rid himself of the two troublemakers who were being sent to Semipalatinsk, with Vasiliev another potential troublemaker, as their security guard.

Still, there was the unresolved question of the documents crammed with statistics on the exile system. They reflected badly on his administration. Bark had told him he had disposed of them, but he might be lying. All the more reason to make sure he was caught and prevented from using them as blackmail. Yes, Bark was now the enemy! He could not get far without obtaining horses. So, it would be easy to track him down. The Gendarmes would be alerted. And a discreet word might be passed on that if the fugitive, who was armed and dangerous, resisted he should be dealt with with the utmost severity.

The Governor-General felt pleased with himself; a fairly common state of mind. He chuckled as he rang the bronze bell on his desk. An orderly immediately appeared. Grigoriev ordered a dinner of Ukrainian borsht, roast boar and a dish of *pelmeni*, to be washed down with two hundred grams of vodka. "Then we'll see about the sweet," he added. It was to be served exactly at two o'clock. He would dine alone. He preferred celebrating his victories by himself. No one else was capable in his eyes of appreciating them, and he would not trust anyone who did.

The Governor-General's digestion was upset and his mood spoiled by a message which was delivered shortly after he had consumed a large portion of pudding The letter bore the seal of the bishop of Omsk province recommending a priest, a certain Father Iosifei, who was the bearer of confidential information for the ears only of the Governor-General.

Grigoriev hardly recognized the man who limped into his office. The wear and tear of travel was one thing, thought the Governor-General, but Father Iosifei looked like a man dragged half way from his parish. His face was streaked with dust, his hair disheveled, his robe torn. He had spent his gold ruble long before covering half the distance to Omsk, handing out alms to whomever asked. Then he was forced to walk, a movement which was not familiar to him, and beg a crust for himself "in Christ's name." At one point he had collapsed and was half-carried, half-dragged to some wretched inn, and unceremoniously dumped in a hay loft by the owner who had conceived a dislike of priests who preached abstinence. After a while he began to conceive of the ordeal as a penance.

Grigoriev waved the priest into a seat and ordered tea. What had driven him to this state? Grigoriev recalled his half-forgotten promise to lift the priest out of his muck hole and appoint him to a city parish. But surely that wasn't the cause of his ruin. Of course, there was the other matter, but hadn't that been Bark's work?

Gulping down the hot tea, Father Iosifei broke into a paraxym of coughing. Tears trickled down his dusty cheeks leaving ugly streaks.

"It all went terribly wrong. I have sinned before God and man," he groaned.

Grigoriev was tempted to shout at him, drive him out of the office until he could clean himself up and control his hysteria. He should have known it was a mistake to get mixed up with the clergy.

Instead he growled coarsely; "Well spit it out!"

Even in his distraught state, Father Iosifei looked offended.

"It was you who set me the task!" he shouted in his turn and then broke down, weeping and crossing himself repeatedly.

"I instructed you to get rid of the wizards and sectarians, nothing more. How in the name of the Trinity did you manage to create such chaos?"

Father Iosifei clenched his hands in his lap and lowered his head. He dropped his voice and began to speak in a hardly audible manner.

"Yes, and it was my pastoral duty to rid the land of the shaman and the skoptsy. But I sought God's help; you pressed me to use man's means. I was weak. You promised to reward me with a parish worthy of my talents. I succumbed to temptation."

"All right, get to the point. What happened there? I thought this was all Bark's work."

"The devil walks the Earth in many forms."

"Please spare me the pieties."

Grigoriev listened impatiently with growing astonishment as the priest haltingly told his tale. He had followed the Governor-General's suggestions. He quoted word for word: "it would be advisable and to my benefit to frighten the shaman, Ivan Fedorovich, so that he would leave the province and also to find some way of ridding the province of that skoptsy scum." Together they would turn the province into a model Orthodox community.

Father Iosif felt the jealousy and hatred he bore Ivan Fedorovich, which he had buried deep in his soul, struggle to the surface. But he bit his lip and said nothing about his inner feelings to Grigoriev. He had long been tortured by the suspicion that his wife and son had fallen under the influence of the shaman, but he would not expose his shame to the world.

"So," he continued, "when I discovered that Father Porfiy had returned—you understand he had become a half-mad wanderer in the wilderness— I decided to make him the instrument of God's wrath. I brought him food, secretly and led him to believe we shared heavenly voices. One day told me in a terribly excited voice that he had robbed the shaman of half his strength by killing his dog. I began to fear I had driven him too far. He said he was beginning to hear the heavenly voices when he was alone. He would not say what they told him."

Father Iosifei groaned and buried his face in his hands. He did not see the look of contempt on Grigoriev's face. When he raised his eyes again, the Governor-General was staring at the picture of the tsar.

"Early in the morning after the great storm, I was along praying in my church for guidance when he burst in. He was covered with blood. He demanded I hear his confession. I absolved him and gave him the heaviest penance I knew. The next day I noticed that all the holy oil was missing. I was astonished when Inspector Vasiliev told me about the castration. I cannot imagine that Father Porfiry had committed this outrage. He said nothing to me about it. Then I learned that the villagers had given Ivan Fedorovich a shaman's funeral," Father Iosifei shuddered. "I persuaded the elder to burn the body. I could not give him a Christian burial but ..." his voice trailed off.

There was silence in the room for several minutes. Father Iosifei looked up; his bloodshot eyes stared vacantly. "I know nothing of any Bark."

Grigoriev imagined he could fill in the rest of the story. But he was not about to tell this priest his secrets.

Chapter Thirty-Five

The next morning, Irina was startled to be woken up early by the prison matron who announced that she should prepare to leave within an hour. When she emerged from the barracks into the courtyard, she saw Letchik seated in a cart drawn by two oxen with a soldier seated in the driver's seat. Vasiliev was standing next to it by his horse, securing a large bag behind the saddle, a faint smile on his face. Irina resisted the temptation to shake her head in wonderment. Vasiliev insisted that the prisoners not be shackled. No one objected. Shortly before they reached the first post station, Vasiliev called a halt. A hot wind had been blowing across the steppe, filling the air with dust and forcing them to wrap scarves around their faces. It became increasingly difficult to see far ahead. Vasiliev ordered them to seek shelter in a nearby gully. He waited until they were out of sight and then, before joining them, removed a sprocket from the wheel of the ox cart.

When the wind died down they started out again. The faint outline of the post station was barely visible on the horizon when the wheel came loose and the cart lurched to one side. Vasiliev was delighted to hear the distinct crack of wood splintering.

The soldier cursed and Vasiliev happily joined in.

"Listen, I can't let these prisoners out of my sight, but I'm damned if I'll sit here while you go off for help. So this is what we'll do."

He ordered the soldier to remain with the cart while he led Irina and Letchik to the post station where he would arrange for help. He handed the soldier a flask of vodka and told him to sit tight.

The soldier watched them go off, Vasiliev on horseback, the prisoners marching ahead of him. Then he unhitched the oxen, sat down in the shade of the broken cart and drank his vodka. The next time he looked at the figures, they were too far away to distinguish one from the other, so he could not see that the woman was now on horseback and the two men were walking ahead of her.

At the post station Vasiliev showed his orders but was told there were no mounts available.

"And what about hiring some from the Kirghiz. There must be an encampment nearby.

"Yes, Your honor but they only lease camels."

"So be it," Vasiliev making an effort to stifle his laughter.

"You'd better send someone out to bring in the cart. Tell the driver to follow us as soon as the repairs have been made." Vasiliev knew the poor fellow would never catch up with the camels!

Within a few hours two Kirghiz tribesmen showed up with a pair of Bactrian camels. They gave instructions to the postmaster who translated for Vasiliev.

Camels fording the Irtysh

"They're not much to look at. But you can hitch them up to the spare *telega* I've got in the courtyard. They'll get you across the steppe and even ford the Irtysh. Vasiliev looked skeptically at the animals with their two drooping humps and long neck. They looked back at him disdainfully. He shrugged, half expecting them to imitate him. But they just moved their thick lips from side to side as if chewing some delicacy. They emitted a strong odor. But they did manage to get their passangers across the Irtysh.

The camels plodded along at no greater speed than the oxen, but Vasiliev finally got them to trot and when the cool breeze of evening came they positively galloped, to the great discomfort of Letchik who was bouncing around next to Vasiliev.

"This can't be the way Haroun el-Rashid travelled," growled Letchik. "Maybe they're getting frisky smelling the desert."

By this time the green grasses interspersed with masses of wild flowers had burned up in the scorching summer heat, and the terrain began to change into the hard, arid semi-desert. As they moved south along the right bank of the Irtysh they passed log cabin villages inhabited by Cossacks where they did not dare to stop.

They kept up a blistering pace until they reached the first Kirghiz encampment, a few circular, grey tents pitched far off the roadway. Apparently the word had reached them — although Vasiliev could not imagine how the news could have travelled faster than they did— and an old man in a red and yellow skullcap greeted them. He invited them into his tent and offered *kumiss*. After they had drunk off a few bowls, he called one of his sons who spoke a few words of Russian. He told them that two foreigners and a Russian officer had preceded them. Serov would be happy to learn the Kirghiz had promoted him, Vasiliev mused. The foreigners had sung some strange songs but one of them had tried to get possession of a little boy's soul by making a likeness of him on paper. The Kirghiz were willing to sell two horses and take the camels off their hands.

The road was good and they were able to move even faster with the sturdy steppe ponies pulling the *telega* while taking turns on Vasiliev's mount. They camped out the first night at an uninhabited oasis around a sky blue lake where a brilliant assortment of flowers engulfed them as they stretched out for the night. As a precaution, they did not build a fire but ate some crusts and dried beef that Vasiliev produced from the saddle bags.

The next evening they saw a brick structure resembling a dilapidated fort; it was surrounded by low, bare mounds of earth.

"It looks like an ancient cemetery," said Letchik. "One of the convicts in Omsk told me about them. Maybe dating back to the days when Scythians roamed the steppe. The chiefs are buried inside the enclosure. Perhaps it's a good place to rest. No one will disturb us there!"

Vasiliev build fire from the poles sticking out of the mounds. "A sacrilege, I know but the nights are getting cold." He unpacked the large bag behind his saddle and handed Irina and Letchik the items of clothing he had bought at the bazaar.

"It's time for you to disappear as convicts and rejoin the human race. So go change in the privacy beyond the firelight and we'll burn your prison wear." Listening to Irina chuckle and the rustle of a petticoat, he felt a surge of desire. How long would they have to wait?

When she stepped back into the circle of light she was still grinning.

"You're a marvel, Vasya, but I don't think I will send you out to shop for me again!"

"Well, yes, the blouse is too tight."

"Oh, and I thought that was deliberate! No, I mean the style, really old fashion."

"Parisian it is not. But you have the look of a country girl and not a noblewoman."

Letchik emerged to applause from both of them. "The perfect student," Irina exclaimed.

"Student, surely, but perfect? I need to cultivate a haughty demeanor and a pince nez to set it off."

"I see where I have failed. But you can't fault the transportation."

All three dissolved in laughter, and at that moment Vasiliev felt that something new and splendid had come into his life.

They solemnly watched the burning of their prison clothes and then sat down by the fire to examine the documents.

"Let me tell you how I've put these in order. The first set is made up of official correspondence, letters from various officials and doctors who attended Alexander I in Taganrog. Incidentally, he supposedly travelled to this god forsaken place for the empress' health. Why he didn't go to the Crimea is a big question; there you can find better climate, more suitable lodgings, palaces and the rest. Then we have the official death certificate duly signed by five men, again high officials like General, Baron Ivan Ivanovich Dibich and the court physician, Sir James Wylie. Then come letters informing the tsar's brothers of his death. Interesting discrepancies show up but a lot is vague. We needn't go over all this now."

"What's the point?" Letchik interrupted.

"*Meno mosso*, my friend. I'm getting there." Vasiliev carefully turned over the pages.

"As Ivan Fedorovich wrote to his friend, if the tsar, Alexander I, did not die in 1825 but lived on as Fedor Kuzmich until 1864 then he was still the legitimate sovereign. The ritual of annointment at coronation can't be simply set aside. So, you could argue that all the imperial decrees issued by his successors down to his death in 1864 don't have the force of law. How about that! What would you revolutionaries make of it?"

"Mother of God!" Letchik exclaimed. "Even the peasants would wake up if this became known. It's a great story too. All powerful tsar runs off to Siberian wilderness to live the life of a *starets*. Can't you see the Western newspapers printing it?"

"And in Russia," Irina added, "newspapers or not, the rumor mill works its magic. The word would spread like wildfire."

"So Ivan Fedorovich was right. He had constructed a bomb more powerful than the one the terrorists used to blow up the Winter Palace. The Decembrists would be avenged in ways they never imagined."

The fire was burning low and they could not read any more.

"Next installment tomorrow— just like a Dickens' novel," sighed Irina. When Irina and Vasiliev stretched out on the bare ground, Letchik said softly. "I'm going to sleep outside the enclosure, just to keep watch." And he stole away into the darkness. Vasiliev remembered the last and only time he had lain beside Irina when they had gone on the ghastly night expedition to exhume the body of Countess Ushakova. Now it was different. She groped for his hand and squeezed it tight.

He raised her hand to his lips. Her fingers were rough and dry. He turned her hand over and kissed the soft palm.

"How strange it all is," she said.

"Yes, but a wonderful strangeness." He felt a wave of tenderness overcome him. He drew her closer.

"Do you think we have wasted too many years?"

"I don't know. Perhaps. If so, we won't waste any more."

He felt her fingers trace the outline of his face.

Suddenly, she began to giggle like a schoolgirl. He smiled at her in the darkness.

"What is it? Have you encountered my crooked teeth?"

"No Vasya, I've always known about them. No, no!" she whispered. "Shall we always remember making love for the first time in a Scythian cemetery?"

She kissed him very hard.

"I'm still a virgin, Vasya, but I promise not to scream."

Chapter Thirty-Six

Bark hated the steppe. It was empty and barren; it seemed devoid of life. The straight line of the horizon never changed. There was no sense of having covered any distance no matter how hard you rode. Nothing changed. His thoughts often turned to the mountains, the high snow capped peaks of the Caucasus. He could never have described them the way Lermontov had, but he felt the same way about them. There was something heroic about their striving to reach the heavens. Or at least the sight of them inspired heroism. This is what explained to him the courage of the mountaineers. Fierce, fanatical heathens, they may have been, but what fighters! Yes, he thought, if life were different he would return to the Caucasus. Instead he was riding through this flat, empty land to an unknown destination.

His only solace was the girl. She surprised him. He turned in the saddle and glanced quickly at her. Pretty, yes, but there was another quality that he found difficult to put into words. Suddenly, it came to him; the resemblance to a Chechen girl he had known. Oh, the complexion was not the same; either was the color of her hair. But the chiseled profile, the set lips, the wisp of hair whipping her cheek. It was more than her looks; the passion and tenderness of her love-making; yes that was surprising. And her skill at preparing a frugal repast over a small fire. She must have bought some herbs at the market as they were riding out of Omsk and concealed them in the folds of her ample skirt. When he ran out of the salted beef and managed to shoot a rabbit, she had prepared a delicious stew. Skinned the animal herself. He looked at her again and she turned to him and smiled. He felt his heart quicken. Was it possible he was falling in love with her? A sensation he had never felt before. He thought he was impervious to sentimental nonsense. She had just been another lay and now he wanted to protect her; take her with him no matter where he was going. He almost laughed out loud and shook his head. The next thing he might imagine was domestic bliss.

He was about to say something to her when he spotted an irregular shape near the far horizon. He pointed with his arm. She shaded her eyes, and then nodded. So her eyesight was as good as his. This too pleased him. As they drew closer, the shape took on the appearance of a ruined fort. She signaled to him and drew a cross in the air. "A nomad burial ground," she shouted.

They reined up at the distance of a rifle shot. Bark looked at the sky. Still a few hours of daylight left. He debated whether to take shelter; it would be better than sleeping again in the open air where the temperature could drop suddenly and a penetrating wind could suddenly spring up. He felt an urge to press ahead. But he was beginning to change his mind about the need to catch up with the Americans. He was toying with the idea that he and Anna should just make for the border and forget the Omsk governor and all his twisted plotting. Only one thing held him back. The statistics might prove useful in getting them across the border, if they ran into trouble. He had already killed for them; but he did not relish killing again, and certainly not Americans. That would stir up a hornet's nest. Perhaps there was another way.

He beckoned to her. "Listen, my dear, I would like nothing better than to bring a little life to this dead ground. But we should take advantage of the daylight. This isn't the time to let up. Once we cross the border we can rest. Agreed?"

Anna was pleased he had asked for her approval. He had not done that before; no man ever had. In any case she could not refuse him anything.

He noticed the weariness in her face, and as a concession, he slackened the pace. But they rode on.

They were dead tired when the next morning they rode into Semipalatinsk.

Bark leaned over to touch Anna's arm. "It's not Paris my dear, but I'll get you there."

She smiled wanly, assailed by the wretched appearance of the town; it was as if a gigantic brush had painted it entirely gray. There wasn't a single tree or bush or blade of grass to alleviate the monotonous dull hue covering the weather-beaten log cabins. Suddenly she felt as though her mount was sinking under her legs.

"Don't worry," Bark went on, "the officers here call it 'The Devil's Sandbox.'"

So that was it, thought Anna. The streets were covered by a thick layer of sand that slowed the pace of their horses, muffling the sounds of their hoof beats. Here and there the sand had drifted up against the walls of the houses. As the sun came up, the temperature rose quickly and she felt as though her skin was drying up. Suddenly she heard a strange wailing, of first one voice and then others. She felt was though she were descending into an alien world that would engulf and never release her.

"We'll go to the eastern district where the Tatars live." He turned to see the startled look on her face.

"Ah! The call to prayer; you'll have to get used to it. Five times a day. Look there is the first mosque. See how the sun catches the top of the minarets. The place is full of them. Besides it's the last day of Ramadan, the period of fasting for Muslims. I remember it well from my days in the Caucasus. No need to be frightened. There'll be a great celebration tomorrow. "

Bark soon found them quarters and provided Anna with a young Tatar woman who would wash her and cook their meals. He hardly had brushed off his uniform and dashed cold water in his face than he left her, promising to return in a few hours. She allowed the Tatar girl to bathe her, wash her hair and dress her in a long flowing robe before she stretched out on a soft divan and fell into a deep sleep.

When Bark returned he was in high spirits and caught her up in his arms, making fierce love to her before collapsing in his turn. He told her nothing of his plans. But she felt a surge of happiness before she too fell back asleep.

Chapter
Thirty-Seven

At breakfast the next morning, Kennan and Frost were complaining mildly about the night noises that kept them awake; the rattles of the night watchmen and the early cries of the muezzins from the minarets. Serov was reminded of the years of the war when he had served with Vasili Vasilevich on the Danube front. There were plenty of mosques in Bulgaria, but many of these had been abandoned or burned by the local Christian population in the communal warfare that wracked the country. He was surprised that here in the depth of Central Asia, the Christian Russians, Muslim Tatars and pagan tribesmen called Kirghiz seemed to live peacefully enough. So much so, that they could even engage in organized contests of strength with one another. The chief of police had invited the Americans to witness a famous annual wrestling match between the Tatars and the Kirghiz.

A large crowd was assembled around an open sandy area arranged in three concentric circles; men squatting on their heels in the first row, men standing in the second row, and behind them horsemen. The chief was greeted cordially as he made room for his three guests in the front row on the Kirghiz side of the crowd. By the time they arrived, the sun was at its zenith and the sand had been stirred up by the early matches. As they watched the contest between two fairly evenly matched wrestlers, a Kirghiz chief was whispering in the ear of the chief of police who turned to the Americans and translated. "It seems the Kirghiz side is taking a licking. Of course, it's all good-nurtured, but still one doesn't want the outcome to be too one sided, or else some of the young bloods might get upset, you understand."

Serov had been studying the wrestlers with the knowledgeable eye of an experienced fighter. As a young serf of Vasiliev's father, Count Vorontsov, he had learned in the village how to wrestle, no holds barred. Then his young friend Vasya from the big house had taught him how to box in exchange for Serov's instruction in the tactics of village street brawls. Serov always believed that the combination of these two styles had enabled him to survive the mass fist fights that the local merchants had arranged among the serfs for their own entertainment. Now he felt himself drawn into the contest, wondering how well he might do in the arena.

Bark too was studying the crowd. The local Tatar champion was resting on the edge of the crowd while one of his compatriots struggled to overcome his Kirghiz opponent. He glanced up and caught Bark's eye. Bark nodded. It was time to challenge the Russian. Bark had paid him well. The object was to break the Russian's leg. Nothing more. That would eliminate the bodyguard and make Kennan and Frost more amenable to surrendering those "damn statistics" as Bark had fallen into the habit of calling his "passport to freedom."

The Tatar got up from his place and strolled over to the Kirghiz side. He bowed to the chief and then in broken Russian asked politely if the Russian officer would enjoy a brief round. The chief shook his head, but Serov touched his arm and explained that he might enjoy the challenge if only to tell his grandchildren about it. The chief shrugged; Kennan raised his eyebrows, but said nothing; Frost was too busy sketching the match to pay any attention.

Serov insisted on wearing the Kirghiz colors. They took him to a tent behind the horsemen where he stripped and donned a blue skull cap and a pair of course cotton trousers with a red sash. Like the Tatar champion he was bare-chested. The Tatar was wearing a yellow skull cap and green sash. The crowd was already excited; the unusual sight of a Russian dressed in the tribal colors of the Kirghiz seemed to drive them into a frenzy. The police chief was frowning; it had been a mistake, he feared, to allow Serov to fight. But he really had no jurisdiction over him, and he did not want to offend the Americans who seemed to be encouraging Serov once he had declared himself. Kennan was leaning forward expectantly; Frost put down his sketchbook.

Serov and the Tatar circled warily around one another, each making a few feints. Serov knew he had to adopt the traditional local style; he could not use his fists. He knew this put him at a disadvantage. But he was sure the Tatar would be overconfident, and if he struck quickly he would gain the advantage of surprise.

As if at a signal the two men rushed one another and grappled together, each one seizing the sash of the other, bending at the waist and keeping their legs spread apart and well back to avoid being tripped. Serov had noticed that the Tatar's key move was to pull his opponent toward him, catch him off balance and then knock him down him with a powerful side blow of his leg. What he did not know was that the Tatar intended to deliver this blow at the knee joint thus crippling his opponent rather than simply tripping him up as he had done in his previous victories.

Serov was ready for the move and when the Tatar backed away suddenly and then pulled Serov toward him, Serov came at him with full force and seizing hold of his opponent's shoulder with one hand while gripping the sash with the other hand he swung both his legs under the Tatar and pulled him forward with all his strength. As the Tatar fell on him Serov launched his entire body backward while pressing both legs against the Tatar's buttocks. As the two men hit the ground Serov completed the somersault by pulling the Tatar over his head, ending up on his feet. He clasped the stunned Tatar around the shoulder and hip, hurling him the ground where he pinned him with a full press. The four masters of ceremonies, dressed in long green *khalats* threw down their rattan wands signaling the end of the fight. Pandemonium broke out among the Kirghiz.

As Serov rose and raised his arms in triumph, the Tatar lashed out with his leg in a desperate move to earn his money. But Serov, whose instincts had been honed in mass fights without rules, had not dropped his guard. He stepped adroitly aside and caught the man's leg at the end of its swing and gave it a mighty twist. The Tatar cried out in pain and fell back in the dust.

The Kirghiz front line rose as one man, crying "foul." Serov shook his head and raised his arms in a gesture of restraint. He then turned to the fallen Tatar and helped him to his feet. As Serov led him limping to his side of the arena, the Kirghiz broke out in shouts of approval.

Serov was embarrassed when the Kirghiz lifted him on their shoulders and carried him off to their encampment where the chief was waiting to greet him as a hero. He had a strange presentiment that his victory was going to have fateful consequences.

Kirghiz encampment

Chapter Thirty-Eight

Serov emerged from the tent of the Kirghiz patriarch feeling bloated from the vast quantity of kumiss that had been pressed on him. He was the honored guest and could hardly refuse, but he would have enjoyed the drink more if it had not been served in a greasy wooden bowl. He had been reluctant to leave Kennan and Frost, but they insisted that he reap the rewards of his great feat, as Kennan put it, and the Kirghiz promised to mount guard so that no one would disturb the Americans. The night air was cool and the only sound that reached Serov was the occasional bleating of a goat, tethered outside one of the tents. He stood for a while staring at the sky where the flickering stars seemed alive. For a few moments he imagined himself back in his village, and only too late realized that he was not alone.

A soft voice came from a darker shadow just in front of him. Serov's hand went to his belt.

"Excuse me, sir! Don't be startled. I am a friend. May I speak with you?"

"What is it you want?" asked Serov brusquely.

"My name is Egor. My sister and I were at the wrestling match today and greatly admired your style." Serov detected a slight accent, but the Russian was pure, if rather formal.

"We would like to invite you to our humble dwelling for a meal. Perhaps tomorrow evening? We live with my old grandmother, but she too is eager to meet you after we told her about your triumph. Let me explain." The voice drew nearer. Serov regretted coming out alone. His first impulse was to return quickly to the tent. But something in the young voice stopped and reassured him. This, he reflected was unusual.

"It is not easy for us to enter a Kirghiz encampment. You see we are *pravoslavnyi*, Orthodox Christians, in fact half Russian, through our father, although our mother was a Kirghiz. Well, I am telling you this so that you understand why I am meeting you here in the darkness. May I continue?"

"Go on."

"Yes, well, my sister, Dunia, teaches at a small school for Christian converts, some Kirghiz, a few Tatars. I am a telegrapher. We live on the outskirts of the village with our grandmother. We see so few Russians here. And as I said, we greatly admired your spirit."

"I'll tell you what," said Serov. "My duties keep me in town but would you and your sister like to have supper with me at the Hotel Sibir? You could even meet the Americans, one of whom speaks excellent Russian. Agreed?"

"You are too kind. But, yes, of course, if that is more convenient for you."

Long afterward Serov wondered what had got into him and finally concluded that you could not distrust everyone and continue to live.

The following evening Egor arrived with a stunning girl of about twenty years of age whose exotic features seemed to Serov an artist's blending of the ideal Russian and Kirghiz beauty. After they had left, Kennan and Frost teased him that she and Serov seemed so mesmerized by one another that the others felt left out. Serov felt the unusual heat of a flush suffuse his face.

The next day Serov found Kennan greatly excited about the prospect of his first meeting with political exiles through the good offices of a Russian official named Pavlovskii. Serov quickly surmised that his presence would be awkward for all and decided instead to ride out to see his new friends, Egor and Dunia. Their grandmother, who had obviously been a great Kirghiz beauty in her youth, greeted Serov warmly. Serov was struck by the taste with which the cabin was furnished with Kirghiz carpets and brightly decorated saddle bags and harness hanging on the walls. She had prepared a bucket of cold lamb, fresh tomatoes, bread and kumiss for them to take with them on a ride across the steppe. Serov was stunned by Dunia's skill as a rider. Egor had brought his grandfather's bow and arrows and gave a display of his skill as an archer. He proposed to teach Serov in how to shoot exchange for learning the art of wrestling. It was dusk when they returned to the cabin.

Dunia and Egor sang duets, mainly Russian folk songs but a few Kirghiz laments as well. Serov listened transformed, seated in an old comfortable chair made by their father of various hides. He had never imagined a life like this. In the Russia he knew, you were either a nobleman whose daughter may have had all these marvelous talents but spoke French, displayed refined manners, and was surrounded by servants: or else you were in a peasant's hut with a bare floor, filled with unpleasant odors and a sick grandfather lying groaning on the stove. So this is what they meant by "democratic" Siberia. He suddenly realized that he had dropped his peasant's accents and was speaking a plain Russian not so very different from Vasili Vasilievich's. And he could not keep his eyes off Dunia, the likes of whom in Moscow he would not dared to have courted even in his head.

Chapter
Thirty-Nine

Vasiliev awoke with the feeling that he had never greeted a more splendid dawn. The sky was roseate in the east and a few wispy arabesques lazily drifted overhead. But of course it was only the backdrop for his deep sense of happiness. Leaning on his elbow he stared at Irina for several minutes, marveling at the change in her features; the stern mask had dissolved. It was as if a myriad of tiny muscles had all of a sudden given up their watchful guard.

He rose quietly and passed under the ruined arch into the open air. Letchik was building a fire and for an instant Vasiliev tensed up, fearing an off-handed remark such as one of his fellow officers might have given on such an occasion.

Letchik did not look up; "She spoke of you every day in prison and exile. I believe I came to know you that way. It was a good introduction."

Vasiliev took the cup of hot tea and sipped it slowly.

"She would have been a good comrade too," he replied.

"None better. She helped me survive the greatest sorrow of my life." He looked up at Vasiliev for the first time.

"I fell in love in the Tiumen Camp with a young woman who was already in the final stages of consumption. At first I thought it was just a case of my own morbidity. But it wasn't that. No need to go on about it. You know how impossible it is to describe a love. I tried everything to save her...perhaps that's not right. There was no chance to save her. Perhaps I was just selfish in prolonging her life. There's no cure, you know, but if I ever get out of this hellish country, I will dedicate my life to finding one." He paused. "I'm sorry to put this on you at this moment. But you should know that the Swan... well I guess we have to call her Irina now ...pulled me out of my despair. I'd like to think there was something of Irina in my Elena. You are a fortunate man, Vasili Vasilievich. But you know this."

"Thank you for telling me. I don't presume to know how you suffered. I can only say that when I last saw Irisha in the Moscow prison, her hair shorn, wrapped in a shapeless grey dress, torn away from me and sentenced to years in exile, I felt something of what you felt when you lost your Elena."

Letchik nodded.

They sat for awhile in silence until Irina appeared, smiling shyly and stretching her arms to the sky.

"We can be in Semipalatinsk in a few hours but the last few miles will be tough with this sun," said Vasiliev. "Best to wrap a cloth over your head and shoulders. The heat can be painful."

As they rode together, Letchik dropped behind, sensing that Irina and Vasiliev had plenty to talk about, years to fill in. Irina spoke first, without any prelude, and began to relate the story Vasiliev had longed to hear but hesitated to ask her about. She had left her comfortable life and ask her family for the revolutionary underground only after she had discovered that her beloved father was, in fact, a cruel disciplinarian who did not hesitate to order the soldiers under his command to be harshly punished for slight infractions of the rule. She had accidently witnessed how a soldier had been crippled by running the gauntlet as her father looked on, and how he refused to speak to her about it afterwards. She had already read and re-read Dostoevsky's *Memoirs of the House of the Dead* and wept over the suffering of the exiles in Siberia. But it was still just a book. What her father had done and continued to do was happening before her eyes. She broke with him. She found good comrades in the Land and Liberty movement. But she would not endorse terror. When she too, like Fedor Mikhailovich, was arrested and sent to prison and exile, she understood better many things in Dostoevsky's book. That there was pure evil but also immense reservoirs of good. But in Russia both good and evil were being thrown together in an abyss of suffering. Sometimes she felt she would go mad; other times that she would die.

She turned in her saddle. "My belief in you kept me sane and alive. I want so much, Vasya, to be whole again."

"I can only promise you one thing, my darling. We will never be parted again."

As they entered the town they could see behind them a great cloud of sand whirling rapidly in their direction. They rode along the banks of the Irtysh River, watching a great caravan of camels laden with bags of grain headed for Mongolia, three hundred and fifty miles to the southeast, Vasiliev asking directions to the Semipalatinsk Prison.

Irina and Letchik were kept under guard in the holding room while Vasiliev presented his papers to the chief of police.

"My instructions were to find the prisoners lodgings in the town. They have already served their prison terms. They will need to find work; both are skilled nurses and should be employed in this profession. After I see to their installation, I would like to inspect the prison," Vasiliev felt obliged to add.

"More inspections!" cried the chief. "Two Americans were here just yesterday with all kinds of documents, giving them access. Decent fellows; the one spoke a good Russian. But foreigners inspecting our prisons? What is the government thinking these days?"

"Ah yes, Kennan and Frost. My assistant Sergeant Serov is accompanying them. Where are they staying?"

"At the Sibir. By the way your assistant made a rather spectacular debut as a wrestler," the police chief chuckled. "He beat the Tatar champion and has become something of a hero to the Kirghiz."

Vasiliev smiled to himself. "I hope he did not create any difficulties as a result."

"Not really. I was happy to see the Tatars taken down a peg. Sometimes they become rather arrogant, you know."

The chief shuffled some papers on his desk. "Well, well, perhaps we can put up your politicals at Lobanovskii's. Since his wife died he'll have an extra room for the female ...what's her name? And the man can double up with Lobanovskii. Since you've brought them this far, if you don't mind I'll just send you over there without a guard. He lives a few versts out of town. We're short on staff these days and most of my men are out handling the caravan. And your inspection...?"

"We can arrange that later."

"Good. You should present your credentials to the governor, General Tseklinsky, and then please come to dinner with my wife and my family. It will be a treat to hear about life in Moscow." And the chief promptly let the matter of the two politicals slip out of his mind. He had more important things to worry about like the caravans and the Tatar bandit who had been raising hell among the Cossack villages.

Chapter Forty

Vasiliev did his best to entertain the chief and his wife, who smiled wistfully at his stories of Petersburg. But his mind was elsewhere. The brief conversation he had had with Serov in the lobby of the Sibir before the dinner gave him plenty to worry about. Serov's Kirghiz friends had confided in him that the Tatar had been paid by a Russian officer to injure him badly. This was clearly Bark's work. With Serov out of the way, Kennan and Frost would make easy targets. The man was ruthless and desperate to boot. He would not hesitate to murder again, if it were necessary to recover the prison records. The road from Semipalatinsk to the Mongolian border was over three hundred and fifty miles, ending in hilly and mountainous country. Plenty of opportunity to set an ambush. If he, Irina and Letchik joined up with them they would probably have to travel more slowly and they could be easily separated. Besides, he thought, they would be the hunted and Bark the hunter, not a role that he relished. Sitting on the veranda of the chief's house, smoking cigars and listening with half an ear to tales about the hardships of the early colonists from Russia, Vasiliev formed a plan.

Much would depend, he knew, on the attitude of the Americans. There was some risk involved for them. Late at night he found Kennan still awake, writing up his notes for the day. Kennan put down his pen and listened attentively. Then the American then grasped Vasiliev's hand. "Of course, I agree." Then a look Vasiliev had not seen before passed over his face. "It won't be easy to part from you, my friend." And then he said something Vasiliev would never forget.

"If you can get across the border and reach Peking, go to the American consul. I will leave him a letter. He's a good man and will get you visas to the United States. We could use men and women like you and your friends on our frontier."

Early the next morning, Kennan and Frost noisily prepared their departure. Frost even went to the telegraph office to send off a telegram announcing their departure to the Governor-General in Omsk. They drove ostentatiously through the town and left on the road southeast on the road leading to the Altai Mountains three hundred miles away.

At the outskirts of the town, the tarantas drew up at a Kirghiz encampment.

Kennan and Frost climbed down and entered one of the tents followed by several young Kirghiz who had quickly unloaded and carried in their baggage. Vasiliev, Serov, Irina and Letchik were waiting for them. They had quietly left the hotel at dawn and ridden out of town on horses provided by Serov's Kirghiz friends. They embraced the Americans hurriedly. Vasiliev whispered to Kennan.

"One last favor! When you write your book I beg of you not to mention any of us, least of all Serov and me. It would only cause trouble for those in Petersburg who had trusted us." Kennan nodded his agreement. He never saw them again, and he kept his promise.

Irina and Letchik got into the tarantas while Vasiliev and Serov mounted two Kirghiz ponies. They rode along side as the driver whipped the horses into a fast trot. Kennan and Frost waited comfortably in the tent of the Kirghiz patriarch the rest of the day, until word came that a Uhlan officer and a woman had ridden past. The Kirghiz boy who reported giggled in his broken Russian.

"They'll not get far on those nags."

Chapter
Forty-One

The Kirghiz had supplied them with their best horses and they made rapid progress, passing through prosperous Cossack villages all along the right bank of the Irtysh River. The heat had soared into the hundreds and they were overtaken by a fierce sandstorm. The atmosphere was suffocating, making it difficult to breathe. Irina got through it best of all, having wrapped herself in white woolens, to the astonishment of Serov, and saved enough water to moisten the face cloth that shield her from the worse on-

Alexsandrovskaia-Severnaia Ravine

slaught of the sand. When they arrived at the station of Cherem-
shanka, the storm diminished and later that day they reached the
foothills of the Altai.

As they entered the Alexandrovskaia-Severnaia Ravine, Vasiliev thought again about the possibility of an ambush.

They would be easy targets in the narrow passes leading out of
the Bukhturma Valley. He hand was never far from his holster. But
it was hard to imagine danger lurking in the country which now
opened up in front of them.Cool breezes blew across meadows of
green grass and mountain flowers; in the distance they glimpsed
the snow peaks of the high Altai. They were enchanted by the picturesque appearance of the Altai Station, a cluster of sturdy Cossack
cabins surrounded by gardens and young birches. In the distance
they could see a group of colored Kirghiz tents. Fresh cold rivulets
of water from the melting snows of the mountains ran through the
village.

To pass the long evenings, Vasiliev took out the documents and
glanced through them again, passing them around. Serov, who was
seeing them for the first time, read them slowly as if committing
them to heart. But he only shrugged when Letchik asked him what
he thought of them. Then he said, "High politics, higher than I am
wont to go."

In the mornings, Vasiliev woke up trying to remember his confused dreams. He began to understand for the first time the peasant utopia of the *belovodye*, the white waters, the land of peace and
freedom, which were supposed to lie beyond the mountain range.
Lying with Irina by his side he felt a strange sadness overcome him.
He was just beginning to discover a different Russia with its vast
natural splendors untouched by the clutter and clamor of modern
life at the moment when he was about to leave it. Lermontov's verse
came back to him:

> Farewell, unwashed Russia
> Land of slaves, land of lords
> And your blue uniforms
> And your submissive hordes
> Perhaps beyond Caucasian peaks (well, in this case Altai peaks!)
> I'll find a peace from tears...

Irina was the first to notice the change in Serov. "He seems preoccupied, even distant. Not like him. What do you think?"

"I'm worried that he feels even more strongly than I do about leaving Russia. I have you, the promise of a new and full life. We speak English, Serov does not. What skills does he have? A good policeman, but without the language…"

"But there is something else," said Irina. "Ever since Semipalatinsk, the change has become more noticeable. He seems actually troubled. But also he speaks differently, somehow, have you noticed? What else happened there besides the famous wrestling match?"

"I don't know. He hasn't told me. It's unusual."

The next morning a Kirghiz rider reined in outside their cabin. Serov immediately went out to meet him. When he returned his face was grave.

"Bark and a woman are closing in on us. They are only a day's ride behind."

Vasiliev stared hard at Serov. "Sergeant you have been holding back on us. What did you arrange in Semipalatinsk?"

Serov stared back. There was no 'begin' your pardon' on his lips. "You had your own arrangements to make. I had mine. My friends agreed to help. We set up a relay service to keep track of Bark. No sense being surprised, is there?"

Vasiliev forced a laugh. "Serov you have unplumbed depths," he repeated and immediately regretted it when he saw the look on Serov's face.

"That's good of you to say, Vasili Vasilievich. And there is another thing. Bad news comes doesn't always come in threes, two are more than enough."

"Something worse than Bark? Surely not!"

"A day or two behind Bark is a small detachment of Gendarmes who are, my friends say, looking for him or for us."

So, Vasiliev thought, Serov gives signs of taking charge. Perhaps he believes I am too preoccupied with Irina. Ah, that's not fair. He always was with me on rescuing her. What is it then?

"I thought we have more time," said Vasiliev when they arrived at Arul the most remote Russian settlement in the Altai closest to the Mongolian border of China. "But here is the place we have to plan to ambush Bark. We'll hire some Kirghiz horses accustomed to climb these mountain paths to the south. Once we dispose of Bark, we will make for the border and cross into China. That won't be the end of our problems, but just the beginning of a new set. At least we'll be free of our pursuers whoever they are."

Irina and Letchik were listening carefully; Serov had lowered his head, resting his chin on his chest. Vasiliev was about to say something to him, but checked himself.

The next morning they made their way cautiously up a steep Kirghiz trail that led to a high foothill behind the village, Serov leading the way.

A breathtaking sight came into view of the snow-clad mountains along the Mongolian border. They passed a few Kirghiz tents dotting the rocky outcroppings. Small herds of goats and sheep grazed on the fresh summer grasses. At one point, Serov leaned over and called to a herdsman, speaking a few words in a language Vasiliev had only recently heard. More surprises from Serov!

The Kirghiz trail

Soon they passed beyond all signs of human or animal life. The horses slowed the pace, picking their way without a misstep over lichen covered rocks. Vasiliev called a halt where the trail narrowed between two immense glacial boulders.

"This is as good a place as any."

Chapter
Forty-Two

Captain Elagin of the Gendarmes did not relish his assignment.
The Governor-General's orders were clear enough. But the idea
of hunting down a Uhlan officer made him uncomfortable, whatever the crime may have been. He had no proofs except Grigoriev's
word which he had learned could not always be relied upon. The
pursuit was proving to be more arduous than he anticipated, and
the shortage of mounts forced him to reduce his detachment to four
men. It was obvious that Bark was headed for the Mongolian border. That meant crossing very rough terrain, much of it unmapped.
For this reason he had decided reluctantly to engage the services of
a young Kirghiz tribesman who allegedly had been born and raised
in the foothills of the Altai. "Well, we'll see how reliable his childhood memories," he had muttered under his breath as he left the
Kirghiz patriarch's tent outside Semipalatinsk.

Once his plan had failed, Bark lost all interest in confronting the
Americans. Their Russian bodyguard was a tough one. And he was
no longer willing to risk a fire fight in order to get those damned
prison statistics. Now that Anna was with him, he felt even more
uncertain about the outcome. Without the documents he and Anna
would have to take their chances crossing into Mongolia at a remote point. Risky, but he knew now she was game.

They were making good time. The girl was splendid, he could
think of no other word to describe her. Their fierce love making
seemed to energize rather than tire him, and they kept a blistering
pace. When they arrived at the Altai Station, Bark had almost decided to give up the chase. Anna insisted they rest a day; she was

enthralled by the sight of the mountains which she had never seen before, and he could not restrain her when she dismounted and ran into the fields of fragrant wild flowers, picking handfuls and burying her face in the blossoms. He felt the fierceness in his soul ebbing away.

The local Cossacks told him his best chance would be to jump off at Jingistai or Arul. They said the going was rough, but he was confident. This would be nothing to compare with the Caucasus where he had learned his mountaineering under fire. He turned down the advice to hire a Kirghiz guide. He just needed to make sure they were mounted on those scrawny looking but sure-footed Kirghiz ponies.

Bark bought the provisions he thought he would need and surprised Anna by suggesting they rest another day. She seemed wildly happy. As they walked arm and arm through the Cossack village, she asked him shyly to teach her how to shoot.

"Mongolia sounds like a wild place," she said. "And I might help if we get in trouble."

He shook his head in wonder. "All right, but we better warn our Cossack friends, or they'll think bandits are attacking them."

Chapter
Forty-Three

Late in the afternoon, Vasiliev signaled Serov across the trail. "I don't think they'll show up now. It would be foolhardy to try to follow this trail as it grows darker."

They had left Irina and Letchik with the horses at their camp in the valley within hailing distance just beyond the crest of the hill where the trail descended sharply.

"Let's wait a bit. Bark seems like a reckless fellow; who knows what he might try. Don't want to be surprised. I'll stay on, if you want."

"Wouldn't think of it, my friend. We'll give it another half hour."

Bark and Anna were slowly climbing out of the valley. Bark kept glancing at the sky, trying to decide how much daylight remained. They couldn't stop and make camp on the trail. He was counting on getting to the crest before darkness; the descent would be easier. There would be a three quarter moon and that would help. They might have to lead the ponies part of the way down.

"Easy now, Anna. Just let the horse find its way."

Elagin and his men had reached the Altai Station the day before. He learned from the Cossacks that a Uhlan officer and a woman had passed through; no one mentioned the other travelers. Why tell a Gendarme more than he needs to know?

Elagin calculated how much time it would take to reach the Mongolian border and worried about losing his man. Then he thought of the pursuit into the mountains and how little honor he would gain from arresting an officer like Bark, a decorated Caucasian veteran. And the Kirghiz boy kept telling him how dangerous the trails were and that their cavalry mounts would not make it; they would have to hire Kirghiz ponies. The very sight of them discouraged Elagin. When one of his men mounted, he looked ridiculous, seated on the high short-stirruped saddle. Elagin clenched his teeth. He couldn't quit just now; too many people knew about his progress in tracking Bark, how close he had got. If he quit now word would get back that Elagin had found the Altai Station just a bit too comfortable to move on.

"Damn it," he swore out loud. "Get me five ponies and let's finish this thing."

As his detachment began their ascent, Vasiliev and Serov had decided to give up their vigil, leave their position behind the glacial boulders and turn to go back up the trail when they heard the clatter of a loose stone. They whirled and saw two mounted figures dark shapes coming toward them out of the shadows. The moon had barely risen and was still hidden behind the crags overlooking the trail.

Vasiliev cursed himself for having been caught in the open. He knew it could only be Bark, Standing in the middle of the trail, he drew his revolver and shouted: "Halt, police, you are under arrest! Dismount and throw down your weapons." Serov dropped off to the side and leveled his revolver as well.

They heard Bark mutter, "Do as they say, Anna. We want no shooting."

Bark slipped his Berdan army rifle off his shoulder and let it drop to the ground. He swung out of the saddle and held the bridle of Anna's pony as she dismounted.

"Your side arms, too," ordered Vasiliev.

Bark unbuckled his holster and let it fall.

"Please don't," Anna cried out and went down on her knees.

"Anna, no! Don't beg…" Bark had no time to finish before the shooting began.

Anna had seized the revolver from the ground and was firing wildly. Vasiliev was hit and fell to the ground. Serov hesitated. He could barely see the woman lying flat out, and Bark falling next to her. Then Serov felt a chip of stone from the boulder slice his face. He reached up to feel the blood pouring into his eyes. Blinded, he fired once and dropped his revolver.

"Quick, Anna, out of here." Bark lifted her into the saddle and quickly mounted. They turned and raced headlong down the trail.

"Vasya!" Serov cried out Vasiliev's childhood name.

"Can you get after them?" Vasiliev groaned. "I'm hit in the shoulder." He staggered to his feet. "The horses, get the horses!"

"I can't see!" cried Serov; "blood in my eyes." He felt for the wound and ripped open his uniform, tearing off the collar of his shirt and pressing it to his forehead. He fought the feeling of shock, sat down abruptly and tipped his head back.

"Just creased me feels like. I'm trying to stop the blood."

"What a mess I've made of this!" Vasiliev was trying to cut off the sleeve of his uniform with his army knife, a stream of mother curses spewing out of his mouth; just like a peasant, thought Serov, forced to smile in spite of his pain.

"Can you stand up and get back to the camp?" Vasiliev asked.

Serov grunted. He remembered his long talks with Letchik about treating wounds. He lay down, applied pressure to his cut and — what was the rest of it? Wait for help. And where is that coming from? He asked himself.

Running and stumbling behind them, Irina and Letchik had heard the shots. Seeing Vasiliev on the ground, Irina stifled a cry and rushed to his side. Letchik knelt down by Serov and opened the bag he had brought with him from the prison hospital. He examined Serov's injury, pronounced it a flesh wound, staunched the blood, swabbed it with grain alcohol and applied a rough bandage.

"Ready to fight another day," he grinned in the darkness.

"It doesn't feel that way," said Serov between his teeth. "Fetch me my gun. See if Bark left his rifle; it should be lying there in the path... Got it? Good! That means they won't be back any time soon."

Irina had improvised a bandage for Vasiliev but she couldn't tell how seriously he had been hurt.

"He shouldn't walk. I'll go back and bring up a pony. See what you can do," she murmured to Letchik. She brushed his lips against Vasiliev's forehead and murmured something the others could not hear. Then Vasiliev's voice rang out, "the healing kiss" and he tried to laugh but coughed instead. Irina shook her head and hurried away.

Letchik examined Vasiliev, searching for an exit wound and swearing when he didn't find it. The bullet was lodged somewhere in the upper arm. Letchik thought of his instruments, just a probe and a long surgical knife. He would have to wait for daylight to remove the bullet, or else chance it by the firelight at the camp. Either way it wasn't going to be pleasant.

For Vasiliev the feeling of humiliation was almost greater than the pain.That he and Serov should be disabled by a woman! When he tried to explain to Letchik what had happened, Letchik tried to quiet him. It was then they heard from a distance the shooting.

"Mother of God, what now!" exclaimed Serov.

"Rifle fire," groaned Vasiliev.

"But I have his Berdan in my hands," said Serov.

The burst of gun fire was followed by dead silence. Serov braced himself against a boulder and aimed Bark's rifle down the trail. But there was no further sound from that direction. After a few minutes, Irina appeared leading the pony.

"What happened? " She asked. "I was afraid they'd come back. But then I realized the sound of the shots was too far away."

No one answered. They managed to get Vasiliev onto the pony and led him back to the camp.

Serov insisted on staying behind. He assumed his position as the immovable column, the *stolb*. He fought to keep his eyes open, and finally gave up, dragging himself back to the camp where he collapsed by the fire.

Chapter
Forty-Four

Letchik was right. It wasn't pleasant. But once Vasiliev had fainted it was easier to dig out the bullet.

"We're lucky. A clean wound. But he'll need to rest. We can't scale mountains just yet," Letchik pronounced as he improvised a sling.

"We're so close," Vasiliev grunted. "A day's ride and we're across the border. I worry about staying here. We don't know about the shooting. Maybe bandits...or else, more likely the Gendarmes. The Kirghiz said they were in hot pursuit, riding only a few hours behind Bark. Either way we're exposed here." He glanced at Irina and then he raised his eyes to the mountain chain. "So close."

Serov's wound had opened again from the exertion of holding Vasiliev down while Letchik performed his small operation. He sat motionless by the fire, the new bandage around his head showing a small dark red spot in the middle. He was reading the secret documents again.

Vasiliev glanced over. "A strange time to be reading up on your history, Serov."

Serov folded up the documents and handed them back to Letchik.

"Not so strange Vasili Vasilievich."

It was that tone again, thought Vasiliev. Not like Serov.

After a night's rest, they slowly made their way to the Rakhmanovsky Hot Springs Station where they stopped so that Vasiliev could recuperate before they had to challenge the mountain passes to Mongolia. Early the next morning, they all bathed in the hot

Rakhmanovskii Hot Springs

springs that sprang from glacial boulders decorated with wooden crosses and bits of colorful Kirghiz shirts and trousers.

After they had dressed, Vasiliev spoke quietly to Irina. "Serov seems so restless; even the hot springs hasn't calmed him down." Irina brushed aside a lock of her hair.

"Yes," she said with a strange catch in her throat. "He is restless." Vasiliev looked at her expecting more. But she turned away and greeted Letchik who had come to join them. "Where is Serov?" Vasiliev asked. "He's taking a last look at the springs," Letchik replied. Vasiliev was about to make a joke; was there a conspiracy being hatched? But something told him this joke would fall flat. He compressed his lips and watched as Serov came up to them.

"If we want a decent breakfast," said Irina, "then we had better gather some firewood." She signaled Letchik, "We'll be back shortly."

Serov stood up and grasped her hand. "Irina Nikolaevna, be careful. I want you to live a long and happy life."

She turned away and hurried after Letchik. Vasiliev looked at him curiously.

"Listen, my good and old friend," Serov began, spreading his hands. "It's hard for me to say this, but it's time for us to part. No!" he gestured, "Wait until I have finished my little speech. You know I'm not practiced in these things. I've been thinking a lot. I can't leave Russia. It was hard enough to leave the village back then when you first got me to join the Moscow police. But to leave everything? No, the three of you have ways— what is the word, talents? to make the jump. Not me. There is nothing for me outside. But until just a few days ago, it seemed to me that without you there wouldn't be anything for me left inside either. Then I met Dunia. So, she is my Irina, Vasili Vasilievich. Yes, I will go back to her."

Vasiliev wanted to interrupt. But Serov's calm and steady gaze stopped him.

"I've learned much from you. How to plan. You know it is not a peasant's way, to plan, but to accept what comes. You have given me something precious, yes, to plan, to think ahead. And so I thought about how you could leave Russia with honor. Does that surprise you? Perhaps not. Perhaps you have also thought about this. But now fate, the peasant's guide, has given me the means to plan."

Vasiliev turned his head, though it pained him, to look in the direction where Irina and Letchik had gone.

No, thought Serov, they will not interrupt us. Irina Nikolaevna is my friend too. That night when Vasiliev was asleep, he had talked to Irina and Letchik about his plan. Irina understood right away but it took a little time for her to convince Letchik. Finally, he shrugged his shoulders and said. "The hell with the Romanovs. They'll get it in the neck one day. I just hope I am still around to see it."

Serov paused before going on. He chose his words carefully.

"You must appear to have died here, Vasili Vasilievich. And your last, heroic act was to save these precious documents so that the honor of Russia may be preserved. Oh, yes, I admit they will also be my passport to a safe exit from this dead end. Now listen please. "

"I am listening Serov, but I am not sure I like what I am hearing."

"I didn't think so. But wait."

"We do not know what the rifle fire meant. But it is unlikely that Bark has survived. Either way, my plan will work. First we will build you a nice looking grave and heap it with stones and a cross. Right here in the valley. And we will place your cap upon it. Then I will go back, by foot to Arul. I'll tell my tale. You and I were tracking Bark. We know nothing about the exiles. We left them in Semipalatinsk. No one is the wiser; my Kirghiz friends will say nothing. Bark and the girl surprised us; you were killed in the gunfight. With your last words you entrusted me with the documents we found on the ground when Bark abandoned them after the fight, along with his rifle. I will ask them to perform a military salute over your grave! Isn't that what our Jewish friends in Kiev would call *chutzpath*!" Serov chuckled and Vasiliev could not help but smile.

"They are a long time gathering wood, don't you think?" asked Vasiliev a twinkle in his eye.

"They are not gathering wood, they are gathering stones."

Vasiliev sighed. Yes, Serov's plan was brilliant. But he was thinking about losing his friend. Why does a man have to lose something he cherishes in order to gain something he may cherish even more?

They sat in silence for a long time. Then Vasiliev drew out of his tunic a paper.

"You have planned brilliantly, Sergeant! But I too have been planning. This is my last will and testament. I wrote it in Semipalatinsk and had it witnessed in the Governor-General's office. In it I leave you my estate, 'The Nettles.' As you know, it was left to me by my father, your former master and owner, Count Vorontsov. You may sell it or run it according to your new 'democratic'principles. Don't object! There's no one else for me to leave it to. Let's say it's my wedding present to you."

There were tears in Serov's eyes as he took the paper. "So let it be, Vasili Vasilievch. I don't like goodbyes. So I will leave now. Irina knows what I intend to do. She will forgive me for my sudden departure. You will have a good life together."

Serov gathered the documents, embraced Vasiliev and mounted his Kirghiz pony. He rode back up the stony path. He did not look back.

Epilogue

An envelope letter bearing a German postage stamp and dated April 10, 1910 was delivered to Mr. George Kennan Esq. in Washington D.C. Inside was a short note and another sealed letter. The short note was written in Russian and read:

> Dear Mr. Kennan:
> I trust you are well. Remembering our short but happy acquaintance, I am imposing on your good nature to send the enclosed letter to the proper address. I have no other way of reaching my old friends. I press your hand warmly,
> Ivan Serov.

The sealed letter bore the simple, brief inscription: "Vasili Vasilievich" and the return address read "The Nettles, Moscow Province."

Kennan took out a fresh envelope and wrote:

"The Hon. Basil Vasil, Sheriff's Office, Duluth, Minnesota." He hesitated a moment and then wrote an illegible return address. Then he placed inside the unopened letter addressed to Vasiliev.

When the letter arrived, Sheriff Vasil brought it home and opened it that evening in the presence of his wife, Irene, their closest friend, Dr. John Letchik and his twin sons, who were just about to enter the University of Minnesota. He read it aloud.

Dear Friends,

Many years have passed and I pray that you have reached the other shore safely. Let me tell you about my life. When I reached Arul, a small detachment of Gendarmes were encamped. A Colonel Elagin was much moved by my story. He promised to pay full honors at your gravesite. He was not happy about having shot down the Uhlan officer and his girl. "They resisted us," he said; "the girl was mad."

Returning to Semipalatinsk I married Dunia and a wild celebration followed. The officiating priest was Father Iosifei who recalled his meeting with you and the tragic events that brought it about. He said he would remember you in his prayers. He had been offered parish in the city but turned it down. He told me that he had just read a pamphlet by Tolstoy and saw the light. He confessed it was he who incited Father Iosifei and not Bark. It's funny how hard it is to get everything right. Father Iosifei then quoted scripture. "What profiteth a man to gain the whole world and lose his soul." Perhaps this planted the seed in me.

I used the reward I received for turning over the documents to pay for the return trip to Moscow with Dunia and her brother. It turns out that they are the children of Ivan Fedorovich. Such is fate!

My mother had died while we were in Siberia. God rest her soul. I began to read more by Tolstoy and all three of us became Tolstoyans. We worked with the elder and the rest of the commune, and divided up 'The Nettles', keeping only a few acres as a garden. Dunia began a school for the peasant children and Egor taught some of the older ones the trade of telegrapher. We have two sons and a daughter. When the terrible events occurred in the summer of 1906, our land was spared. The commune protected us.

So, as Lev Nikolaevich truly said, in the end a man only needs enough land to be buried.

Always your friend, Serov

On Fact and Fiction

Most of the characters in this book have been invented except, of course, George Kennan and his travelling companion, the artist George A. Frost. I have woven the adventures of Vasiliev into Kennan's famous two volume narrative, *Siberia and the Exile System*, (London: James R. Osgood, McIlvain and Co., 1891) in which the author, true to his promise, does not mention Vasiliev in order not to compromise his friends in St. Petersburg! I have also relied on Feodor Dostoevsky's *Memoirs from the House of the Dead*, trans. Jesse Coulson (Oxford: Oxford University Press, 1968) based on the original Russian published in serial form in 1861-62 in order to evoke the life of the prisoners and exiles. Readers who wish to pursue this theme may turn to Leo Tolstoy's *Resurrection*. There is no good recent history of the Decembrists in English; Anatole Mazour, *The First Russian Revolution. 1825 The Decembrist Movement, Its Origins, Development and Significance* (Berkeley, University of California Press, 1937) is, however, servicable. The literature in Russian is enormous.

The term Kirghiz has been used as Kennan used it to designate nomads who today would be called Kazakhs or Mongols.

A sample of my own views on Russian historical detective fiction may be found in "A Tale of Three Genres," *Kritika*, vol. 15, no. 2, (Spring, 2014).